/0/1

The Last

Timucuan

Fredric M. Hitt

Illustrations by
Linda Silsby Hitt

This book is a work of fiction. Any resemblance to actual events or persons, living or dead, is entirely coincidental.

"The Last Timucuan," by Fredric M. Hitt. ISBN 978-1-60264-290-4 (softcover); 978-1-60264-291-1 (hardcover).

Published 2008 by Virtualbookworm.com Publishing Inc., P.O. Box 9949, College Station, TX 77842, US. ©2008, Fredric M. Hitt. All rights reserved. No part of this publication may be reproduced, stored in a retrieval system, or transmitted in any form or by any means, electronic, mechanical, recording or otherwise, without the prior written permission of Fredric M. Hitt.

To The Old Ones,

Your spirits walk among us

touching us with the breeze,

whispering in the rustle of leaves.

Lexicon of Timucuan Words and Phrases

Timucua- Indian tribe inhabiting North Florida and South Georgia, 15th through 18th centuries. Subgroups include Mocama, Salt Water, Potano, Utina, Yustaga and others, speaking ten dialects of Timucuan language.

Atichicolo-Iri - Spirit warrior

Cacique - Ordinary chief

Cimarron (a) (es) - Outlaw, runaway

Holata - Regional chief

Holata Aco - Chief of Chiefs

Inija - Chief's next in command

Isucu - Herbalist, medicine man

Jarva - Shaman, sorcerer

Nariba - Term of respect, old man

Niaholata - Woman chief

Paracousi - War chief

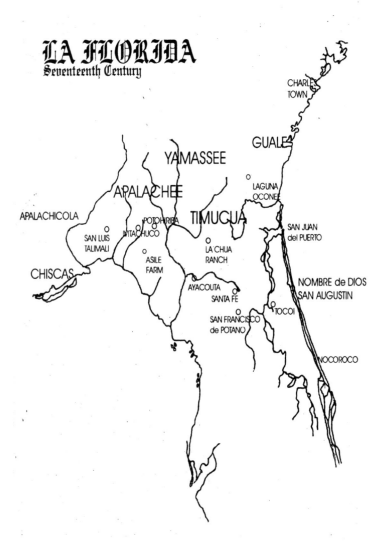

LA FLORIDA
Seventeenth Century

CHARLES TOWN

GUALE

YAMASSEE

APALACHEE

LAGUNA OCONEE

APALACHICOLA

TIMUCUA

SAN JUAN del PUERTO

POTOHIRIBA

SAN LUIS TALIMALI

IVITACHUCO

LA CHUA RANCH

ASILE FARM

CHISCAS

NOMBRE de DIOS

SAN AUGUSTIN

AYACOUTA

SANTA FE

TOCOI

SAN FRANCISCO de POTANO

NOCOROCO

Prologue

Convento de Santo Domingo
Guanabacoa, Cuba
May 23, 1768

To: Monseñor Pedro Agustín Morell,
Bishop of Santiago de Cuba
Havana

Your Excellency,

Greetings from your Christian brothers of Convento de Santo Domingo, whose lips move endlessly with prayers to God in Heaven for your good health. May our loving Father bless your boundless spirit and sustain you in your great work.

When last we spoke it was the occasion of the conclave of the Council of the Indies, at which you so ably represented the Church and testified as to the circumstances, including failures of leadership, which led to the loss of La Florida to England four years ago.

As a mere Franciscan friar, it was perhaps presumptuous of me to appear at such an august meeting of my betters, but I attended for the sole purpose of speaking to you concerning certain recent discoveries I have made which may be of historical value, as they relate to the Indians of La Florida and their treatment at the hands of military and civilian authorities of Spain.

So much time has passed, and, notwithstanding your acute memory, perhaps I should remind you of the details of our conversation. I reported to you the discovery of what appears to be a trove of historic native writings originating in La Florida.

I mentioned the papers to you, recalling that five years ago, while Cuba was occupied by the English and you were exiled to San Augustín, God quickened your heart to the suffering of the natives and made you an instrument for saving the lives of the few surviving Indians of La Florida and transporting them here to Cuba at the end of the war.

Knowing of your love and compassion for these poor, wretched souls, it occurred to me that the writings in my possession might be of interest to you. My cursory examination suggested that they might have historic value, and shed light on the suffering and ill treatment of the Indians of La Florida during the mission period.

You asked me to further investigate the content of the documents and to send to you, in readable form, those that appear to have significance. I began the process immediately upon my return to Guanabacoa, but I feel that you are due an apology for the extraordinary length of time it has taken for me to respond to your request.

The records, as you shall see, are voluminous. I estimate there are no fewer than 800 mixed pages of paper and parchment, some of fair quality and some of poor. Many of the documents are dated more than 100 years ago.

The oldest papers have become dry and brittle with age, and require the gentlest handling lest they fall to pieces. They are written in the Timucuan language. Therefore, I have taken the time and gone to the expense of having them translated and rewritten by a certified government interpreter and scribe. The man is a Taino Indian, having, therefore, a native tongue similar to Timucuan.

What I am sending to you with this letter is but a small selection of the documents at hand: those that appear to be the most ancient in origin. Before I commit more time and money to the project, I would like to hear what you have to say about their possible value.

These documents were found among the last effects of Sr. Juan Alonso Cavale, a Timucuan who died without family here at the age of 54. Although he registered at The Church of Our Lady of the Ascension when he came to Cuba in 1763, there is only one record of his having attended Mass. Those few Indians who knew him said he was a Christian while he lived in San Augustin, but that he chose to live in apostasy, away from the influence of the friars, from the time he immigrated to Cuba.

Sr. Cavale lived and died in a hut on the side of a steep hill half a league east of town and near the harbor. In the beginning, he cared for an elderly Indian whose name was Manuel Riso. The older man died within two months of their arrival here in 1763, and the church ledger reflects his age at death as ninety years. Riso was laid to rest in the church pauper field, and now he is joined in death by his friend, Juan Alonso Cavale.

For some reason, these men had little in common with the other Indians from San Augustín and lived as hermits apart from the others. Perhaps it is because they are Timucuans, and their neighbors were of the Surruque, Yamassee, and Guale cultures, whose languages and customs were different.

Because they did not attend the mission, I fulfilled my priestly duties by sending a widow to check on their wellbeing from time to time, and to carry bread and corn to them so they would not starve.

The woman reported the death of Manuel Riso. Likewise, she came to me on the fourteenth day of November last with news of the passing of Cavale. I went to his house to say the prayers and prepare the body for burial and to inventory his possessions. I was shocked to discover the squalid, flea-infested condition of his existence.

By the looks of him, he must have sold whatever he had and exchanged the proceeds, and his meager earnings as a farm laborer, for strong drink. He was emaciated in the extreme. What little food remained in the larder consisted of stale bread and a piece of moldy goat cheese. Beside his cot, I found an empty bottle that smelled of cheap rum. Other bottles were scattered about, inside and out. As it has been with so many other Indians who emigrated from La Florida, the poor, sad man drank himself to death.

Those who knew him called him Alonso, and, at the Funeral Mass, they eulogized him for his devotion to the old man, Manuel Riso, and for his love of flowers. Amongst the litter of broken rum bottles, Cavale had planted and tended an impressive variety of seasonal flowers, including a flourishing stand of the native plant the Indians call October daisies.

His possessions consisted of tattered old clothing, and they had been patched and worn so often that they barely covered his nakedness. He had nothing else of value. Not a single garment was fit for reuse by the poor people of Guanabacoa, and I burned what was left.

I decided to burn his bed, also, to kill the vermin. When it was moved, underneath I discovered a leather trunk containing the papers. I dragged it home with me to the convento.

What struck me at first was the fine quality and workmanship of the leather. I wondered why Cavale had kept the trunk, and not bartered it for rum, as he had everything else he owned.

When I looked through the writings I discovered that some of them were skillfully wrought, as if prepared by a scribe. When I inspected the oldest document, the one at the bottom of the stack, I saw that it dated back well over 100 years.

I puzzle over such an encyclopedic collection of high quality documents in the hands of an otherwise unremarkable soul. Perhaps the answer to this riddle can be found within the writings themselves.

My state of curiosity and amazement was only enhanced by the discovery of numerous pen and ink drawings scattered among the pages of manuscript. Although they were primitive by European standards of art, they were cleverly done, and appear to be of recent origin. It is my belief that the drawings were done by Cavale himself, and meant to illustrate the events depicted in the earlier writings.

I must confess that this has become an obsession for me, trying to decipher and make sense of the words and emotions of Indians who suffered under Spanish rule for so many generations.

I cannot, however, overemphasize the burden, in terms of time and finances, that this effort has placed on your brothers here at Convento de Santo Domingo. The services of a Timucuan translator do not come cheaply, and the time and effort required to preserve the old paper and parchment, and to reproduce them into a more durable form, is daunting.

Transmitted with this report are reproductions of approximately one forth of all the writings. If when you have read them, your curiosity is satisfied, and you find them of no historical value, please advise me and I will refrain from further effort. If continued, this work could require my attention for two years or more.

I leave you to peruse, as I have, the words of an Indian named Coya, who cried out to the Church for relief from the repression of a harsh governor, many years before you or I were born. Perhaps by studying his writings, we can learn of the mistakes that led to the demise of the Timucuan people, the collapse of the Catholic missions, and the abject failure of Spain in the colonial province called La Florida.

As always, I remain your devoted and loving servant and Brother in Christ.

I kiss your ring.

Fr. Manuel de Soto
Chaplain of the Convento Santa de Domingo

Western Timucua

Chapter 1

Fortress at San Augustín
July, 1655

*T*his is not a bad prison. I have stayed in worse places in my life. My cell has a window at eye level so I can look out at the hillside to the north. The metal bars allow sufficient light for me to write on this paper given to me by the prison chaplain.

The old *jarva* in the dungeon next to me has no window to the outside, but lives in a perpetual gloom: too dark to read and write, even if he knew how, and yet too light during the day for him to sleep. He has only the light from the window that the guard uses to look in on him, and from cracks in the outside wall.

A word about the construction of this fortress: it is built on a sloping hill, and the floor of my cell is more than a meter below the level of the ground outside. When I look through the window, I see the feet and legs of workmen standing nearby.

The walls of the fort are made of pine, probably because it is plentiful. If the governor knew to use cypress, the fort would last forever. The pine logs are already rotting where they are sunken into the dirt, and rats and other animals can easily dig their way into the prison.

Two nights ago I had a visitor. An opossum came looking for something good to eat. He was a picky eater, and turned up his pointy nose at what was left in my bowl of gruel. He was suspicious of me, and went back through his hole before I could grab him. We get no meat here, but only rotting vegetables, thin soup, and moldy bread.

———————

I was here for five days before Fr. Medina took notice of me. Each morning he comes to the prison and stops at each door of the 17 cells and speaks a prayer through the window. Then he asks if I have anything to confess, before he returns to the convento. Yesterday he asked the guard to open my door and let him come inside.

He carried a three legged stool and sat down next to where I lay on my bed.

"Are you who they say you are, the *Cacique* of the Utina?" he asked me.

"My name is Coya," I said. "When I was a young man I was called Coya Ayacouta Utina, and yes, I was *Holata Aco.* I am a private man now, merely the head man of Laguna Oconee, and of no importance."

The priest sniffed the air and looked around. "Has something died in here?" he asked.

The smell is with me every day, more so when it is hot and there is no breeze coming from my window. "Perhaps a rat died in the wall," I said. That seemed to satisfy him.

"But what are you doing here in prison, amongst murderers, thieves, and scoundrels? I have never heard of a high chief being locked up unless he sponsored a rebellion."

I laughed out loud. "No rebellion, I can assure you. Just a misunderstanding with the governor."

The priest reached out his hand and grasped mine. "As chaplain, it is my duty not only to address the spiritual needs of prisoners, but to insure that their imprisonment is just," he said. "Perhaps I can help you get back to your people."

———————

I told Fr. Medina as much as I could about the unfortunate events that led me to prison in San Augustín.

In February, Oconee had a visitor, a sergeant from the presidio who carried an order from Governor Diego de Rebolledo. In it, his Excellency insulted us by saying the people of Oconee were *cimarrones*, ragtag outcasts of diverse villages, and criminals. He said that we have no legitimate claim on the lands we occupy, and that the king desires that we move to Misión Nombre de Diós, which is more than five days hard journey.

We asked the sergeant, "If we are such wretched people, why would the king want us, and why would the governor require that we come to San Augustín?"

He had no answer to that, but said we had 14 days to collect our things and prepare for the journey, and that he would return with a squad of soldiers to accompany us and make sure we did not lose our way.

I sent a letter to the governor by way of the priest of Laguna Oconee. In it I did not challenge his order, believing that would result only in punishment and retribution. I asked simply that the move be delayed three moons so that we might harvest what little maize we had planted, and have food to eat on the journey.

"Governor Rebolledo reacted badly to the letter," I said. "He sent the soldiers to collect us immediately. My people now live at Nombre de Diós, and I am here in the prison."

"That is all? There was nothing else?" the priest asked excitedly. He began to write in a notebook he carried with him. "Governor de Rebolledo was clearly out of line, and reacted inappropriately."

When he looked up from his writing, I said to the friar that there was something else he should know. "There was a second letter. I wrote it to the bishop in Cuba and asked him to intercede on our behalf. In it, I said that we are all good Christians, and that the people of Oconee are too old to be leaving our home to go to work in a strange place."

Fr. Medina sighed heavily and closed his notebook.

"The letter was never sent," I said. "I still had it when the soldiers came, and they took it from me."

The priest stood up and walked to the window and looked out, deep in thought. He turned to face me. "So that is the reason. Rebolledo is punishing you for merely asking a bishop for help. This is even more outrageous than I thought."

Before he left, the friar said that he would help me secure my freedom, and that he would bring me paper and ink so that I might write my petition.

"If the governor will not grant your freedom, we, the Franciscans, will direct this to his superiors. The Council of the Indies does not allow abridgement of the rights of the Indians. Nor would they condone punishment for the mere act of communicating with the clergy."

——— —— ———

I did not tell the jailhouse priest the whole story, or how I truly felt about the order to move from Laguna Oconee to San Augustín, nor would it have mattered. This was not the first order for relocation I had seen. Many years ago, when I was the paramount chief living at Ayacouta, I received an order from Governor Benitez Ruíz de Salazar. He commanded that I send a militia of my men to the village of Oconee to collect the people who congregated there and take them to Ayacouta so they could work as porters to carry produce to San Augustín.

He did not insult them, as Governor de Rebolledo did, by calling them bad names. He simply required them to work.

The greatest and most painful failing of my life was my response to that order. I sent a squadron of men, accompanied by a soldier, to bring the people to the south. Most of them were old people, but some were younger men who had worked as burden bearers and had sore backs and were crippled from the work. My *paracousi* counted 45 people who were rounded up. As they left Oconee, the soldier burned their houses so no one would return.

There are no good trails between Oconee and Ayacouta, but many ravines, jungles, and deep rivers. Nine of the old ones died on the trail from the heat and exertion. When the survivors struggled into Ayacouta, I knew how Judas felt with his 20 pieces of silver. I saw the anger and disrespect they felt for me, their chief. I was shamed by what I had done to these innocent people. Four more died at Ayacouta from broken hearts, bodies, and spirits.

I prayed to God for guidance, and my heart was quickened to their suffering. I looked the other way and ordered my men to do the same, as these people once again walked out of Ayacouta and moved to the north. At first, one or two slipped out of the village at night, and then whole families would go in the daylight when they realized they would not be punished.

Soon, all the people who survived had returned to Oconee. Then others of my people began to leave. They could no longer bear the burdens the Spaniards placed on them, and wished to live a better life.

I had lost the respect of my people and had failed them. When my first wife died, my heart died with her. My first son, Lucas Menéndez, is now *Holata Aco* at Ayacouta. I followed my people to Laguna Oconee.

We now had no intention of obeying the order of Governor Diego de Rebolledo. We would die first or head north to the mountains to hide. It was a mistake to wait, hoping for a miracle. We should have run away when we had the chance.

Chapter 2

*T*he enthusiasm of the friar for justice has waned. He said to me yesterday that it is a complicated matter, to involve the Council of the Indies in internal matters of the Province of La Florida, and that it may take more time to secure my release.

Each day Fr. Medina comes to attend to my needs and to help me with my prayers. He brings me paper and ink, and urges me to write something each day. He says it will relieve me of the boredom of my captivity and keep my mind alert and active, so that when the day comes that the governor releases me to return to my people, I will be fit to lead them.

This quill from a turkey is strong and withstands a firm stroke without bending, but it feels strange to my fingers after such a long time.

Perhaps the writing will also distract me from worries about my youngest children. Juan is seven years old, and Carlos was born two years later than his brother. They have no mother. She died giving birth to the youngest. I know that their uncle, Big Bow, will protect them and keep them from trouble in San Augustín. Big Bow said that Juan is practicing his writing at the mission, and the friar is pleased with his work. Of course, Carlos is more interested in fighting with other children and playing war games, at his age.

The reason I am content in this cell is because I have been here many times before. The room looks much as it did in the days when I used to visit my grandfather, Marehootie. It is where he died, more than 30 years ago. I can feel his presence, still. It is very comforting. Though I wish they had not whitewashed the wall upon which he painted a mural.

One thing that is different is the smell. Not always, but sometimes I can smell a bad odor. It is not outside the window, because the grounds around the fort are cleaned each day. Something may have crawled into the walls and died there, but it does not really smell like a dead animal. It is a sickly-sweet odor and worse on the hot days.

My people, from Oconee, live among the Mocamans at a village not far from here. Big Bow serves as my *inija* and looks after them, and comes to see me each day to tell me of their condition. Those who are able work on the fort, and sometimes I recognize their voices outside my window. They laugh a lot in the mornings, and it cheers my heart to hear them. Later in the day, when it is so hot outside, I hear them groaning and laboring under the burdens the Spanish put on their backs. It is hot enough in here, where the ground protects me. I can only imagine how it must be above ground, where the sun beats down from above and glares off the white sand in the work yard.

Yesterday a guard dog went mad from the heat. It was killed by a soldier's bullet after it bit the neck of one of the workers. These Spaniards take no better care of their animals than they do the Indians.

Fr. Medina says he is working for my release, appealing to the governor to relent and set me free. He believes that I will be turned loose soon.Fr. Medina also suggested that everything I write here be in the Timucuan language, so even the guards who are literate will not understand what they are looking at. When I was *Holata Aco* of Utina, I wrote some of my orders to my chiefs in the Timucuan tongue, so this is easy for me. There are some times when Spanish would be a better language. There are many words in Timucua that have different meanings when spoken, depending on how they are said, how loudly or softly, or even depending on the look on the face of the speaker. When they are written, their meanings might not always be clear to the reader.

It was Fr. Pareja who took our words and put them on paper so they could later be read aloud exactly as they were spoken the first time. At first we thought there was magic in the paper, that it could capture the words. The priest of San Juan also taught us to read and write in Spanish. That was very exciting to the boys at the convento.

When I remember Fr. Pareja's love for us, and how hard he worked to make us good Catholics, my eyes water. I do not think the priests they have now are as good as the ones in the early years.

I should be ashamed for writing that. Fr. Medina is working hard to have me turned loose. He even warned me that there are people in the governor's employ who are skilled in reading and interpreting Timucuan, and that I should take care in what I say, and hide my writings where they will not be found.

I do not know who I am writing this to, or why. I will never show it to anyone. Perhaps my penmanship will improve if I concentrate on the task of organizing my rambling thoughts. But it is tiresome. My hand cramps from holding the quill so long, and my eyes do not focus well. Even with the window above my head, there is not enough light here in my cell. Now that the sun is setting, it is getting too dark to write more today.

I remember the light as being brighter when my grandfather, Marehootie, was here. Perhaps a palmetto bush has grown up and blocks the sun from the window. I will ask Big Bow to cut it down.

———————

I was awakened during the night by shouts from the next cell. An old Tacatacuran, a *jarva,* was having a bad dream, or maybe he was frightened by a vision. It has happened before but is very disturbing. I do not understand him, just a word or two here and there. In the daytime I have tried to talk to him through the cracks in the wall, but he never answers me. Maybe he does not like Utinans.

Fr. Medina told me the old man has been locked up four years. He was convicted of plotting against the king. "Sedition," he calls the crime. I cannot imagine what an old man like that could do to hurt someone who lives in Spain. *Jarvas* can cast spells to harm their enemies, but I've never heard of magic strong enough to cross an ocean.

Maybe he was plotting against the governor. That is a plan I could support.

There I go again, assuming that no enemy will ever decipher what I am writing down and hold me to account. It is perfectly safe to think what you want, unless they are impure thoughts. It gets risky when you write them down.

———————

The friar came to see me early today. It is Sunday and he has to prepare for Mass, so he did not stay long. He sat on a wooden stool while I sat on my bed.

I asked him about the noise from outside. Since daybreak, the soldiers have been shouting orders and marching about, beating drums and firing their weapons in the air.Fr. Medina said there is bad news. "The king has warned the governor that the English war boats have attacked the island of Hispañola and seized Jamaica and might come to San Augustín next," he said.

Sergeant Major Adrían de Canizares was busy organizing the soldiers to send to the north, to San Pedro and San Juan, to watch for invaders. Six soldiers went with Governor de Rebolledo on a visit to the Ais, where the governor buys amber so he can sell it for a profit.

"If a business trip is more important than the English, I do not think Rebolledo feels we are in any real danger," Fr. Medina said. "Only 75 men are left here at the presidio, but they are on high alert."

The friar asked to see what I have written, and I handed it to him. He does not read Timucuan, and after looking at the two pages he handed them back to me and asked if I would read to him. I answered that they contained my private thoughts, and that many of my musings concerned my family. He pursed his lips and I could tell he was unhappy, but he smiled as if he were content.

"Your penmanship leaves much to be desired," he said. "You should form your letters more carefully and write more slowly."

"It is the light in here," I answered.

"There is nothing wrong with the light," he said, placing his hand on my knee. "Yours is the only cell in the fort with a window. Do you not remember?"

I could tell he was still peeved.

Fr. Medina said he had heard nothing from the governor concerning when I might be released, and he had very little else to say. We prayed together.

As he prepared to leave, the priest asked if I would like him to return later in the day with the sacraments of the Lord's Table. I said that if it were convenient, I would look forward to it. Then he asked if I would also like him to hear my confession.

My answer was that I had nothing to confess, having very little opportunity to sin in this dungeon. I thought that would make him smile, but it did not. I believe he wanted to find out about what I had written down by asking me in Confession. He is as wily as a raccoon.

Apparently it was not convenient for him to bring the sacraments, as he did not return today.

———————

Big Bow came to see me this morning. He brought fresh water and hickory nut bread baked by the women in the village. He watched me while I ate. "There is nothing wrong with your appetite," he said.

Later, after I had finished, the brother of my first wife became serious. He looked through the window of the door to insure the guard was not nearby, then sat on the floor next to my cot so that we would not be overheard.

"There has been trouble in the village," he said. "One of the Yamassee from Oconee drank wine, and fought with his wife. I sent him away before his wife's brother could find out and kill him."

"Was it Yalu?" I asked.

Big Bow nodded.

"Where would Yalu get wine?" I asked.

"Maybe he traded for it with a Spanish sailor. There are merchants who sell wine in San Augustín, also. But Yalu has no money or much to trade. If you are asking what I think, I think it was communion wine, and he stole it from the priest."

"You did the right thing in sending Yalu away," I said. "In a week or so, his wife will welcome him back and it will be forgotten. At least until he gets drunk the next time."

At Tocoi, on the river, there are many drunks among the men who ferry people back and forth. This is the first time I have heard of it among the people from Oconee.

"No one else is drinking wine," Big Bow said, as if he were reading my mind.

"How are my boys/" I asked.

Big Bow hesitated before answering. "They are doing well. Juan works hard on his studies, and does more than his share of work in the village. Carlos, of course, is all boy."

"Meaning?"

This time my brother-in-law was even slower to answer. "He struck another child in the head with a stick. It knocked him senseless."

"A stick?" I said.

"It was more like a club. The boy's father asked me to tell you."

I stood and walked the three steps to the window. The sun was one hand above the horizon. It was time for Big Bow to join the others in the workyard.

"Carlos misses his father," Big Bow said.

"I can do nothing about my present predicament," I said without turning from the window. "What do you think it would take to make the injured boy's family happy?"

"Perhaps an apology and a gift to the boy of Carlos's knife or something else he values."

"Take care of it for me, Big Bow. You are a good uncle."

"I can convince Carlos to part with his knife. He knows that I will make him another. But it may be harder to get him to apologize. He does not think he did anything wrong. Sometimes he does not know when the war games are over."

We were both quiet for awhile. I watched the sand swirl in the wind and dance across the yard.

"Some of our people want to go home, Coya. I hear them talking among themselves, saying that you may be locked up here until spring, and they will miss the planting time at Oconee. I have been very firm. I tell them that they should be patient. That if they try to leave, the soldiers will bring them back and lock them up, also."

I turned to him. "What you really mean is that if they try to escape, it will only result in me being locked up longer," I said.

Big Bow did not answer.

"Ask them, for me, to wait until the next new moon."

Chapter 3

*I*t has been four days since I have seen the priest. Sometimes he gets busy and will not come for a day or two, but after four days I wonder if he is still angry that I did not read him what I have written.

Big Bow is here each morning with fresh baked bread and spring water. He also brought bad news today.

The young bucks from Oconee are tired of waiting. They say they will leave soon for home. If the Spanish pursue them, they will just keep moving toward the mountains until the soldiers give up the chase. Big Bow is a *paracousi*, and they respect him for his knowledge of war. But he is not a chief, and the young men are unmoved by his arguments that they remain patient.

"Do you know there are only 75 soldiers left at the presidio?" I asked.

Big Bow had been gazing out the window, and he turned to me. "Are you saying that this would be a good time to leave for home?"

"If you left quickly, and in small groups going different directions, I doubt that they would bother to chase you. The priest tells me that their greatest concern is to guard the presidio from the English."

Big Bow stepped to the door and looked for the guard. He came back and sat next to me on the bed.

"I have a plan" he said, and he told it to me.

There is an ox used by the Spanish to pull a cart loaded with timber for repairs on the fort. It is kept in a pen, and other than when they feed it, the soldiers are never around at night. It would be a simple matter to bring the beast behind the fort and use a chain to pull the bars from the window. The opening would be wide enough for me to slip through. We could be miles away before morning.

"Even if the guard did not hear the chain rattling, he looks in on me sometimes and would sound the alarm," I said.

Big Bow dropped his head in thought. Then he looked at me askance and lowered his voice. "If he were able. Blue Eyes always opens the door when you call him, and he is watching you at night. I could slip a knife to you through the window after it is dark."

This was not a choice I wanted to make – my freedom at the expense of an innocent life. Yet my weakness and poor decisions in the past had cost many lives. I did not answer Big Bow for a long time. I prayed silently for God's guidance.

Finally I said, "Tell the people to leave the village in small groups on Saturday night, two days from now. When they are all gone, hand me the knife through the window before you collect the ox. We can meet the others at the river crossing at Tocoi at midnight."

Big Bow breathed in deeply, and let the air out. "There are soldiers sometimes at Tocoi. The plan is already made. We will rendezvous at the crossing to the north, at the old village of Picolata."

I leaned forward on the edge of the bed and held my head in my hands. "If I do not take the knife when you hand it through the window, you must go without me."

———————

Sleep did not come easily last night. So many fears jarred me awake each time I began to find peace. Then the *jarva* screamed, and I was wide awake.

There was no escaping his rantings. I also heard a falsetto voice, as if a spirit were arguing with him. I could make out a word or two. And then he cried out, "Coya! Coya!"

I slipped out of my bed and crawled to the wall between us. I listened at the hole where the rat comes in and out, but the *jarva* had fallen silent, as if he knew I was listening.

After a time, I crawled back to my bed. I pondered the meaning of the *jarva's* outburst for a long time. And then he began to rant and rave again. I heard him say, "Lucas," and I knew he was talking about my oldest son, the *Holata Aco* of Utina. "War," he said in a loud voice, and then repeated it three times, each time louder than the last.

Blue Eyes scraped his metal cup across the bars on the *jarva's* door and hollered at him to shut up.

Jarva stopped jabbering, but I could hear his deep, raspy breathing.

I did not sleep.

I have only one piece of paper left, and the ink well is almost dry. Today is Friday. Perhaps Fr. Medina will visit me and bring more paper and ink.

———————

Fr. Medina brought both good gifts and bad, late in the morning. Even before he spoke, I saw on his face that pinched look that betrays his unhappiness even when he is smiling.

"I have spoken to the governor, and there are certain complications," he said as he stood before me. He paused, and then he sat next to me on my bed. He never does that. He always sits on a stool in front of me, or remains standing.

Sitting beside me, he could not look me in the eye. "There are problems west of the river. Rebolledo blames your son who has much influence over the other chiefs. The governor ordered the chiefs and principal men to come to San Augustín in case they are needed to fight the English. Lucas refuses to come, unless someone else carries his burdens."

I said nothing, though I marveled at what I was hearing. The *jarva* had said there would be war.

"Until Lucas agrees to honor the order, Governor Rebolledo says he cannot turn you loose. You are a pawn in a game of chess, one might say."

The friar had brought with him a carrying bag, and now he picked it up off the floor and set it in his lap. From it, he withdrew a stack of papers, a bottle of ink, and two more turkey quills. Then he offered me two small candles and a flint box. My hands were full of the other items, so he set these last on the blanket between us.

"I do not write after dark, but I thank you for the candles," I said.

Fr. Medina cleared his throat. "You are being moved to the room on the other side of the *jarva*. It has been used for root storage, but it is being emptied now. I will help you move your things when the guard tells me it is ready."

I picked up a candle and looked at it. Then I inspected the flint box.

The priest turned to me for a moment, then looked straight ahead again. "It has no outside window, only the small opening in the door, as in this one. You will need candlelight to see. The governor said it is a question of security. Perhaps he fears that your son will come to take you away."

Fr. Medina waited with me until the guard informed him that my new room was ready. The priest promised it would not be as hot, because it had no window, and because it was dug three steps deeper into the earth.

In the middle of the day it is almost completely dark with the door closed. Only a little daylight comes in through the window in the door. When the sun goes down, the guard's oil lamp reflects on the wall of my cell. If he carries it away to look in on other prisoners, it is impossible to see my hand before my face.

It is damp, and the air has an unhealthy chill. Only part of the dirt floor is dry. A pool of water stands along the back wall.

There is a strong odor, a cloying, sickening smell. Even as I write this, I cannot describe it. It is the same smell I noticed in my first room, the one with the window, but here it is overpowering. As my eyes adjusted to the dark, I saw an old dilapidated basket that had fallen apart in the pool of water, spilling its contents of rotting sweet potatoes.

Before he left, the priest promised to complain to the sergeant major and ask that the filth be removed from my room. That was many hours ago, and no one has come to clean it. Fr. Medina left me his bandana to tie over my nose. It helps a little bit.

As I write this, it is dark outside, but not as dark as here.

I am writing this by candlelight. When I look directly into the flame, it appears too bright and hurts my eyes. I see a halo around it, as if I were looking at a painting of

Mary, Mother of Christ, or some other saint, on a church altar.

The only other light is the reflection the candle makes in the red eyes of the rats that come to feast on their meal of potatoes.

I no longer wish to write, and my candle melts away. If I sleep, perhaps I will wake up in Heaven.

Chapter 4

Laguna Oconee,
January 27, 1660

I do not know that the date I have written above is correct. It is not our way to worry about the day of the month, as if something memorable or important were about to happen. We know the change of seasons, and when it is time to plant maize, and we remember to mark off the seven days of the week for those of us who pray and do no work on the Sabbath. When we had a friar, he did that for us, and he also kept track of the day of the month.

I wish I had started this differently, by telling the amazing things that have happened, but if I make a mistake and ruin even one page, my father will skin me like a squirrel. Let me start over.

Twenty-seven days ago, I was called to the Oconee council house, where the men were warming themselves with the cassina drink and discussing, with my uncle Big Bow, who would prepare the fields for planting and who would hunt or fish, and other important matters. I am only 11 years old, and I was happy to give up my warm blanket to be with the men so early in the morning.

A trader had come to Oconee, carrying a packet of two Spanish documents, a letter and a parchment. We have no friar to translate, and none of the men can read. Big Bow knows a few words in Spanish, but he is not a reliable translator. I am the only one in the village who has been taught by the friars to read and write in Spanish, so they called upon me.

The light in the council house was dim. Big Bow held a torch so I could better see the parchment. Some of the men gathered around, looking over my shoulder, while others remained on their benches and listened to hear what I had to say.

The parchment was beautifully written, the work of a scribe, with large, flowery letters, so ornate that they were hard to make out. At the top of the page, the words "Pardon of the Crime" appeared in big letters. Within the body of the document my father's name, Coya, appeared seven times. Once he was referred to by his formal name, Coya Ayacouta Utina.

Big Bow, whose understanding of Spanish is imperfect, believed that the parchment announced the death of my father, and that the Spaniards felt bad about it, and were seeking forgiveness.

The second document, the letter, was from a priest named Fr. Medina, and when I looked at it, the meaning and nature of the formal document became clear. They have a new Spanish governor, Medina wrote, and he had decided that the imprisonment of my father by the former governor was illegal and stood to be corrected .The new governor was pardoning Coya of his crimes as a gesture of good will for the new year. The priest was asking that we come to San Augustín to collect my father and carry him home.

When I stood before my elders and told them what I thought, a loud argument broke out. One man said it was a clumsy trap set by the governor to lure us back, so we could be punished for going home without permission. After all, soldiers had twice before rounded up the people of Oconee and taken them away. If we returned to the presidio voluntarily, it would save them the trouble.

They did not ask me what I thought on the matter, but I spoke up anyway. I said I did not believe a Franciscan friar would write a letter to help a lying governor fool the people of Oconee. That gave the men something to think about, and their voices became quieter, and softer.

When Big Bow said he was going to San Augustín, only two men volunteered to go with him. Big Bow is only head man of the village, and not respected as a chief. He could not order men to accompany him against their will. Because I could speak Spanish better than anyone else and since it was my father we were collecting, Big Bow said that I would also go to San Augustín.

Let me say that I was honored to be treated as a man, and no longer a child. My brother, Carlos, was too young to go, and would stay at Oconee with the women.

When I begin to write again, I will remember to tell what happened in San Augustín.

———————

It is a five day journey from Oconee to the river crossing at Tocoi, and over very rough territory with ravines and thick woods. There are no trails to speak of. Four years ago, when we fled San Augustín, we stopped to rest in the village of Chichiro. This time we planned to stop there again to sleep.

The two men with us are hunters, and they moved through the woods as quickly and quietly as Big Bow. For me, with my short legs, it was a struggle to keep up.

There was a wooden Spanish sign nailed to a tree, warning of sickness and death ahead in Chichiro. It was still daylight, and as we came close, we could see no people at all in the village, and although it was a very cold day and the sun was setting, there were no camp fires. We circled around Chichiro, crossed to the other side of a creek, and went on our way.

We crossed the river at Tocoi, paying for our canoe passage with squirrel skins the hunters had collected along the way. The heavy woods between the river and the town had lost some of its trees in the four years since I was last in San Augustín.

The priest's letter told us to come to the monastery when we reached San Augustín. Big Bow and I went inside, through the heavy, wooden double doors. The men with us feared it was a trap, and remained outside.

The monastery was very large – not as big as a council house or a church, but bigger than a regular house, or even a convento. It had furniture, such as chairs to sit on, and tables with fine saucers for eating. I also saw pictures on every wall, and statues of the saints. The floors were made of polished wood planks. I have never seen such a beautiful place.

Fr. Medina greeted us warmly. He said that he wanted to talk to us before we saw Coya. We sat at a table, on wooden chairs. I had sat on many benches in my life, but I felt like a king sitting up so high my toes could barely touch the floor.

When he spoke, the priest looked at both of us, instead of looking only at Big Bow and ignoring me. He said that my father had not been well, that his health had suffered in his captivity. He said that Coya had lost his sight. The priest spoke so quickly, I did not fully understand his meaning.

Fr. Medina talked of other things: the wickedness of the old governor, and what a blessing it was now that

Governor Alonso de Aranguiz had proved to be a just man and was making things right. To tell the truth, I do not remember much of what he had to say after he said my father was ill and blind. I will ask Big Bow what he remembers and write more about it some other time.

The priest took us into a room with white walls, where there was a bed, and an old man lying on it. It was my father Coya, but not as I remembered him. His eyes were covered with a white glaze that looked like scum that sometimes covers the still water of a pond in the summer.

He was thin as a reed, and frail. Fr. Medina touched his arm and said that his family had come to take him home. Coya turned his head toward us, as if he could see. He reached out his hand, his fingers no thicker than twigs of a sweet gum tree. I held back, afraid to touch him. Big Bow stepped forward and took Father's hand, kneeled down, and kissed him on the head.

"We have come to get you, *Nariba*," Big Bow said, using the term of ultimate respect. Tears ran down Coya's face. When he smiled, I saw that he had no teeth in his mouth.

"I have brought your son," Big Bow said. Then he reached back, grasped my tunic, and pulled me down beside him next to the bed.

My father looked puzzled. He pulled his hand away from Big Bow's grasp. "But Lucas is dead," Coya said. "My son is dead, murdered by the Spanish."

————

It took eight days to carry my father home to Oconee. He could not walk more than 100 meters without losing his strength, and was so frail that Big Bow feared he would fall and break his bones. We carried him on a litter, with each of us holding one corner. For a young man not yet 12 years old, and not having my full growth, it was a struggle. I did not complain.

When we were half a league from home, we stopped to rest and to bathe in a stream. We dressed Coya in a deerskin match coat, and fixed his hair high on his head with holly and mistletoe. He looked fine for his homecoming.

Coya said he would walk the rest of the way to Oconee. He felt his way along with a carved maple walking stick, a gift from the priest at San Augustín. Big Bow was on one side of him, and I was on the other to make sure he did not stumble over a root, or walk into a tree.

The people of Oconee knew we were coming. We keep lookouts at a distance from the village, and runners to spread the news when visitors approach.

The whole village was there to greet him, rushing forward to touch him and kiss his feet. His blindness was obvious, and they were gentle so as not to knock him down. The high pitched chattering of the women's greetings, and the deep-chested harumps of the men, echoed through the village and the surrounding forest.

For the rest of the day, Coya sat under a tree sipping cassina and accepting the gifts that were offered. He could not see, but he recognized every voice, and it became an entertaining game. He would listen, and then say who it was who had spoken. He knew even the older children by the sound of their voices.

As the sun was setting, Coya looked around as if he could see, and asked, "Where is Carlos, my youngest son?"

I went looking for him and found my brother in the forest. He had not been at home to greet our father, and seemed not to care about his return. He had killed three squirrels with his bow and arrow, and was stalking a fourth. He would not come with me until I threatened to break his bow.

Then Carlos ran back to the village to see our father. I picked up the dead squirrels he had left behind, and carried them with me. I skinned them and gutted them and gave them to the cook to add to the dinner pot.

There was a banquet, and the dancing and celebration went on until the sun came up again. Father slept through most of it.

———————

Big Bow gave up his house to Coya, and built another for himself.

I live with my father, along with my younger brother, although Carlos prefers to spend his time wandering through the woods with other children, playing war games, rather than tending to the needs of his father.

Coya has recovered his strength and his health has improved. The women of the village feed us well. We have a medicine man, an *isucu*, who has herbal cures for whatever ails Coya. I pray to God each day and give thanks that my father's health is restored. The medicine man has no cure for blindness. He says the old prayers, and although they would be condemned by a priest as the words of the Devil, we have no priest here, so we allow it.

The friar in San Augustín gave us a collection of paper and even a few pieces of fine parchment upon which Coya had written during the early days of his imprisonment. He also gave us a bottle of Spanish ink, enough quills to feather a turkey, and a stack of Spanish writing paper. He intended that Coya continue his writing upon his return home.

I looked at the old papers. They were well written, but the more recent ones were harder to read, owing to the sickness that was robbing father of his sight. I offered to be my father's eyes and hand, to write down the words he told to me. I am young and my hand is steady.

Father had another idea. He said that I should use the paper and ink to practice my letters, to write them down over and over again until they become beautiful. Since the mission in Oconee is closed, I have no other way of practicing the penmanship that I was taught as a child by the friars here and in San Augustín.

I did what my father said. Each day I practiced writing the alphabet. I studied how the scribe had formed the letters of the governor's pardon, and how the priest had written the letter in a less formal hand. I tried to master both techniques of writing. I used each side of the paper so I would not run out.

Finally, I told Father that I was bored just writing the letters, and that I thought they were just as good as any Spanish scribe could write. Of course, Father could not see them, and no one else could read. So he accepted my judgment.

He said that it was time for me to start writing whole words and sentences, and expressing myself like an educated person. He gave me permission to write down the story of his homecoming from San Augustín, and that is what I have done.

Chapter 5

*T*oday, I read to my father all that I have written. Big Bow was with us, and said he had nothing to add to what I remembered about what the friar said concerning Father's health.

We sat at the edge of the forest late in the day, and while I read the papers, we watched the birds flying through the trees with nesting material in their beaks. Father could not see them, but he could identify the birds by the flutter of their wings.

Father seemed pleased with my writing. He did say I got something wrong. He said he had not cried when we came to get him at the monastery, but that his eyes sometimes shed tears because of his sickness and not because of strong feelings. Sometimes what you write can be embarrassing to others.

I have read what Coya wrote while he was in the prison cell with a window. I asked him to tell me about the years he spent in darkness with the rats. He will not answer my questions. The only thing he will talk about is the death of Lucas, and how he heard the news from a shaman in the next cell.

He learned of Governor de Rebolledo's death much later, when the priest came to take him from his prison cell to the convento.

By now it was growing dark, and Big Bow and I wanted to go home because the mosquitoes had found us. It is always dark for Father, and he had more to say.

"That was the most disturbing news since the death of my son," he said. Father's hands shook and his voice grew louder. "I stayed alive in that rat hole so I could live long enough to avenge Lucas and kill de Rebolledo, myself."

Big Bow tried to change the subject, but Father went on. "With God as my witness, I will follow him to the gates of Hell."

Later, Big Bow said to me that it is too upsetting to Father to ask him to talk about the past.

———

I returned today from Misión Santa Fé de Toloca, two days to the south. The friar there is Pedro Mendoza de Palma. He was the first priest we had at Santiago de Oconee. He is also my godfather who gave me the name Mendoza. Of course my first name, Juan, honors my father who was baptized Juan de Coya.

Fr. Mendoza first came to Laguna Oconee soon after Coya gave up the chiefdom at Ayacouta and moved here. It was Father who convinced the Custos of Missions that Oconee deserved a friar. Even though he was no longer a great *Holata*, Coya was respected by the priests in San Augustín.

Fr. Mendoza married my father and mother. He also educated me, teaching me to read and write in Spanish as well as the Timucuan tongue. He was also the priest who catechized and baptized me into the faith.

There was another priest, Carlos Lopez Anguinano, who came to help Fr. Mendoza, but he was sick. The custos had sent us a dying priest whose chest rattled when he breathed. He was so weak he only conducted Mass on Sunday, and sometimes taught the children. All the rest of the work, the traveling about to the six other towns, fell to Fr. Mendoza.

Fr. Lopez was there during the terrible time of my mother's death, when she gave birth to my brother. The birthing woman made a mistake. I was not there, of course, but heard from others that the birth cord was wrapped around Carlos's neck and his face was blue when he was born.

He lived, but my mother did not. Coya, being Christian, would not allow a *jarva* to attend the birth. Fr. Lopez was there. He heard mother's confession while she bled to death, and he gave her the last rights.

Two days later, Fr. Lopez died in his own bed. Coya named my brother Carlos to honor the memory of the sickly priest.

———

Again, I have made a mistake with my writing by allowing my thoughts to drift into sadness and painful memories. I meant only to explain why I went to the mission at Santa Fé.

Medicine men have always known how to make inks of different colors, using wood beetles, plants, flowers, and berries. Inks are used for tattoos for chiefs and warriors, but it works as well on paper and parchment. I believe it is better than Spanish ink in holding its color over a long time. The *isucu* of Oconee taught me to make ink, so we never run out of it.

There are turkeys enough to keep us in quills forever. The only thing we lack is paper. We had neither paper nor parchment to write on. I had used it all. Coya sent me to Santa Fé, where Fr. Mendoza has writing paper for the children who are taught at the convento.

The friar was happy to see me, and invited me to eat with him at the convento. We sat outside at a small table while the cook's children served us boiled corn and hickory nut cakes. Fr. Mendoza knew of Coya's imprisonment and of his release. He did not know of Father's blindness. He promised to burn a candle at Mass and say a special prayer for his improvement.

Fr. Mendoza was pleased that I was writing, and he made me show him my talent by writing a few words on paper. He said that some day I could move to Misión Santa Fé de Toloca and help him teach the children.

The priest stopped smiling when I told him the reason for my visit – that I had come looking for paper or parchment. He went to his room and returned with six sheets of paper for me to take to Oconee. I handed him a silver chain from my father, one he had received as a gift from the governor when he was an important *Holata*. When he saw the gift, the friar went and found 12 more pieces of paper for me to take. Paper is dear to the Spaniards, but things made of gold or silver are valued even more. To them, that which is decorative is better than that which is useful. It is a strange way of thinking.

I forgot to say that Fr. Mendoza was at Misión Santiago de Oconee in 1655, the day the soldiers came to arrest my father and to take the people to San Augustín. The priest distracted the soldiers, arguing with them while many people slipped away into the woods and escaped. But it did no good. The soldiers had an order from the governor. Fr. Mendoza went from Oconee to Santa Fé de Toloca, and has been the priest there ever since.

When Coya returned from prison to Oconee, he told the village council that we do not need a priest. "They are good to have, to teach us the Gospel," he said, "but they attract soldiers."

———————

It has been half a year since my father came home. His eyes are no better. He says he can tell light from dark, but nothing else. I sometimes close my eyes and imagine how it must be for him. With my eyes shut tight, if I face the sun I see its brightness, and when I look away it gets darker.

His health seems better, although he is still thin and frail. He can move about outside with his walking stick, but stays most of the time in the house and does not even go to the council house in the morning to drink cassina with the men. Sometimes he sits outside under a tree with the sunlight warming his face.

Coya talks very little and is sometimes rude to old friends who come to see him. He was by himself for so long in the prison, I believe he has learned to be comfortable alone. Big Bow says to him that he should visit with the others more, but Coya is not interested.

I notice also that Big Bow is getting older. He was once a very big man, taller even than Coya. Now he is hunched over, and he carries one shoulder higher than the other. When he walks, he moves sideways, like a crab. He is not embarrassed by his looks, and sometimes makes fun of himself.

When he was in Ayacouta as my father's *paracousi*, he worked with the other men, carrying bundles to San Augustín, more than 30 leagues away. Each man was ordered to carry three arrobas of corn on his back. If someone was injured or sick, Big Bow would carry part of his load, also. One day, a tree he was cutting down fell on him and broke his back, and even after he learned to walk again, he could not stand straight.

———————

We have a storyteller, a widow who came here from another village while Coya was still in prison. She entertains the children during the day while their parents are working or hunting or fishing. Her name is Mara, which is the same name as Coya's first wife, the mother of my brother, Lucas.

I should say that Mara is a pagan. When Coya learned that the village storyteller had not been saved, he was unhappy. "If we had a priest, he would never allow this to happen," he said. "She should be telling stories from the Bible, not stories invented by the Devil."

Coya tried to catechize her, but she was not interested. "I have my stories. I do not need your God" she said. From that day, Coya has tolerated Mara, but he does not respect her.

Mara sits under a maple tree four meters from our house, telling the Story of Bread, the Story of the Eagle and the Bear, and all the other stories that were taught to the children before the priests came. Sometimes there are only two or three children, and other times close to twenty will be there, sitting on her lap or laying around in a circle.She is an entertaining performer and has the talent to mimic the animals. She has one voice for the raccoon, and another for the eagle, and a different one for the fox.

Mara can also change her face to look like the animal in the story. She puts charcoal circles around her eyes when she is a raccoon, and she widens her eyes and turns her head all the way around when she is an owl. Her best animal is the rabbit. She wiggles her nose up and down and hops around in a circle. Even the adults in the village come to see her perform.

My favorite story is the one about Thunderbird, and how he flies out of his cave and high into the air. The beat of his wings is thunder, and his eyes flash with lightning, frightening the towering clouds and making them cry. For such a small woman, Mara's voice sounds like the rumble of thunder. She told it one day in the summer just as a storm was building, and the children were so afraid they ran home screaming.

My father has told me that in his childhood, an elder would listen to the stories and correct any mistakes the storyteller might make in the telling. Nowadays, the stories are just entertainments for the children, like the ghost stories the men tell around the campfire on dark nights, but Coya listens from inside our house. He moves his seat close to the door, where he can hear more clearly. I see him nodding his head up and down, or wagging it in disagreement.

One day he was sitting under the storyteller's tree when she came. He did not interrupt her, but waited until she told the last of the three stories she had to tell.

"That was an ancient story, and very well told," he said.

The storyteller thanked him for the compliment. The children stood up, and were ready to return to their play.

"Would you like to hear another story, one that is not ancient, but just as exciting?" he asked. One by one, the children sat down again. The storyteller leaned forward to listen.

My father told a story of two brothers. One was a medicine man, an *isucu.* He was also a Christian. The other was a warrior of great strength and courage, but a pagan. Their life quest was to save the Timucua from evil people who would enslave them. One he called Marehootie. The other was Crying Bird. The younger children did not understand and became restless.

Two days later, Coya was there to follow the storyteller's performance with his own story. He told another story about the same two brothers. This time, only one or two older children stayed to listen.

When the storyteller returned the next time, there were more of the older children than the young ones. When the storyteller was finished with her tales, my father began to speak. All of the older children stayed. Even my brother, Carlos, was nearby, listening, pretending to be busy carving an antler into a knife handle.

The next day, Carlos sat directly in front of our father as he told a large group of people of the great heroism of Crying Bird when he killed three criminals who ambushed him in a forest of oak trees.

Before our father was finished, Carlos interrupted him. "Was he *Noroco*?" he asked.

Coya dropped his chin to his chest in thought. "If you are asking if he killed enough men to join the highest rank in the warrior class, I would say yes. He was *Noroco* many times over. But he was no murderer. He never killed a woman, a child, a priest, or an innocent person, only those who threatened his people and those who deserved to die."

Carlos was excited, and he pressed on with his questions. "Did he kill Spaniards?"

Coya felt for his walking stick, and rose unsteadily to his feet. "Enough storytelling for today," he said. Then he made his way to our house, and disappeared inside.

I know who Coya is talking about when he tells the stories of Marehootie and Crying Bird. I have heard those stories from my uncle, Big Bow. Coya is talking about his grandfathers, not mere legends. They were the men who taught Coya to be *Holata Aco* of Utina, the most powerful Indian in the world.

Chapter 6

I have no time to write anymore. I spend my days chasing after Carlos, trying to persuade him to sit down and learn what I have to teach about reading and writing.

It would be better if this were a mission and not a village of mixed Christian Indians and pagans, and if I were a friar and not a mere slave to my father's wishes. When a mission Indian child runs from the priest, he will be whipped.

But that is not our way, Coya says. "You must be gentle with your persuasions. A leader knows how to make his followers want to do the right thing. Attract the bees with the sweetness of flowers, not the stink of rotten fruit."

Sometimes I want to say to my father that because he was a great chief he should use his powers to attract Carlos to his lessons. But that would be disrespectful. It is better to write it down than to say it out loud.

Every day it is the same, but getting worse. Carlos wakes up early and is gone by the time I come outside. He no longer goes into the hunting woods where I can find him and make him come home with me. He has found better places to hide, like in the high branches of a tree, or a cave along the creek bed, and it takes me half a day to find him.

Sometimes he would listen and pretend to work hard on his lessons. We could study only inside the house, because if he was outside he would be distracted by the other children, by a passing dog, or the flight of a bird. I would point to a letter and sound it out for him, and then form the letters into short words.

Finally, after many months, I would challenge him to read short sentences by moving my finger along the line on a page from the breviary, or from a Spanish letter, and reading what was there and then asking him to read the same sentence.

One day he read for me. I was surprised at how well he did, and I took him to Father so he could hear him read his first words and be proud. When Coya asked Carlos to read from another page, he could not get even one word right. Carlos had memorized the words on the first page and pretended to be reading.

Instead of Carlos receiving the scolding, I was the one who felt the lash of my father's tongue. "You have a student who is bright enough to memorize everything you read to him," he said. "You are a poor teacher if you cannot teach him to read."

Carlos sat nearby. He was smiling.

A few days later, Carlos seemed to be doing well with his reading, and asked me to take him to Father so he could listen. I have enough coyote blood to smell a trap. My brother has a mean streak in his character.

———————

If Carlos was difficult at first, he is now impossible to teach. Big Bow tried to help me teach him, putting his hand on Carlos's shoulder to help him concentrate. Father listens sometimes, but nothing seems to work.

Three days ago, I went looking for Carlos and couldn't find him anywhere. He did not come home, even when it became dark. Coya was upset and worried. He blamed me, saying I had been too harsh with my brother. Big Bow defended me by insisting that it was Carlos who was the problem and not me, and that if a child of 11 would not learn, there was no teacher ever born who could teach him.

In the morning, he still had not come home. Coya went to the meeting in the council house and told the bad news. Big Bow organized a search. He sent everyone in different directions and told them to go as far as they could, but to turn around in the middle of the day and take a different route home. If Carlos returned on his own or was found, a conch shell would be sounded to let everyone know.

The best hunters went into the thickest woods, and the fishermen divided up and went to the two lakes to the east and south of Oconee, in case Carlos went swimming and drowned.

Big Bow told me to go west to the edge of the swamp, and to follow it to the north. Another boy was told to go with me, but turn south at the swamp. Big Bow said that we should watch for tracks and for beaten down grass to see if Carlos had come that way. "Do not go any farther into the swamp than you can see out," he said. "If you do not find him before you reach Cedar Creek, turn around and come home."

It was I who found Carlos. When I reached the swamp, the mosquitoes made a banquet of my blood. I had a salve of wax myrtle leaves and bear grease, and rubbed it on my body, but these mosquitoes liked the taste. They left me alone only after the sun climbed high, but by then the day had turned very hot, and I felt dizzy from the heat.

I was about to turn around and go home, or at least find a shady place to rest, when a tall man stepped from behind a palmetto bush. He had a spear with a dangerous spike on the end, one like people use to hunt frogs or small alligators. He pointed it at me. I was too frightened to run. I thought he might chase after me and stick me with his spear.

He directed me at spear point to where Cedar Creek runs into the swamp. We walked into a camp with 10 or more dirty, rough looking *cimarrones*. They had with them one woman. She looked meaner than the men. Their leader demanded to know why I was spying on them. I said I was searching for my lost brother, but they did not believe me. They looked in my packet to see if I carried anything they wanted for themselves. They took the dried venison I carried for my meal.

A boy walked into the camp, carrying drinking water from the creek. He was just as filthy as they were and reminded me of a camp dog, slinking around, getting in nobody's way. When he came close to me, I saw that he was Carlos, my brother.

Carlos was no friendlier to me than the *cimarrones*. He cursed me for coming to look for him and said he would beat me if I ever did that again. The men all laughed at that, and wanted to see us fight. Carlos is a head shorter then me, and not nearly as strong.

"I would not bruise my hands on this coward. It is enough of a disgrace to him that he fears me so," Carlos said. He flipped the back of his hand against my nose, making my eyes water, and then he told the others that I was crying like a woman.

When we would not fight for their entertainment, the *cimarrones* ordered us to leave. They said that if they ever saw my face again, they would kill me, but they told Carlos to come back any time.

It was late in the day when we got home. Father embraced Carlos and held him close for a long time. He had nothing to say to me.

I took Big Bow for a walk in the woods and told him about the *cimarrones*. At daylight he sent a dozen armed men to the creek to chase them out of the territory.

"Those are evil people who belong to no village and no clan," he said to the men before they set out. "They move around looking for people to rob. There was a man who farms corn two leagues to the north. He was murdered last year, and no one knows why. These may be the people who did the crime."

The men of Oconee returned. They had found no *cimarrones* on the creek, nor any sign of a camp.

"They are good at covering their tracks," Big Bow said.

———————

A letter came to Oconee today, carried by a trader who traveled from the Misión Santa Fé de Toloca. It was addressed to Coya and was written by the friar, Fr. Mendoza.

Before I speak of the letter, I need to write down some startling news that the trader had to tell.

He said that English pirates came ashore at San Augustín and attacked the town at midnight, when only the guards at the fort were awake. The governor and the other Spaniards were chased from their beds, and ran to the fort or fled into the woods to get away.

Nobody knows how many pirates there were, but there must have been many of them. The soldiers came out to fight, but by morning there were so many pirates in the town they went back into the fort and bolted the door shut. The pirates plundered the houses, the church, and the government offices. They hauled away as much as they could carry from the storehouse.

The worst part was that at least 20 Indians were taken away, and some blacks and half breeds. The trader says they were probably taken to Charles Town where the English have a slave market.

Big Bow said that it was not all bad news. "It proves how weak the Spaniards are, to run away and hide from a boatload of Englishmen."

———————

Much has happened since the letter from Fr. Mendoza arrived with the trader, and today I am writing in a new place. It was a long letter, from one old friend to another. It had no bad news at all, no demands of any kind, which is unusual. Fr. Mendoza blessed Coya and said he prayed daily that God would restore his sight, and that the people of Oconee were constantly in his thoughts and prayers. He said that things were going well at Misión Santa Fé, and that it had been five years since the pestilence had come to kill the people.

Then he got to the reason for the letter. I will write down the friars exact words.

"I have need of someone with Juan's talents to teach the children of Santa Fé to read and write in Timucuan and in Spanish. I have seen Juan's writing, and it is good as any scribe the governor ever had. Children love him, and his patience will make him a wonderful blessing to me."

Further down in the letter, Fr. Mendoza said that Chief Antonio of Toloca raises horses for the Menéndez-Márquez family, and that he needed a boy to help with the animals.

"I know your first son Lucas was a caballero when he was a boy, and I wondered if you wanted the same thing for Juan."

Before he signed his name at the end, Fr. Mendoza said this: "I have no way of paying for Juan to come here to teach. Chief Antonio is paid two reales a week for each caballero he hires. The chief knows Juan, and speaks highly of you and your family. He will send the money to you, if Juan will come and herd horses for him in addition to teaching at the convento."

My father had me write his answer to the priest. He agreed to the terms, so long as I was fed and clothed and had a place to sleep, without expense to him. He also said that I must be allowed to return to Oconee every three months for ten days, to attend to my duties here, and to carry the reales home.

Coya signed his answer, and the next morning I set out for Santa Fé. Before I left, my father kissed me on the cheek, and his eyes leaked a little. He said that I should not mention to Fr. Mendoza my failure to teach my own brother to read and write.

Big Bow was also upset to see me go. He seemed more stooped over than usual. I did not say goodbye to my brother. Carlos did not come home the night before, and did not know or care that I was leaving.

Chapter 7

Rancho de Santa Fé
July 13, 1671

I have neglected my writing for three years, here at Santa Fé, and Coya always asks me to read to him when I go home to Laguna Oconee. My duties at the mission are so demanding of my time that I have a good excuse not to write, but father says that, apparently, I am not working that hard here at the ranch, and he is right.

Fr. Mendoza warned me that my boss at the ranch would be a problem for me. Valdez is a soldier, but he was so disruptive at the presidio that the sergeant major sent him out here to where he would be out of his sight. His job is to manage the horses and, when they are trained, to provide them to the ranches owned by the Menéndez and Florencia families in Timucua and Apalachee. Valdez is a fair hand as a caballero, but he is a drunk.

If the sergeant major believed that moving Valdez away from San Augustín would deprive him of strong drink, he underestimated Valdez's devotion to Cuban rum. Whenever he delivers a horse to the farm at Asile, he always returns drunk and belligerent. On those trips, he gets rum from Cuban traders who travel up the San Martín River near Asile.

Valdez has me deliver horses that are going to La Chua. That may be because there are no Cubans at La Chua Hacienda.

We presently have eight breeding mares, four bays and four sorrels. There is one stallion, a black horse with a blaze on its head. Valdez named him Cimarron because he is so wild and disagreeable. The horse no longer tries to bite or kick at me, but he hates the Spaniard. When I say to Valdez that he should be gentler with the animal, he ignores me. Neither of us has ridden on Cimarron.

When I am at the mission for two weeks of the month I live in the convento in a storage room where I make my bed. I take my meals in the kitchen. Fr. Mendoza uses me to assist him at Mass, and has trained me in the preparation of the Lord's Table. When he travels to the visitas in the four surrounding villages, he puts me in charge of both the church and the convento. I hold the keys until he returns.

Most of my time at the mission is spent with the 11 children who are in my charge. I get up early in the morning to supervise them in sweeping the grounds, weeding the friar's garden, and running errands for the cooks. Fr. Mendoza does not allow the children inside the church unless he is present. He says that they break things on the altar if left unattended, but I think he is more concerned that they might be tempted by the Devil to steal.

In the afternoon, I teach the children to read and write in Spanish. We usually work in the convento where there is a room for us. Sometimes, when it is pleasant outside, we sit under a tree for our studies.

Late in the day I teach the older people at the council house to read and write in Timucuan. Most of them are as smart as the children and proud that they can write letters to relatives and friends who live in other places.

Fr. Mendoza read me a letter from the Custos of Missions in San Augustín, praising me for my success in teaching the adults. The custos suggested that it might be more useful to teach them Spanish in the future, instead of Timucuan. In my opinion the people do not seem as enthusiastic as they were in the beginning.

———————

I should write more about the horses and how we train them. My father has done many things in his life, but riding a horse is not one of them. I ride almost every day. We keep two mares in the corral, just outside the hut in which Valdez and I sleep. We use them to ride around the ranch to make sure none of the other horses have wandered away and gotten lost in the forest or stuck in the mud in the swamp.

I sometimes carry a shotgun in case I find signs of predators that might be stalking the mares. Last month, after we lost a colt, Valdez and I hunted down a pack of wolves. We killed their leader, and the others scattered and have not come back. Bears frighten the horses, but otherwise do no harm, so we leave them alone unless we want to eat bear meat.

Valdez prefers the taste of deer, and there is a plentiful supply. Early in the morning and just before dark they feed in the open among the horses. They like to graze the pasture grasses that grow here year round. When we hunt the deer, Valdez has me use my bow instead of the gun. The arrow is silent, and does not spook the horses.

The abundance of grass was the reason the Chief of Santa Fé chose this place for the ranch. Our hut sits on a hill. We look out at the pasture below and can usually see all of the horses from here. There are lots of oak trees, and the horses use them for shade during the summer. Beyond the pasture are a deep swamp and a spring-fed creek that flows from it. To either side, the forest is thick and presses in against the grasslands. The horses have everything they need here and no reason to wander off unless they are frightened. It is a perfect place for a ranch. Most of the time, our job is an easy one.

Valdez does most of the training of the young horses. Seven were born this spring and summer. I said that Valdez is rough in his treatment of the black stallion, but when he is sober he is good with the young ones. He talks to them softly and moves slowly to keep them calm.

It takes two years to train a horse for a saddle and a rider. First we teach the horse to accept the bit in its mouth. It takes both of us to put on the saddle.

I remember how excited I was and how hard my heart was beating the first time Valdez jumped onto the back of a horse to break it of its spirit. The horse bucked him off, but Valdez got up and chased it around the corral and got back on.

Sometimes it takes three or four days to break a horse, but usually it takes only one day. I have broken three horses by myself, without being hurt.

This morning I smelled rum on Valdez, but he is outside now working with the black. He just called me to come out and help him. I will try to write more when I am done.

Misión Santa Fé de Toloca
July 15, 1671

Luckily it was my left arm and not my head that struck the top railing of the corral. I won't be climbing on Cimarron's back again any time soon.

Valdez said I should ride one of the mares to the mission, but I couldn't figure a way to get on its back with a broken arm. I walked to Santa Fé. When I told Fr. Mendoza what had happened, he suggested that, in the future, I should ignore orders Valdez gives me while he is drinking. The priest bound the broken bone with wooden staves from an old bucket and made me a sling out of an old sheet. He said that if I keep my arm in this sling for a month or two, it should heal straight and be as good as new.

I am of no use at the ranch until I heal, and Fr. Mendoza says I should go home to Oconee to see my father. "Your father is getting old," he said. "You should see him any time you can." I will go visit my father for two weeks, then return to the mission. When I am fully healed, I will go back to the ranch.

Fr. Mendoza saw the papers I carried from the ranch, the ones I had recently written and was taking to my father. I told him there was nothing important in them, but he asked if he could read them anyway.

"This is well written," he said when he had finished, "and your thoughts are organized as well as those of an educated man." I thanked him for his kind words, and, as you can see, I wrote them down also.

I will leave Santa Fé in the morning and take only the trails easy enough for a one-armed man to travel. The priest warned me to watch for *cimarrones*. I think he was making a joke, to remind me of the horse that broke my arm. There are no real *cimarrones* in these parts, as far as I know.

Chapter 8

There are many ways to go north from Misión Santa
Fé de Toloca. Usually I take old paths and game
trails that lead through ravines and swamps, but make it a
shorter journey. With a broken arm, I went the long way
home on trails that zigzag from village to village.

I made good time until I reached the river that runs
red with clay. From there on, there is no easy way to go.
The creeks cut deep into the earth, and the swamps, with
their water moccasins and hungry alligators, are
dangerous to wade. That may be why Oconee does not
attract a lot of people. It took me four days to get home,
two days longer than usual.

It was springtime when I was last in Oconee, and I
can see that things have changed. There are fewer people
here now. Big Bow said some of them have gone to
Charles Town, a settlement of English traders to the
northeast. Some of the houses have fallen into disrepair,
and there is not as much laughter in the village as I
remembered.

But it is my father who worries me most. His age
shows on his face, and his cheeks are sunken in because

he has no teeth. He no longer pins his hair up on his head and decorates it with feathers or flowers. It has turned white, and hangs limp to his shoulders, like a woman's.

Mara was tending to him when I came close. They were sitting under the storytelling tree, and she was combing the tangles from his hair. When I spoke, Coya said nothing, but cocked his head, bewildered.

"I am Juan," I said.

"Have you seen Carlos?" he asked.

Big Bow came out of the house and welcomed me. We walked to the creek where we could speak privately. He had no good news to tell me. I am tired now and need to rest.

———————

I slept through the night in my father's house. Big Bow was there, and also Mara who lives with them now. It was crowded with so many people, but I slept soundly until late in the morning.

Big Bow told me yesterday that Coya is losing his mind and is preparing himself for the next world. Coya has dreams of my dead brother Lucas and says that he has visited with him, and that Lucas has finally found peace in the Village of the Dead where he is again *Holata Aco*. There are no Spaniards there, Coya told Big Bow, only Timucuan warriors and their clansmen.

"Your father is bedeviled by ghosts who torment him by saying that your younger brother Carlos is in prison and is damned," Big Bow said to me as we walked by the creek. "Coya imagines Carlos in his old cell, with the darkness and the stink and the rats. Your father will not die in peace until Carlos comes home."

"Does he ever dream of me?" I said, and immediately felt bad for asking it.

Big Bow had an answer. "You are still part of this world, for him. There is no reason for him to worry about you, as he does Lucas and Carlos."

Today I sat with my father under the tree as the sun went down. Mara was there also, feeding him sips of broth and wiping his mouth when the soup dribbled between his lips. I read to Coya what I had written at the ranch and at the mission, about my life and about how I got the broken arm. Mara laughed at the story of the horse, but Father was not listening. I wondered if he had gone deaf as well as blind.

When I put the papers back in the leather case in which I carry them, Coya finally spoke. "I want someone to get Carlos out of that black hole and bring him to me."

———————

Big Bow went with me the next morning, looking for my brother. We walked to the north and to the east until we were far from Oconee, entering the land of the Yamassee. I wanted to go by myself, thinking Big Bow would slow me down, but he moved very well for an old, stoop-shouldered man. His legs are still long and powerful. He also knows the Yamassee country, and I do not.

Big Bow had his long bow and a quiver of arrows slung over his shoulder. I asked him if he was hunting buffalo. He told me why he was armed. There had been trouble from the Yamassee, and we were going to their territory. The *cimarron* band that Carlos had joined lived among the Yamassee, and there were reports from traders of raids on innocent Timucuan villages to the east, and of killings, and of women taken as slaves.

I carried a bow for hunting rabbits, birds, and other small game. It was comforting that Big Bow was so well armed.

We made our beds near a creek on the second night. This was hilly country, and mosquitoes were not a nuisance, because of a steady breeze from the south. We traveled light and made no fires. We carried dried venison to eat, and picked fruit and nuts we found along the way. The creek water was clean and sweet.

Big Bow shook me on my good shoulder to wake me in the middle of the night. It was dark with no moonlight, and the wind had moved to the east. "Smoke," Big Bow whispered, pointing to his nose.

We found the camp fire by following our noses. Big Bow is still agile enough to climb a tree. When he came down, he used his hands to talk, instead of his voice. There were about thirty men, and two of them were awake, standing guard. There were no houses. It was a camp of *cimarrones*.

The sun had risen and the men in the camp were fully awake. I walked into camp alone with a pleasant look on my face, holding my good arm up to show I carried no weapon. It is not wise to startle people out of their sleep. They looked at my left arm in the sling, and seemed satisfied that I was no threat.

Cassina was brewing on the fire, and the smell of it made me hungry, but they did not invite me to eat with them. Three men guarded me, one with a bow and the others with long knives. The rest went about their personal matters, washing the sleep from their faces and relieving themselves in the bushes.

I heard Yamassee spoken, and Timucuan. There was a white bearded man with them who spoke a language I had never heard, but I knew what he was. He was an Englishman, a trader, and the rest of them showed him great respect. They recognized me as Timucua from the way I was dressed.

A man interpreted for the Englishman, who wanted to know who I was, and where I came from, and whether I was alone. I answered the first two questions, saying that my name was Juan Mendoza, and that I came from Oconee in search of my brother.

The Englishman carried a shotgun with a short barrel. When he heard my answer, he struck my head with it, knocking me to the ground. I landed on my bad arm. Pain shot up it, through my shoulder and into my chest. My head was spinning, both from the pain in my arm and the blow from the gun barrel. When I tried to regain my feet, he stuck me again, this time in the face. I feel to my knees. Blood poured from my nose, and when I grabbed it, I knew it was broken.

At that moment, Big Bow stepped from behind a tree. He stood less than 20 meters away. His bow was poised and he was ready to unleash an arrow pointed directly at the chest of the white man.

I stayed on my knees, not sure of what to do next. The sun was not yet over the trees, and I already had blood running down my face. This was not starting out to be a good day.

Big Bow's right arm shook from the effort of holding the arrow cocked. The *cimarrones* had no ideas either, and for a moment we just looked at each other.

"I know these men," someone said. "They are who they say they are." A short but powerfully built man stepped forward. He had fierce markings on his face, and his lips were stained the color of blood. He wore eagle feathers in his hair. I had not seen him in two years, and would not have recognized him were it not for his voice. It was Carlos, my brother.

The Englishman said something in a loud voice, and his interpreter translated. "Who are they, Calesa?"

Carlos did not answer immediately. He stood there glaring at me with his eyes full of scorn. The white man was content to wait for his answer.

Fredric M. Hitt

"This one with the lame arm works for a priest at Santa Fé. He fancies himself a rider of horses. The old one is the head man of Oconee."

I looked at Big Bow. He did not even glance at Carlos, but stared directly at the chest of the white trader. I hoped that the arrow did not slip from his fingers and kill the Englishman, as long as there was a chance we could leave peacefully. I stood up.

"I am this man's brother," I said, "and this is his uncle. We come in peace to take him home to his dying father."

There was laughter among the ones who understood Timucuan. "You want to take home Calesa?" somebody shouted. They all laughed at that.

Carlos moved close to my face, but he was short, and the top of his head reached only my chin. He spoke loudly enough that everyone could hear. "I have no brother, I have no uncle, and I have no dying father." Carlos spit into my face and turned his back on me as if I were a coward who would accept any insult and not fight back.

Now that I think of it, I should have used my good arm to snap his neck. But I did nothing.

He spread his arms wide and waved them about. "This is my only family, and I am Calesa, their leader."

The Englishman walked away to the other side of the camp, carrying his gun with him. He must have had better things to do than waste his time on us.

Big Bow and I backed away slowly, together, with me looking behind for ambush. I retrieved my bow from behind a tree where I had left it. I pointed it at the *cimarrones*.

"Do not threaten them with that puny thing," Big Bow said. "You look foolish."

They let us escape without following. We could still hear their laughter. They had no respect for us. Nor did they think it was worth their time to kill us.

We stopped at the creek to wash the blood from my face and to make a poultice of moss and spider webs to stick up my nose to stop the bleeding.

"I have never heard the name Calesa," I said. It was the second day of our journey home. Neither of us spoke at all the day of the encounter at the *cimarron* camp. There was nothing to say. We had failed in our duty to bring Carlos home to see Coya.

"It is a bad word," said Big Bow, "not the sort of thing you would hear among civilized people. You know how the Spanish like to curse? How the soldiers have harsh words to insult each other? If we Timucua wanted to curse, we might say, 'calesa.'"

I thought about what Big Bow had said. "Why would he call himself something so terrible?"

We must have looked like an odd pair, Big Bow and me, one with a broken arm and the other with a strange gait. Big Bow thought for a long time before answering.

"I can think of two reasons. He considers himself so fearsome that only a curse works to describe him. Or, perhaps, that is the way he feels about himself, and he has no self-respect."

"Your first answer fits him best," I said. "He imagines himself a great warrior, a *Noroco.*"

"You will find no *Norocos* among that bunch, only murdering thieves," Big Bow said.

We walked a long way through some dry, hilly country before I said "What should we say to my father?"

"I've been wondering about that, myself," Big Bow answered. In awhile he spoke again. "Did you see a man who calls himself Carlos?" Big Bow asked. "If not, you must say that to your father. Do not tell him you saw an animal who calls himself Calesa and looks like your brother."

"Is it better that Father believes Carlos is in prison than running about the country killing innocent people?" I asked.

Big Bow did not bother to answer.

Chapter 9

Rancho de Santa Fé
May 13, 1672

Again I have neglected my writing. Since Father no longer listens, there is no one else who would be interested. Maybe I will write today to annoy the drunk. That's how I think of him now, as a drunk.

I should tell the story of what happened in March, when I returned from delivering a horse to the Menéndez people at La Chua. At the creek I unsaddled the horse I was riding and let it run free while I walked up the hill to our hut.

Valdez was near my bed with his back to me. He was looking though the papers I kept under the bed.

"What are you doing with those papers?" I asked.

He turned toward me. I could see the surprise on his face.

"I know what you're doing," he said. "I know how you spy on me and write lies about me."

I did not believe Valdez could read, and this proved it. There was nothing about him in the papers he held in his hand. They were what I wrote last, about my brother and the trip to Oconee.

I stepped into the hut and faced the Spaniard. He is a head shorter than me, but heavier. His eyes darted back and forth, as if he were looking for a way to escape.

"Read me what it says that offends you," I said.

Valdez looked back at the papers. His hands were shaking. I could smell the rum. "The penmanship is so poor, nobody could read this," he said.

I took the papers from him and pushed him away so I could put them with the others in the leather case. "Until you learn to read, you have no interest in my personal matters," I said.

When he saw that I had no desire to attack him, Valdez let go of his fear. "Perhaps I should spy on you and tell the chief how you neglect your work," he said as he retreated to his side of the room. I laughed, but said nothing back to him. Both of us know who it is who neglects his work.

August 27, 1672

Last night Valdez returned late from delivering a horse to the Asile farm. He should have been here two days ago, and his absence caused me to miss going to Mass on Sunday.

I heard him come in, but pretended to be asleep since he was trying hard to be quiet. He was drunk, as usual. There was a sloshing sound, and I heard him lay something heavy on his bed.

This morning he had a terrible story to tell me when he came out of the hut and joined me in the corral where I was walking a colicky horse.

After he left the new horse at Asile, he said, he was riding though a forest and was attacked by wolves, which killed the mare he rode. He escaped them and walked for two days to get home.

"There was nothing I could do to save the bay," he said, sadly.

I knew he was lying.

He asked me to write a report for him, and he would tell me what to say. Then he said I should take it with me tomorrow, when I go to Mass, and give it to the chief, so he could send it to the sergeant major at the presidio.

"That will explain the loss of the horse," he said, "and perhaps they will give me a medal for my heroism."

"Write it yourself," I said. "Today is Monday and not Saturday, and I doubt that the priest is preparing for a Tuesday Mass."

Valdez went to the creek later for his bath. After he has been drunk, his smell must be as offensive to him as it is to me. While he was gone I looked inside his trunk. There was a keg of rum in it.

I think I know the truth about what happened to the horse. He traded it to a Cuban for the rum. Then he walked for two days, carrying the keg. I thought about pouring it out, but decided that he might kill me in my sleep.

He is watching me as I write this. I am not afraid of him in the daylight, but I will not risk telling him what I think happened to the horse.

Misión Santa Fé de Toloca
November 4, 1672

I have time to write, now. Fr. Mendoza says it will do me good to unburden my heart, that it will help me heal my soul. He counseled me on my grief and heard my confession. I feel better now that my penance is done.

Where shall I start? It is painful to think back.

I had again been to La Chua to deliver two horses. Those were all we had that were trained, and it would be the last delivery until spring. A day after my return, while Valdez was sleeping in the middle of the day, I discovered a paper he had hidden away in a pot in which we keep sugar cubes for the horses.

It was from Fr. Mendoza of Santa Fé and was addressed to me. I stepped outside to read it in the light.

"Juan, there are reports of trouble at Laguna Oconee. A soldier is on his way to investigate. You should go home immediately. My prayers are for Coya and the others who live there. St. Christopher will protect you on your journey."

I folded the letter and put it in my shirt pocket, then went back into the hut. I shook Valdez, but he was so drunk he only moaned and rolled over. I would have written him a letter, but he cannot read. Instead I drew a map showing the direction I was going. Where the trail meets the river that runs red, I drew the picture of a tree with a horse tied to it. When he sobered up, he would understand.

As well as I get along with the stallion, he never lets me ride very far without scraping me off against a tree. I needed a horse under me that could cross some very difficult country and take me all the way to the river. It might have killed a mare. Cimarron understood how serious this was, and he allowed me to mount him without a saddle and to turn his head to the north.

We reached the river at full dark. The last hour, Cimarron was lame in his right front leg, but we slowed down and kept going. I tied him to the tree, waded across the river, and went on foot the rest of the way. A day later

I approached Oconee. Before I got there my nose picked up the smell of an old fire.

Nothing could have prepared me for the sight of the devastation. Oconee, the place I was born and where I spent my childhood, was destroyed. Every house, storage shed, and barbacoa had burned to the ground.

I found the corpses of my father and my uncle. They had died in the fire, in their house. To honor them I cut off my hair in the old fashion. I buried them where the old mission church had once stood, close to where I remembered the altar.

I prayed to God for Coya, using the words I had heard Fr. Mendoza speak at Christian funerals. I confessed later to the priest that I said a Timucuan prayer for Big Bow, as he would have wanted.

I sat for a day under the storyteller tree. There were 10 other dead people yet to be buried. The others had escaped or been carried away as slaves. A few Oconee people came out of the woods, and other people from another village came to help bury the dead.

Mara was with them, and she sat with me, shrieking and pulling at her hair. She loved my father and Big Bow also. She, too, had lost her family, and we held each other.

The next day she told me of the cowardly attack. It happened at nighttime, and the killers snuck around cutting peoples throats in their sleep. When the alarm was sounded, a man with a shotgun killed some people trying to flee into the woods.

The *cimarrones* took Mara, along with the younger women, and they went north. Mara is old and could not keep up, so they left her on the trail.

She said that the *cimarron* who carried the gun called himself Calesa. But she knew him. It was Carlos.

I asked Mara to come with me and find safety at the mission in Toloca, but she would not. She went with the other people, the ones who hid in the woods. She may be dead by now.

———————

Fr. Mendoza heard my confession in the church. He now knows the whole story about Calesa, and who he is, and what he did. He said that praying for the death of another, especially a brother, is a great sin.

"When you have wished it in your heart, you have done it in your soul." But he said that it was not so uncommon, and that he had heard of that sin before. He told me to fast for a day and say 50 Hail Marys as my penance.

The priest asked me if there was something else on my mind. He said I should confess it or carry it on my soul.

"I did not tell you the entire truth about how I broke my arm," I said. "I drank the soldier's rum and fell off the horse."

Whether it was the lie or the rum, something about my confession was more disturbing to the friar than praying for my brother's death. He ordered me to say 100 Hail Marys, and to fast for a second day.

Chapter 10

Rancho de Santa Fé
July 5, 1673

C imarron has done his duty with the mares, and the crop of new birthed horses has been abundant. I have six new foals and nine one- and two-year-olds in training.

My responsibilities give me little time to rest. I have not attended Mass in half a year, nor have I written a word in that time.

At least having Valdez here gave me some respite from the work: a day off to go to church once in awhile. Now that I am alone, I have no time to relax, and with all this breeding going on around me, I miss the company of the young women in Santa Fé. If for no other reason, I regret the Spaniard's death.

This reminds me, I want to write about how he died.

Upon my return to the ranch in February, at the end of the grieving time for my father, I found Valdez sitting on the ground in the corral, propped against a post. It was as if death were following me wherever I went.

His limbs were not yet stiff, so I knew it had just happened that morning. His head had bled and his nose was broken. The black stallion was there also, with a rope still tied around its neck. Valdez's whip was lying in the dirt. The horse's flanks were scarred by it and bloody. The stallion must have tired of the beating and kicked Valdez in the head.

I used the salve medicine to dress the horse's wounds and gave it an ear of corn I carried from the mission. Then I turned Cimarron out to the pasture, and he galloped away to find his wives.

I carried Valdez to the table behind the hut, the one we use to butcher deer, to save him from the ants and bugs on the ground. Already, flies were buzzing around, and I draped a blanket over him. Although the weather was chilly, I knew I would have to carry him to Santa Fé for burial soon.

When I went inside the hut, I found some of my papers torn and scattered about. Valdez had spilled rum on them, and the ink had blurred. I laid them out in the sun to dry and weighted them with rocks so they would not blow away. I carried the rum keg out into the woods and emptied what remained of its contents.

When morning came, Cimarron refused to let me tie Valdez on his back, and I respected his wishes. One of the mares was happy to give the Spaniard his last ride into Santa Fé. I did not stay for the funeral, but rode back before dark so the horses would have protection from the wolves.

Fr. Mendoza honored Valdez with burial in the first row under the church floor, nearest the altar. Valdez had no religion and had never been in that church in his life. But he was Spanish, and a soldier, so he was honored. Chief Pastrana, whose men built the church 40 years ago, lies in the second row, and the same row will be used for Chief Antonio's resting place when he is dead.

Chief Antonio of Toloca came to the ranch in June and brought his daughter's oldest boy with him. His grandson wants to learn the horse business, and will live with me. Being alone out here with so much responsibility, I can use the help.

The boy is only 12 years old, but in a few days I had enough confidence in him to go to town for the day and leave him to watch the horses. He is small to handle the shotgun, but his aim is good and the sound of the gun would scare off any predators.

I would not tell this to the chief, but his grandson is afraid of the stallion. He knows what happened to Valdez, and tries to win the horse's friendship with bits of sugar cane. Even the mares frightened him in the beginning. He wants to work with the foals, but he is useless as a caballero. When it comes time to break the two-year-olds, I will need a man's help.

Misión Santa Fé de Toloca
August 14, 1674

Three days ago, when it was very hot, the chief's grandson and I were sitting under a tree outside the hut, where there was a breeze to keep us cool. We saw two soldiers in the pasture. They were putting ropes around the necks of the mares and the horses we were training. They knew the foals would follow after their mothers. The horses were standing in the shade, and did not run away, but allowed themselves to be tied together. The black stallion stood at a distance, snorting and scraping the ground with his hooves.

The soldiers walked toward him, but Cimarron walked away, staying just out of range of their lassos. When they began to chase after him, it was comical to watch how easily he eluded them. The black was much more agile and swift than the Spaniards. He would lead them in one direction, then quickly move the other way, leaving them stumbling and cursing. Soon the men were red faced and out of breath, leaning over and holding their knees. They finally gave up and brought the other horses in a herd to where we waited.

"We are taking these horses to La Chua where they will be well cared for by a Spanish overseer," the older of the two said. He showed me his orders, signed by the sergeant major from the presidio. I had no choice but to let them go with the horses.

"Can you help us with the black?" he said.

The chief's grandson spoke. "That is a wild horse. Neither of us can control him." I will have to remember to praise the boy to his grandfather. He will make a wise chief when he gets a little older. The soldiers left without the stallion after I said I would try to catch him and deliver him to La Chua.

With no horses, there was nothing to keep us at the ranch. The boy and I walked to the mission the next morning. We carried our possessions, but they were so few we did not need a pack horse. The last night at the ranch we burned Valdez's clothing and his other personal possessions. I threw the rum keg in the fire and it burned a long time with a blue, hot flame.

Cimarron watched us leave but made no move to follow. The grass is good there, and the water is clean. He may hope a few mares come along some day, looking for a place to stay.

———— ——— ————

Misión Santa Fé de Toloca
January 22, 1675

There is very little for me to do here at the mission. There are fewer children being born that need to be taught, and nowadays we only teach Spanish writing, and not Timucuan. I tend the friar's garden, but he says I have no talent as a gardener, other than pulling weeds and scaring away the crows.

Maybe I could do more to help, but since I lost my job on the ranch I have no ambition. I am 26 years old, with no family and no plans for the future. There are three or four girls of marrying age in the village, but none of them interests me. Nor do I interest them, except for the daughter of the woman who sews clothes. She is a nice girl, but she does not smell as sweet as some women do.

Fr. Mendoza, probably because he is my godfather, allows me sleep at the convento. I eat with the other workers who help around the church. I hear them talking among themselves. They say I do not earn my keep.

I told the priest today that I need to go seek my family. My father, of course, is dead. So is my uncle. I never knew my older brother Lucas who was chief, and I try not to think about my younger brother who went bad.

I will go to Ayacouta where both Coya and Lucas were *Holata Aco* of Utina. Maybe there are people who still honor them and will accept me, or perhaps Lucas left children or nephews who can be my family. I feel like the thorny tree without roots, the one in the legend the storyteller tells. It was condemned to wander the earth with no place to stay.

———————

Chief Antonio sent his grandson to fetch me, and I went to his house. He said that he wished me well in looking for my family. While we talked, he sent his grandson on another errand. When we were alone, Antonio rummaged among his belongings and brought out a leather bag with a draw string. Before he opened it, this is what he said:

"Juan, you are a wealthy man. When your father died, there was nowhere to send your pay for tending to the horses. I have two years of pay that I saved for you, almost one hundred reales."

He spilled the coins on the rug between us. I had never seen so much money in one place.

"It would be dangerous for you to take it all, traveling alone. I do not know if you will need it unless you deal with Spaniards, but you should take some with you in case you get in trouble."

I thanked him and picked up 10 of the coins.

From there, I went to the sewing lady who has the daughter who smells bad. She sewed a pocket inside the waistband of my work britches, the ones I also wear for traveling. Thieves would take my medicine pouch, but they might not think to look in my pants.

I will travel light, with just my clothing and an extra tunic, my bow and arrows, a good knife, and a sack of pemmican, dried venison, and fruits that the cook has promised me. I will leave my writing papers here with Fr. Mendoza, since they would get wet in the rain and might be ruined.

I leave at first light. This will be the last I will write, unless I give up looking for my family and return to Santa Fé.

Chapter 11

*A*yacouta was not hard to find. I had a map with me,
one my father Coya made years ago when he said I
might need it some day. No one lives there anymore. The
roof of the council house had fallen in, and only one wall
of the church remained standing.

Cimarrones had made a camp fire in the church, not
realizing that people were resting under the floor. That
was sacrilegious. I think the priest would be angry and the
spirits of those buried would be greatly vexed and
troubled. I removed the burned wood and swept the floor
clean. I sat outside and ate my meal under a tree.

On the other side of the river, I found three men
whose job it is to ferry people from one side to the other.
They were Yustagans, and they were there on the orders
of their priest and the chief at Potohiriba. They gambled
among themselves to pass the time, using Spanish coins.
They asked me to join them, but I said I had no money.

I asked them what happened to the people of
Ayacouta and if there were any of them still living. They
told me that a few Utinans still travel the river, but that

they prefer to live away from the Spanish trail where they would not be forced to work.

Two leagues north on the river, I discovered a small village of Utinan fishermen, and I stayed there one night before taking a trail to the west. They remembered my brother, Lucas Menéndez, as a great leader, and they fed me in his honor. They recognized the name of Coya, but none of them ever met him.

For the next two months I went a long way and met many people. I do not remember today all the names of the villages, but I was at the mission at Ajohica and the big one at Potohiriba. The Yustagans get along well with the Apalachee on the other side of the river, so I kept going toward the setting sun.

The hilly countryside west of the river was covered with rich red soil that grew more corn than I had ever seen. My father had told me about it. He was the first Utinan Chief ever to travel there. I passed several villages until I reached a town called Talimali that was situated at the foot of a large hill.

The people were pleasant to me, and it took me only two days to be comfortable speaking their language. They warned me not to climb the hill to the mission, saying the Spanish soldiers would put me to work building a fort. Many of the Apalachee never go up the hill, except to Sunday Mass, when the soldiers are forbidden to grab them. Of course, the soldiers come looking for them at other times.

When the weather turned cooler, I headed back to the east and crossed the river into Yustaga to make my way home. I wanted to avoid strangers who might be *cimarrones*, as I had been trained to do as a child, so for three days I traveled through thick forests, following only game trails.

One day I encountered a bear and her cub. She stood on her back legs and growled at me, pawing the air until I backed slowly away. My puny bow would be useless in a fight with a grown bear or wolves. I killed rabbits and squirrels and birds and picked berries and fruit and had enough to eat that I did not get very hungry.

When I worked at the ranch I had much time to myself, especially before Valdez died, but there I filled my time writing and not thinking. Without paper and ink, I had time to think about my life and what I might do. I want to find a good-smelling woman and marry her in the church and make a family. Maybe I should go back to Oconee and find the people I knew when I was a child.

At night I listened to the birds calling back and forth: the whippoorwills and the owls. I thought about the old stories, about how the call of an owl was an omen of death. If you hear it once, you will die. If you hear it a second time, the owl will show mercy. These are false legends, of course, the kind the friars condemn as the words of the Devil. I never believed they were the words of the Devil, just stories the Indians tell their children. I believe in God, but the Bible doesn't even mention the owl.

One night I heard a barred owl just as I was finishing my evening prayers. I lay awake waiting for the second call, but fell asleep before I heard it. The next morning I was sick with a fever. I got as far as Tarihica and could not go on. I had a dizziness that made me clumsy on my feet, and I vomited up everything I tried to eat.

I went to the mission priest in Tarihica and told him I was sick, and that I was the godson of the friar at Santa Fé. I asked for a place to sleep out of the weather until I was better. He would have turned me away until I said I had one reale with me that I would be happy to put in the mission poor box. He took my money and gave me a pallet in the storage room.

In three days I felt hungry and wanted to eat. I gave the priest another reale for my food and for this paper and ink. I feel well enough to travel today, but promised myself I would finish writing before heading further east toward Santa Fé.

Chapter 12

Misión Santa Fé de Toloca
October 8, 1675

*T*here was so much excitement in Santa Fé, no one paid me any attention when I returned from a journey that had taken more than nine months to complete.

A large new house was being built next to the convento, but it was round, instead of straight-walled like a Spanish building. It was daub and wattle, with clay floors and a thatched roof. There was no hole to let smoke out, and the workers had fashioned windows with shutters and a large door. It was neither Indian nor Spanish, but a little of both. I had never seen anything like it. They were almost finished building it.

I asked Fr. Mendoza about it. He said they were in a hurry to finish it, and that he would be living there for awhile, and that I could stay there also. I asked him why he was moving out of the convento.

He looked at me with surprise on his face. "You have not heard?" he said. "The bishop is coming to stay here, and I am giving him the use of the convento so he will be comfortable."

Before I could ask more, he rushed off, shouting orders to the workmen.

Through the crowd of workers I spotted a man whose regal bearing was unmistakable. It was Chief Antonio, and he was talking with a group of village chiefs who were his vassals. When he saw me approach, he left them and wrapped his arms around me with a warm embrace.

He said the new house was built in only three days from the time a runner came from Solomototo with the news that the bishop would be here on Thursday. His name is Gabriel Díaz Vara Calderón, and he is the Bishop of Santiago de Cuba.

"He is so important, he knows the Pope," Antonio said.

There were other things going on. Musicians were blowing on their flutes and ringing their bells, some of the young women were dancing, and from inside the church I could hear the women practicing religious hymns.

I stood in the churchyard marveling at all the excitement. The friar stopped to speak to me again and said that I should look on his desk and read the scriptures he had written on a tablet. "Memorize them so you can help in the welcoming ceremony tomorrow."

"The priest from Tarihica sends you his greetings," I said, as Fr. Mendoza rushed off on another errand. I do not think he heard what I said.

The Bishop arrived at noon with his secretary Pedro Palacios. They also had five men with them, each carrying on his back a bundle as large as an arroba. Behind them stood two pack horses, each more heavily laden than the men. They had walked all the way from San Francisco de Potano where they had spent the previous night.

Fr. Mendoza had arranged a very nice welcome for the bishop. We were all quiet and standing still in our places. The holy man walked into the village and stopped, looking about uncertainly, puzzled by our silence. When Fr. Mendoza nodded to me, I stepped forward and recited what I had memorized. The first scripture comes from Chapter 66 of the Book of Psalms.

> *Make a joyful noise unto God, all ye lands:*
> *Sing forth the honor of his name:*
> *Make His praise glorious.*

As soon as I said it, the singing, dancing, and music burst forth. The bishop smiled broadly and beat his foot on the ground in rhythm with the sound. He swayed, mimicking the dancers and raised his hands to Heaven, urging us on.

When the music ended and the dancers finished, I spoke once again, this time quoting Chapter 28 of the Book of Matthew:

> *And Jesus came and spake unto them saying,*
> *All power is given to me in heaven and in earth.*
> *Go ye therefore, and teach all nations,*
> *Baptizing them in the name of the Father, and of the*
> *   Son.*
> *And of the Holy Ghost:*
> *Teaching them to observe all things whatsoever I*
> *   have commanded you;*
> *And lo, I am with you always*
> *Even unto the ends of the Earth.*
> *Amen.*

Fr. Mendoza stepped forward and embraced the bishop and then kissed the ring on his hand. The two men kissed each other on the cheek. I could see tears flowing down the friar's face, and I felt happy for him. These priests are isolated, living among Indians all the time. They seldom see others of their own kind.

Bishop Calderón spoke a long prayer, and he did it beautifully. It was much better than the prayers we hear from Fr. Mendoza at Mass. Calderón's voice was dramatic, like that of a storyteller, and he did not stand still, but moved around waving his arms to the heavens.

I thought to myself, this is a wonderful man, as unforgettable as my own father.

Fr. Mendoza showed the bishop around the village, and he took him inside the church where they stayed for a long time. Later, he took Bishop Calderón to the convento where the bishop could rest from his journey and be prepared for the celebration planned for the council house that would begin two hours before dark.

I helped the porters deliver their bundles to the convento while the others were in the church. Pedro Palacios inspected the room where the bishop would sleep, and unpacked his clothing for him. He laid out on the bed the bishop's formal robe, the color of autumn leaves. I have never seen anything as beautiful in my life.

———————

During the council house celebration, Chief Antonio's grandson came to me and said that Fr. Mendoza wanted me to come to dinner at the convento. You can imagine my surprise. Why should I be invited to have dinner with a bishop? I turned to watch Fr. Mendoza and positioned myself where he could see me as he talked to the bishop on the highest seat in the house. I looked at him with a question on my brow and pointed to my chest. The friar smiled and nodded quickly, and then went back to his discussion with the bishop.

There were five of us in the council house dining room. Chief Antonio was there, Fr. Mendoza, Sr.

Palacios, and the bishop. The table was set with the mission's best plates and saucers, the ones formed and painted to look as if they were from Spain. It was nighttime, but there were candles and lamps all over the room. The food was served by the children of the mission cooks.

Neither Antonio nor I could think of what to say, so we sat quietly and listened to the Spaniards talk while we ate a very good meal of venison and fish.

Palacios described the purpose of their trip: to inspect the missions and the condition of the Indians so that needs might be met and inequities cured. He told us where they had been, saying that there were almost no Indians still living at San Francisco de Potano.

The condition of the Indians at Nombre de Diós was poor, he said, but things were satisfactory at the river mission of Solomototo.

"We will stay here for three more days," Palacios said, "and then go to Ayacouta to ask the Indians about reestablishing the mission there. It was closed fifteen years ago."

Perhaps I should have stayed quiet, but I spoke up. "No one lives there anymore," I said.

Palacios looked annoyed, as if I had contradicted something he had said. Fr. Mendoza looked at me with a frown, shaking his head. Only the bishop seemed interested in what I had to say. "You have been there? Tell us about the place," he said.

Fr. Mendoza was no longer frowning, so I answered. "Ayacouta was once the most important village in all of Timucua," I said. "My father was *Holata Aco* there, although that was before I was born. It is now empty. There are three Yustagans on the other side of the river who ferry people across."

Bishop Calderón looked at Palacios. "Perhaps we would be chasing a wild goose by going there. I think we may go next to the mission at Santa Catalina."

Palacios seemed to be in agreement. "Then we can go to Ajohica, Tarihica, and Guacara before reaching Potohiriba," he said.

"Nobody stays at Guacara, either," I said. Again, all eyes were on me and I was embarrassed for being so disrespectful.

"Juan seems to know a lot about the places we will be going," Bishop Calderón said.

I liked it that he remembered my name. "I just returned from Apalachee," I said. I would have said more if Fr. Mendoza had not changed the subject.

He wanted Bishop Calderón to know how poor we were at Santa Fé, and how the government money never arrived, and about the needs that went unfulfilled. He said that there was never enough adequate wine for the Lord's Table, and that he watered it down to make it last. There were but two church candles left, and none in San Augustín to replace them. Busts and statues of the saints needed to be replaced, or at least painted, and there was not even money for paint.

"The people are so impoverished that widows prostitute themselves with soldiers on the road," he said.

That was the first I had heard of it. I suppose a priest hears a lot at Confession, and I wondered which widows they might be.

"Juan here is an excellent caballero," said the priest. "Until a year ago, he tended horses for the soldiers. He was paid for that work, and it made it possible for him to work at the mission for free. He is literate, and an excellent teacher. He writes as well as any scribe, and is fluent in many languages."

"A talented man," the bishop said.

"And I fear we are losing him," the friar said. "I cannot afford to feed and house him any longer, unless we receive at least five additional reales per month."

Bishop Calderón leaned over to Palacios and cupped his mouth to speak privately. The rest of us spoke among ourselves, trying not to listen. Palacios nodded his head in agreement.

Bishop Calderón said that the hour was late, and he was tired. He wanted to speak privately to Fr. Mendoza about church matters.

Chief Antonio and I thanked them and walked out, he to his house and me to the new house that had just been built.

I could not sleep, but lay there on my pallet thinking about the wonderful experience I had meeting a friend of the Pope. I was still awake when Fr. Mendoza came in to go to his bed.

"Are you awake?" he asked.

I said I was.

"You are a lucky man," he said. "Bishop Calderón is taking you with him. You will be his guide and will handle the horses." From the tone of Mendoza's voice, I did not think he was happy.

I was still awake later. "You leave with him in three days," he said. "You could use some nicer clothes."

———————

I went to see Chief Antonio in the morning. I still had a few of the reales he had given me a year before, but asked if he would give me ten more. Antonio handed me the whole bundle and said it was time for me to be responsible for my own money.

I counted it. There were 80 reales.

The sewer of clothes said that I would need new britches, since the pair I had were patched and worn. She also wanted to make two shirts for me. She had two large pieces of Spanish cloth she got from a trader. I wondered how she could afford such a luxury, and if she might be one of the women the priest had talked about at dinner.

She told me it would take her three days to complete all the items. I asked how much it would cost.

She looked up and drummed her chin with her finger. "Two reales or two deer hides would be fair," she said.

"If you do good work and finish in two days, I will pay four reales," I said.

―――――――

When I returned to the seamstress today, she had finished the new clothes. Her daughter was with her. Before I could leave the house, the woman also gave me a coat to keep me warm in the winter.

"It belonged to my dead husband," she said. She began to weep. Then she pulled out a pair of deer skin moccasins and handed them to me. She made them for her husband while he was sick, and they had never been worn.

I have never worn anything on my feet, because shoes look uncomfortable. I took them to be polite.

I had my arms full of new clothing and was ready to leave. The woman stopped me at the door and placed her hand on my arm and whispered something in my ear.

"Would you like to take my daughter? She is of marrying age," she said.

I was afraid she might say something like that, so I had my answer planned in advance. "The bishop would not allow it."

―――――――

Fr. Mendoza told me to gather all of my things for the trip. I have bundled my new clothes. When I finish writing this, I will put all of my writings in the leather case. It is possible I may not be returning to Santa Fé any time soon, and I want to have them with me.

The last thing I shall do is to go to the friar's room and hide the reales under his pillow. Fr. Mendoza needs the coins more than I do. He can use them to buy wine and candles for Mass, and paints for the statues of the saints, and to support the widows so they will stop being prostitutes.

I will keep 10 reales for myself. I have everything I need in life. I do not need to weigh myself down with silver.

Apalachee

Convento de Santo Domingo

Guanabacoa, Cuba
November 18, 1768

To: Monseñor Pedro Agustín Morell
Bishop of Santiago de Cuba
Havana

Your Excellency,

The warmest greetings of your brothers in Christ of Convento de Santo Domingo and of the Church of the Lady of the Ascension here at Guanabacoa. May God sustain your boundless spirit in His work.

First, I would like to express to you our appreciation for the kind words you spoke at the recent conference at Havana. Your acknowledgement of our efforts to translate and make sense of the Cavale manuscript was so effusive that it made us blush. Though perhaps undeserved, your praise has motivated us even more to devote our best efforts to this scholarly work.

That said, I would like to acknowledge your cautionary instructions that we guard against the temptation to edit or revise what we find. Nothing had been edited, altered, amended, or abridged. Except for minor differences of opinion between our translators on the meaning of certain passages, understanding that which is written is not difficult. More problematic is the condition of the original papers, some of which have deteriorated badly over the years, become soiled, and exposed to water causing the ink to run. Still others are so old they fall apart with anything less than the most careful handling.

Fortunately, the individuals who wrote down this material frequently include the date the document was written. Where there is no date recorded, the context of the stories sometimes makes clear the chronology. One exception is a two-page letter written by an Indian to a Spanish woman who appears to be his lover. I have inserted it where it appears to belong, along with my own parenthetical observation.

For clarity of organization, I have divided the entire manuscript into three different books. First, there is the earliest work, which is already in your possession and appears to have been written by two or more individuals, but all of which concerns events in that part of the Timucua nation which lies west of the River San Juan. For that reason, I captioned it as Western Timucua.

The current transmittal is much longer, containing more than 200 pages. All of these writings originated in or concerned events which occurred at Apalachee, the province west of the Aucilla River. For that reason, I captioned the current volume as Apalachee.

The final submission appears to have been written in San Augustín between 1706 and the surrender of the province to the English in 1763. Accordingly, once that portion has been fully interpreted and copied, it is my intention to designate it as San Augustín.

Rest assured that the original documents are being stored and preserved here at Santo Domingo, pending your instructions on how they are to be to be handled in the future.

Because of the approaching Christmas season, it may be several months before our work is done here and the final volume is delivered to you. Fortunately, that which was written in San Augustín is in colloquial Castilian and presents few of the problems of the earlier writings that were written in a variety of native tongues and dialects.

As always, I remain your devoted servant and Brother in Christ.

Kissing your ring,

Fr. Manuel de Soto
Chaplain of the Convento Santo Domingo

Chapter 13

Ajohica, 15 leagues from Santa Fé
October 12, 1675

I asked Palacios what it is he writes each day. He carries a journal book, and whenever we stop to rest he sits under a tree and inscribes something in it.

"It is history I am writing, Juan," he said. "No bishop has been this far west, and I make notations to help him remember what he has seen. When he returns to Cuba he will write of his experiences in reports to the Council of the Indies and to the Pope."

What Palacios said has inspired me. I, also, will write the history of the bishop's travels. My duties are as an interpreter for the people we meet and as a caballero for the horses. But the animals are docile, and as long as they are fed and watered and not overburdened, they are no trouble for me.

We went to Santa Catalina, but nothing important happened there. I showed the bishop the desolate village of Ayacouta, and he said a prayer for those buried beneath the floor where the church once stood.

But here, in Ajohica, we experienced something that surprised and alarmed the Spaniards, but was only amusing to us Indians who have seen it happen before. I shall tell it.

Soon after daylight, while I was tending to the horses, a raucous shout was heard from the far side of the village. People came out of their houses, hollering at each other and running every which way. Palacios stepped out of the small convento, looking worried and carrying a pistol.

"What is it?" he asked me. "Are we being attacked?"

I held up my hand to silence him so that I could listen to the noise. There was bellicose laughter mixed with the shouts of alarm, and it was coming toward us.

"Put away your gun," I said. "And fetch the bishop, quickly."

Palacios went inside and, moments later, came out again with Bishop Calderón who was wiping the sleep from his eyes.

No longer than it takes to spook quail, a man dressed and painted as a raccoon burst into the mission yard, jumping and running in circles, pursued by children of the village. He eluded them by darting away, and running around the barbacoa and storage shed, then shinnied himself up a tree as if he were a real raccoon, and not just a man pretending to be one.

The Chief of Ajohica stood outside his house trying to look serious, with his arms folded across his chest. His *inija* stood next to him, laughing, and urging the children to take their sticks and knock the raccoon from the tree.

When everyone in the village was there watching, the chief raised his hands for silence so that he could listen to what this wild man-raccoon had to say.

"Cowardly Ajohicans!" he shouted. "Women in men's clothes! You stink so bad not even the vultures will eat you." The raccoon was standing and bouncing up and down on a branch barely strong enough to support his weight, and holding onto the limb above.

Some of the young men circled the tree, waving knives in the air, and hurling insults as filthy as those of the raccoon.

"You pathetic people are challenged. The warriors of Tarihica declare war on you," the raccoon shouted. "Unless you are young girls in your taboo time, you will come to Tarihica in three days to defend your puny selves. Bring with you your women and your wealth. We of Tarihica will enjoy both, after the battle is won."

The *inija* answered for the chief. "Will a raccoon challenge a wildcat? Does he invade the den of a bear looking for a fight? You are a fool, just like the other foul-smelling skunks of Tarihica."

Laughter echoed through the village. Some people shouted, "smelly skunk, smelly skunk."

"Your challenge is taken," the *inija* shouted. "But you may leave your ugly women in their houses. We have no use for them." Again, laughter drowned out the insults.

The raccoon was satisfied, and jumped from the tree. Again he ran in circles with the children pursuing. They chased him out of town.

When I translated for the bishop the essential part of what had been said, he and Palacios were alarmed. "We cannot allow a war to break out!" the secretary said.

"It is not a war, but only a ball game," I said. "We call it the 'little brother of war.' It is an entertaining way to settle disputes without killing each other, although that does not guarantee that people will not get their bones broken in the playing."

Bishop Calderón turned to Palacios, relief spreading a broad smile across his face. "We are going to Tarihica, anyway. I would very much like to witness this 'little brother of war', and perhaps enjoy once again the antics of the raccoon man."

From the concern that creased the secretary's face, I did not believe Palacios was happy with the decision.

―――――――

Each morning, whether we are on the trail or at a mission, the bishop must have a hot beverage before he is ready for the day. Palacios takes a handful of beans from a sack, and grinds them using a mortar and pestle. He says they are not beans at all, but berries that have been roasted. After he crushes them, he boils them in water.

"They come from Kaffia, in Ethiopia," Palacios said. "Merchant ships sometimes come to Cuba, and the bishop has me check each manifest to see if they carry any kaffia beans."

Bishop Calderón was standing near the fire, trying to get warm, listening to what Palacios said. "Will you try some?" he asked, smiling at me. I answered that I would try anything once.

The drink was served hot, like cassina, but it had a bitter taste. I handed the cup back to Palacios, and said that I did not like it, and that I preferred cassina.

The next morning I waited outside the convento until Calderón and Palacios came out. I had a small pot of cassina sitting in the edge of the fire, staying hot.

"Try this," I said. "It is called cassina. Some people call it the black drink."

Palacios did not want the bishop trying something new. "He has a weak stomach," he said.

"Well then, you will sample it for me," Bishop Calderón said, laughing and handing the cup to his secretary. "Juan was brave enough to drink your kaffia. You should be willing to try his beverage."

Palacios's face had a sour look, even before he put the cup to his lips. He sipped a little, then opened his eyes as if he were appraising the taste, then took another small swallow. "Not bad," he said. "A little like tea that has been too long on the boil."

Bishop Calderón took the cup and soon finished what was left. "Not as good as kaffia, if you are asking me," he said.

"We have only four days supply of kaffia beans left in the bag," Palacios said.

"Fine!" the bishop said. "We will drink kaffia as long as it lasts, and then make do with this cassina drink until we get more beans."

I think he liked the taste more than he wanted to admit.

The journey to Tarihica was only two leagues, but it was made difficult by the multitude of people from Ajohica on their way to the game. They moved faster than we could go, and passed us on the trail, shouting and singing and frightening the horses.

Palacios walked beside the bishop, protecting him from the sunlight with a palmetto frond, and fending off those people who came close and might collide with Calderón. The people were more excited by the challenge of a game than the historic event of a bishop's visit.

The priest of Santa Cruz de Tarihica failed miserably in a suitable greeting for the bishop. His people, also, were more interested in the battle that would occur the following day. After the kisses were exchanged by the holy men, the scripture read, and the prayers voiced, the priest took the bishop and Palacios into the convento for their dinner.

I was not invited to go with them, so after I tended to the horses I went to the council house to watch the festival that always happens the night before the game. On one side sat the people of Tarihica on benches and low cabanas. On the other side sat a smaller crowd of people from Ajohica. Some of both groups were dancing.

Two rows of benches were arranged on either side of the central hearth where a fire roared. To one side were 40 players for Tarihica, and on the other side, the men of Ajohica sat quietly, as a shaman visited each one, blessed him, and marked his forehead with charcoal.

The Tarihicans had their own shaman, and he had a bag of magical herbs that the men rubbed on their hands to make them better players. The men sipped cassina, but sat subdued and reflective with all the noise and celebration going on around them.

The Chief of Tarihica spoke to his people, loudly extolling the unmarried women to welcome the attentions of any of the other team's players who wished to be with them during the nighttime. "Weaken them before sun-up tomorrow," he said. "Otherwise we may all lose what we have gambled on the outcome."

I looked around to see if the bishop had arrived. He was still at the convento enjoying his dinner, and I was relieved that I did not have to interpret for him what the chief had said to the young women. I am sure he would have considered it sinful.

The game began at noon. The friar of Tarihica had arranged a place of honor for his guests, and Bishop Calderón and Palacios sat comfortably under a tree where they could watch all that happened. They asked me to sit with them and answer their questions about what was to occur. I explained the object of the game: to kick the ball so that it landed in the eagle's nest at the top of a tall pole in the center of the playing field.

"If the ball lands in the nest, the team of the man who kicked it gets two points. If it merely hits the nest or the pole, one point is awarded. When one team has eleven points, the game is won."

"It is not possible," Palacios said. "No one is skillful enough to kick that tiny ball with such accuracy. Why, it is no bigger than a persimmon or a large walnut."

Bishop Calderón was more interested in what was happening in the crowd than on the playing field. "Do you see those men?" he asked, directing Palacios's attention to gamblers who were taking wagers and collecting the animal skins, beads, mirrors, and other treasures that were being bet by the people.

"Money changers!" the bishop shouted over the noise. "Shall I chase them from the temple?" He was only fooling. He was enjoying the pageantry and having a very good time.

At the beginning, the ball was thrown into the air, and before it could fall to the dirt there was a collision of men going for it. One fell atop the other, and before long they were a mass of flesh, kicking, biting, and scratching each other indiscriminately, each one looking to possess the ball that had by now disappeared. On they fought, until some were hurt and dragged aside by their comrades.

One sneaky fellow stood up and looked about as if puzzled by the disappearance of the ball. I watched the way he backed away from the pile. He held his mouth closed with his hand, as if his teeth had been kicked. When he was clear of the others, he reached into his mouth and pulled out the leather ball. He dropped it to the ground, and kicked it, but missed the pole completely. In less than a heartbeat, the others were on their feet again and chasing after it.

The game continued until just before dark, when the chiefs got together and decided on the outcome. Tarihica's players were better than the Ajohicans. Perhaps it was because of the magical herb they used on their hands the night before. They had a score of seven, to the Ajohican's three.

Many people felt cheated that the game was not played through the night in the dark until one team had a winning score. But tomorrow would be Sunday. The priest of Santa Cruz de Tarihica stood firm on the ruling, and the Ajohicans went home angry and poorer than when they arrived.

Chapter 14

San Matheo
November 7, 1675

*D*espite my intentions to record everything that occurs, I lack the discipline to write every day. If I had a table upon which to lay the papers it would be easier than sitting on the ground and holding the paper on my knees. Palacios asked the friar of San Matheo if he had a place for me to work, and the priest said I could sit at the table in the convento until the women come to put down the dinner plates.

It was as I said about Guacara. No one lives there anymore. The land gave out and would no longer produce crops, so they moved their village two leagues north.

San Pedro de Potohiriba is an important place with a large church where two friars teach children in the convento and adults in the council house. That is the way Fr. Mendoza and I used to teach at Santa Fé de Toloca.

We stayed at Potohiriba eight days and visited five nearby villages served by the mission. Bishop Calderón would not travel on Sunday, and this way he got to conduct Mass two times in the large church. Everywhere he goes, the friars ask him to do Mass for them. When I look in their faces during the ceremony, I can see that it is an honor for them to hear him.

We saw the old fort at Machava, the one the Timucua built when they fought against the Spaniards in 1656. I did not tell the bishop that it was my brother, Lucas, who led the revolt, but he knew. The Chief of Machava showed us the place where the rebel chiefs were executed by the soldiers. He pointed to a spot on the ground. "This," he said, "is the very place where Chief Lucas was choked to death."

At that, Calderón put his arm around my shoulder.

We arrived here at San Matheo two days ago, just in time for the burning of the fields and the winter hunt. Bishop Calderón wanted to see it, since he has an interest in the agriculture in these parts.

These people are Yustagans, and although their tongue is somewhat different from Utinan, I can understand everything they say. Their customs are different from other Timucuans, and the chiefs and leading men paint their faces black.

They also burn their fields before every planting, and since they grow maize twice each year, they are very efficient at the burning. Before the fires are lit early in the morning, they know exactly where the deer will run to get away from the flames, and they are waiting for them with bows, arrows, and spears. The chief told us that not so many years ago they killed bison the same way, but that they no longer come this far to the east.

Bishop Calderón, his secretary, and I stayed upwind of the fire where we could watch the hunt but avoid the smoke. I had my bow and arrow with me, but other than a rabbit that hopped by, nothing came close to us that was worth killing.

A bear loped out of the field and the men chased it into the woods and killed it. They gave the skin to the chief, as it is his due. He divided the bear meat and four deer among the people in the village. A flank of venison was given to the friar, and he served it for our evening meal, yesterday.

——— ——— ———

Today we remain in San Matheo. The bishop's secretary Pedro Palacios fell ill two days ago, during the hunt, and is unable to leave his bed in the convento. His Reverence Bishop Calderón first said it must have been the smoke from the burning of the fields that made him sick. Today, he thinks it is something more serious that afflicts Palacios, causing him chills and sweaty fevers. I have learned to stay away from sick people, but I am told that Palacios has red blotches on his face and chest.

The friar of San Matheo suggested that a medicine man be called to administer herbal cures, saying to Calderón that he had witnessed many people who regained their health after being visited by the *isucu*. The bishop asked the friar if the *isucu* were a Christian, and upon being told he was still a pagan, he refused to let him treat Palacios's illness.

"We must set an example for these people. If it is God's will that Palacios be saved, it will happen through our prayers. A shaman's magic is the Devil's work. Palacios, if he were in his right mind, would prefer to die than to lose his soul."

——— ——— ———

We have been here at San Matheo for three more days. Bishop Calderón has not slept through the night, but stays with Palacios, praying for him and wiping the sweat from his face. The bishop says his heart is strong and his breathing regular, but he has no way to tell how long it will be before Palacios is fit to travel. But Bishop

Calderón has obligations. He wants to complete our work in Apalachee and return to San Augustín in time for the Christmas celebration.

"We will leave him here and go on to Apalachee and visit those missions and the ones to the west. By the time we return to San Matheo, I am sure he will be better, and that God will have placed his hand on him and made him well."

I am not sure the bishop believed his own words. He gave his secretary his last rites today, in preparation for our departure tomorrow. Perhaps it was just a precaution.

Calderón said that, from now on, I am to perform Palacios's duties of writing in the journal. He told me to study what is written there, and each day to record the name of the village we might be in, and the names of the friar, the chief, and the principal men of that village.

He also said that I should count the people in the village and write down that number, and to find out from the friar how many are Christian and how many are pagan. He said that I should write the distance, in leagues, between the towns. I have no idea how to do that.

I am convinced that Bishop Calderón sees into a man's heart. He knows my doubts and my fears. He embraced me and said that God would show me the way.

I will put away my own writing. God has for me a higher purpose, and he will lift me up and sustain me in it. But I must do my part by studying that which is written in the secretary's journal.

Chapter 15

San Luis de Talimali
December 14, 1675

*I*f I ever looked upon a Spanish priest as weak or afraid of hard work, it was a serious misjudgment. His Reverence has shown a fierce determination and stamina to complete his survey of the Indians and missions in these parts, and the last month has been harder on me and the horses than on him.

I look at the journal and see written there in my own hand the names of nine missions and twice that many minor villages we have visited, and some of them I do not even remember, we traveled so fast.

On the second day after we left San Matheo, we crossed the river into Apalachee where we went to five missions, and then we crossed another river to where the Indians are called Apalachicoli, and we visited three more small missions there.

The Apalachicoli refuse to bury their dead under the floor of the church, saying that the sky should be open to the spirits so they can ascend to Heaven. Bishop Calderón had me write in the journal that these people are unrepentant pagans, and that some of them may be cannibals.

Now we have returned to the mission called San Luis de Talimali. I have been here before on an earlier journey; although that time I stayed in the village at the foot of the hill and never came to the top where the council house and mission church are built.

This is a busy place, with more Spaniards than I have ever seen away from San Augustín. Many soldiers, and Spanish gentlemen, and artisans live here. I have seen two Spanish women and many children.

I will try to describe the town. There is a large, round playing field for the ball game. The soldiers use it for practicing their marching. The field is surrounded by wooden crosses, 14 of them, representing the Stations of the Cross.

At one end is the largest council house I have ever seen. The Apalachee *inija*, a man named Bip Bentura, took me into it and said that it holds as many as 3,000 people for dances.

"I have never seen that many people in my whole life, let alone in one place at one time," I said to him.

On one side of the field is the church, with its doors opening toward the east. Fr. Juan de Paiva, the mission friar, bragged to Bishop Calderón that the church is built to the exact dimensions of the one at San Augustín, and could contain five hundred people at a single Mass. There is a large and beautiful convento, where Bishop Calderón sleeps, with gardens outside his window.

The bishop's porters and I are quartered in a hut close to the convento, so we will be near the bishop in case he needs us.

North of the field is the house of a Spanish officer, Juan Fernandez de Florencia. He is the Deputy Governor of La Florida and is the boss of the Spaniards in

Apalachee. His brother, Pedro de Florencia, lives with him, along with Pedro's wife and young daughter named Juana.

Beyond the governor's house is a barracks that houses a garrison of fifteen soldiers and three officers. There are three other Spanish houses. Bip Bentura said that they are for other members of the governor's family, and that most of them are named Florencia.

The chief's house is near the top of the hill, next to the council house. Just below him on the slope of the hill are six or seven smaller houses in which Bip Bentura and other Indian officials live. The main village of Talimali is at the bottom of the hill. It is where I stayed while I was here more than a year ago.

———————

I was interrupted in my journal writing this morning by shouting and laughter outside the convento. It is a miracle! Palacios lives! God be praised! Bishop Calderón always told me that his secretary would survive his illness, but I thought it was wishful thinking. Now I can hardly contain my joy and excitement at the wonderful news.

Palacios is weak and has trouble standing for a long time, but God carried him all the way from San Matheo to San Luis de Talimali. If my calculations are correct, that would be more than 20 leagues.

Bishop Calderón ordered Palacios to bed to rest from his long ordeal. Palacios did not want to go, but followed the bishop's orders when Calderón promised him that he would be awakened in time for the dinner planned tonight in the deputy governor's house. I will be there also. I will wear my new Spanish shirt for the first time.

Before I went to dinner, Palacios came to see me. He asked that I return to him the journal.

The evening at the deputy governor's house started out well, but did not end well for me.

The governor has a fine house and a banquet table large enough for eight people, and it was full. I remember the names of all who where there: Deputy Governor Juan Fernandez de Florencia and his brother, Pedro de Florencia; Fr. Juan de Paiva; Bishop Calderón and his secretary Pedro Palacios; Chief Matheo Chuba of Talimali; *Inija* Bip Bentura; and me.

I do not prefer to eat inside where it is so crowded. Florencia and his brother smoked cigars after the tasty meal of sea bass and corn. Chuba and Bentura walked outside to breathe clean air, and then returned. I wanted to go with them, but thought it would be disrespectful to leave while the deputy governor was speaking.

When Spaniards get together they sometimes talk too fast for me to keep up. As an interpreter, I stop someone who speaks too fast, and ask him to repeat what he has said so I will get it right. But that would be impolite at a dinner among friends, so I smiled and said nothing.

Florencia asked Calderón for what impressions he had formed during his travels through Timucua, Apalachee, and the land of the Apalachicoli.

"I find the Indians to be well developed in their stature, but disinclined to do hard work," he said. The other Spaniards laughed at what he said.

"They are, however, clever people who can imitate any art they see. Their rendering of scrollwork on the church doors is particularly well done."

As the bishop described his impressions of the Indians for the benefit of the others, Bip Bentura watched me from the corner of his eye.

"One Indian in particular has been a delightful surprise," the bishop said, and he turned his head to look directly at me. "Juan Mendoza has been a blessing to me beyond measure. He is bright, industrious, and as good a scrivener as I have seen this side of Madrid. He is also widely traveled and an excellent interpreter."

Every head turned toward me, and I suddenly felt the warmth of the room. Deputy Governor Florencia looked at me closely, as if studying my features. Fr. Paiva leaned forward, looking down the table at me.

"I could use him as parish interpreter," the friar said, laughing, "except for the fact that he is previously engaged."

Calderón looked at Palacios, and then turned back to the friar. "Since my secretary has returned, and because I am done here and going back to San Augustín, perhaps he is available after all."

The deputy governor raised his hand before the friar could speak. "There are no appropriations in the budget for a parish interpreter," he said.

Fr. Paiva slumped back into his chair, defeated by the man who controls the purse strings.

"On the other hand, I have need for a scribe," Florencia said. "The one who was coming to work for me drowned crossing a river on the way from San Augustín." The deputy governor looked across the table at Paiva. "Perhaps we can share him. That way, everyone is happy."

No one asked if I was happy with the decision. The deputy governor proposed a toast to seal the agreement between church and crown. A black slave poured a little wine into the drinking cups of the Spaniards. None was offered to Bip Bentura, Matheo Chuba, or me.

If there is any good to be found in my dismissal from the bishop's staff, it is that I have now found the time to write for myself the history of his travels through Western

Timucua and Apalachee. God forgive me if I have allowed my personal disappointment to color my account of his miraculous works.

Chapter 16

Bishop Calderón departed for San Augustín this morning with Palacios and two fresh horses from the farm at Asile. I recognized both of them as colts I had trained at Rancho de Santa Fé. As I helped with the packing, one of them nuzzled me playfully in the ribs.

"That horse seems to know you," Calderón said. He was watching the loading.

"Horses love me," I said simply. If I said that this horse and I were old friends, the bishop might think I was appealing to his sympathy because I was disappointed not to go with him to San Augustín. That would be true, but I was no longer needed, and I respect the bishop too much to use trickery to get my way.

Fr. Paiva, Bip Bentura, and I watched the bishop's caravan as it went down the hill and headed east. They traveled with twenty men who were carrying corn to San Augustín, and two soldier guards. I pray they will be safe.

Fr. Paiva went to the church to supervise the preparations for the Christmas celebration, but before he left he said I should find a place to sleep in the convento. He also said he wanted to meet with me after the evening meal to bless me for my new work and to explain the duties of parish interpreter.

———————

Bip Bentura also had matters to discuss with me. We sat on a bench near the ball field and watched the children at play.

"What do you know of Florencia?" he asked after we had sat a long time and there was no one else within earshot.

It was a strange question. Bentura had been with me two nights before, when I was first introduced to the deputy governor.

"Nothing, except that he in a wealthy man and a generous host," I said.

The *inija* proceeded to tell me what was on his mind. "Juan Fernandez de Florencia is not the first Deputy Governor of Apalachee Province," he said. "That honor belonged to his father, whose name was Claudio Luis de Florencia."

I recalled a story told by my father of a revolt by rebel Apalachee warriors before I was born. My father led an army of 500 Timucuan fighters who helped the Spanish soldiers put down the rebellion. It was one of Coya's favorite stories, one of the few good things he felt he had accomplished in his life.

I now understood what it was Bip was trying to say to me. "It was Claudio Luis who was the first to be murdered by the Apalachee," I said.

Bip Bentura looked around again, and slid closer to me on the bench and lowered his voice to a whisper. "His mother was also killed, as well as two of his sisters and his baby nephew. Two priests also died that day."

The crime happened almost 30 years ago at Bacuqua, to which the deputy governor and his family had been lured, ostensibly to attend a festival. Bip Bentura said that what happened that day was remembered with such great shame by the Apalachees, and such fear and grief by the priests that no one ever speaks of it.

"We leaders of Apalachee need to talk about it now, at least among ourselves," he said. "A man weaned on revenge now has the power of life or death over us."

————————

I met with Fr. Paiva at the church. It was after the evening meal but before dark. Even so, the friar lit candles around the altar and they flickered against the walls and high ceiling and off of the faces of the saints who looked down on the little ceremony. He had a prayer to recite to bless and dedicate me to my official duties. As I listened to his words, I understood better what it means to be the parish interpreter.

I am to faithfully interpret between the Spaniards, the Apalachee, and the people who speak the Timucuan tongues. Beyond that, I have a special responsibility to the friars.

"We Franciscans have come to this frontier of Christendom to save the souls of pagans," Fr. Paiva said, "and to free them from the influence of Satan. For us to measure our success, we must understand more than just what the Indians choose to say to us."

Paiva was studying my face. He paused in what he was saying, as if waiting for my response. I did not understand his meaning, so I said nothing at all.

Finally the friar went on. "We want you to tell us what is in their hearts, the things they say in private that they might not say in the presence of a friar, and the things they do in secret that are contrary to Christian beliefs."

"Do you not ask those things at Confession?" I said.

Paiva cleared his throat and rearranged the folds of his robe before answering me. He looked me in the eye and placed his hand on my shoulder. "Juan, there are limitations to the benefit of the Confessional. It can save souls by exposing sin lurking in the darkest recesses of an evil heart, but if the confessor hides his sin or fails to recognize it, his soul may well be lost."

"And you want me tell you their secret sins," I said.

"Not for me," Fr. Paiva answered. "You are now parish interpreter. It is God who requires it of you."

Fr. Paiva said it should not be a difficult task. He already had in mind something I could do to help him and the other friars better understand the Indians.

"It was suggested to me by Bishop Calderón that we examine the ceremonies the Apalachee and the Timucuans observe in connection with the games they play. He was curious about the ball game he witnessed in Tarihica and wants to know more about it."

After Christmas and the New Year celebration, I was to learn everything I could about the ball game and tell it to the priest. "In particular, the history of the games and the customs and ceremonies they observe," he said. "There are already questions we ask at Confession about those games. Perhaps when you have told us more, we can improve on those questions."

———————

December 25, Christmas Day, 1675

I attended Christmas Mass today. Since it was my first at San Luis, and because I was now an officer of the church, I wanted to look my best. One of the Spanish shirts I bought before I left Santa Fé had never been worn. It was a beautiful dark red, with fancy stitching at the collar.

I also wore the moccasins for the first time, the ones the seamstress had made for her dead husband. They looked good on my feet, and felt more comfortable than I expected. My hair was pinned up and decorated with mistletoe and a ribbon.

The church was full, with women to the right, or Epistle, side of the altar. The men were on the left, with an open aisle between men and women. The Spaniards were in the very front. Because of my position, I stood next to the aisle, directly behind two rows of men of the Florencia family. Bip Bentura and Chief Matheo Chuba were on the same row with me.

Everyone stood in silence as the bell outside was rung. When it finished, Fr. Paiva remained standing in front. He was waiting for something else to happen before beginning the Mass.

I looked around to find the reason for the delay. Proceeding slowly down the aisle, with great dignity, the wife of Pedro de Florencia approached the altar. With her was her daughter Juana Cathalina de Florencia.

The girl looked at me as she passed by, and she smiled. As never before in my life, I was struck in my heart with a woman's beauty.

———————

January 3, 1676

The agreement between the crown and the church with regard to my duties did not survive the coming of the New Year.

The deputy governor was new to Apalachee, having come here only weeks before my arrival with the bishop. My first major duty as scribe, he said, was to help him survey the entire province of Apalachee, from the Aucilla River in the east to the Ochlockonee River in the west, from the Gulf of Mexico in the south to the land of the Creek and Chacato Indians in the north.

I told Florencia that the friar wanted me to devote the first month of 1676 to asking questions about the ball game, so that he could send a report to Bishop Calderón in Cuba.

"You may help the priest when your duties with me are done," he said. "It is I who pay for your services and not Fr. Paiva, and you had better not forget what I have said."

When I told the friar what Florencia said to me, Paiva reminded me that it was he who provided my bed and fed me, and that my first duty was to God. I am not good at scripture, but I remember that Jesus said a man may not serve two masters, for he will love the one and hate the other, or cling to the one and despise the other. That is not an exact quotation. I do not have a Bible.

January 10, 1676

We returned last night from Ayubale. After counting the people who live there, Florencia and I spent two days searching the surrounding countryside to discover who might live nearby. He said it was important that we account for all the Apalachee people, not just those who live in the mission village. We had the friar of Ayubale with us, and three soldiers.

If the deputy governor could read the signs, he would know there were many people hiding from us in the woods. We walked into a small village where all the houses lay flat on the ground. Florencia thought it was an old, deserted village. Even the soldiers new better, and I could see them laughing behind his back. In one place, you could still smell smoke from the fire, but no one was there, so no one was counted.

I carried a journal book and used it to write down what Florencia was told by the friar and the Chief of Ayubale. He wanted to know the total number of Apalachee in the area, how many were still pagan, how many babies were born in the past year, and if there were any people from other tribes among them. He also asked the chief if he had ever seen an Englishman, or if he knew of any Indians who carried firearms.

We only traveled eight or ten leagues, and some of it was circling around, but the trip was exhausting to Florencia. He is not old, but he lacks the strength to go far or move fast.

I met with Florencia again this morning at his house, and he read what I had written in the journal about Ayubale and the surrounding country. He had me change some things I had written. He also thought of some other questions we should have asked, such as whether they have a shaman in the village, and whether the shaman has authority over the people.

When Florencia was satisfied, he said that now that he has shown me what is needed in the census and the questions to be asked, it is my responsibility.

"I want you to count everyone in Apalachee, and to visit every mission and the surrounding countryside," he said.

I have come to believe that Spaniards are charmed by numbers. They examine them and compare them, turning them over in their minds as if they were precious stones. Florencia wants to know, "How many are there?" When I worked for the bishop, he would ask, "How many leagues from here to there?" Indians are satisfied to know they outnumber their enemies, and that they are close enough to get home before dark.

"You do not need a soldier escort," he said. "These people are peaceful, and happy to cooperate. And do not forget to ask about Englishmen and weapons."

Florencia told me that he would give me 60 days to cover the entire province. I could do it in half that time, but did not say that to him. I have a plan. While I am conducting the census, I will spend time with the village chiefs and *inijas*, and ask about their customs concerning the ball game. Perhaps I can, after all, serve two masters at once.

* * *

January 14, 1676

My journey to San Marcos was uneventful. There is no mission, although there are two villages of fishermen who net fish and harvest oysters from the waters of the gulf.Now that I travel by myself, there is no reason for people to hide in the woods. I believe I counted all 61 of them. They are too busy fishing to play the ball game, the chief told me.

There are also three soldiers assigned to live at the port of San Marcos to guard the mouth of the river from pirates, and to collect taxes on goods brought into the province on Cuban boats. Sometimes the soldiers get drunk on the rum the Cubans give them as a bribe, but even the Cubans know better than to give rum to the Indians. It is said that it is possible to obtain Spanish guns, if the price is right.

As I was returning to San Luis yesterday, I saw Pedro de Florencia's wife and daughter picking berries along the creek. They are always together whenever they leave their house.

I hid in the river cane and watched them. Juana Cathalina is about 13 years old and not yet married. Her hair is long and as black as her skin is white. Her arms are thin and graceful like the legs of a fawn, and her neck looks as long as a crane's. I was not close enough to see her face, and she did not turn her head my way, but my heart remembers the smile she gave me on Christmas Day. I wonder if she smells as sweet up close as she looks at a distance.

She is a fine looking woman.

Chapter 17

January 22, 1676

Today began as many other days begin, sitting with Fr. Paiva at his desk in the convento, sipping hot cassina, and discussing what I have learned about the origins and customs of the Apalachee ball game. There is so much to tell that interests him, especially the legend of the first time the game was played.

When I finish talking with the chiefs and *inijas* in the province, he wants me to organize what I have learned and write it down. He will study what I have written, and then show me where I have made errors and make suggestions on changes in composition. The final report, the one that he will send to Bishop Calderón in Cuba, will bear Fr. Paiva's signature.

He asked me to tell him how the Apalachee game is different from the way I have seen it played in Timucua Province, but before I could answer, a messenger arrived. Usually we know in advance of visitors coming to San Luis, but this messenger was a runner and we had no warning.

He came directly to the convento and handed Fr. Paiva a sealed document. The friar thanked him and told him where he could go to get a meal and find a bed to rest in before turning back to San Augustín. Paiva sat back down at his desk and reached for a letter opener to break the seal. His hands were already shaking. Messages that come suddenly never bear good news.

From where I sat across the desk, I could see that the single page of parchment had a black border around it. The friar's lips moved as he silently read. Suddenly, tears welled up in his eyes. He laid down the letter and covered his face with his hands, sobbing.

"Leave me, please, Juan. Leave me," he said.

I wanted to touch him or comfort him in some way. Instead, I picked up my papers and walked out of the convento into the churchyard and found a bench to sit on in the sunlight. Two soldiers were wrestling with each other in the center of the ball field. The sound of the blacksmith's hammer at the stable echoed through the naked trees. Otherwise, all was quiet in the chilly air.

In a while, Fr. Paiva came out of the convento and walked to the church. He carried a hammer, and he nailed the message he had received to the door. Then he went inside the church and closed the door.

Others had seen him. One of the soldiers was curious. He released the hold he had on the other soldier's neck and walked toward the church. A man who had been breaking the ground in the friar's garden in preparation for spring planting dropped his hoe and hurried in that direction also. I was closest, and got to the door ahead of the others.

The large print at the top of the parchment said, "Notice of Death." At the bottom was the signature of Pedro Palacios, Secretary to the Bishop. I wiped the tears from my eyes so I could read, but more tears sprang up in their place. It took me a long time to read the notice, although it was a short one with a simple message.

Gabriel Díaz Vara Calderón, Bishop of Santiago de Cuba, died at Havana, Cuba of an illness contracted on his recent mission to La Florida.

I tried to open the church door, but it was locked from the inside. I could hear the friar's sobs, and the broken prayers he lifted up to God. I came back here to the convento and sat at his desk, waiting for Fr. Paiva to return. In time, I used his ink and quill to write an account of this terrible day. I cannot stop thinking about the day I found my dead father. Father Calderón filled the emptiness of my loss of Coya. I loved them both.

———

The sun was setting and the friar had not come out of the church when the girl appeared at the convento. She stood in the doorway, looking at me. She was dressed all in black, which made the delicate features of her face look even whiter and lovelier.

"I have a message for the priest," she said. "My uncle wishes to meet with him in the morning to plan a suitable Mass of Remembrance for Bishop Calderón."

I stood up awkwardly, almost knocking over my chair. I tried to answer her. I wanted to say that the priest was grieving in the church, and that I would give him the message when he came out. But the words stuck in my throat. I was dumb.

She stepped into the room and moved closer to me. "You are shy. I saw you the day you were hiding in the cane by the creek. Now, you won't even speak to me."

"I am not usually shy," I said. "You startled me. That is all. It has been a very bad day for me."

Juana Cathalina stepped even closer. I tried not to show my discomfort. The room felt much warmer and smaller. "Does your mother know you are here by yourself?" I asked.

"I do not need a chaperon just to look for the priest."
The girl's lower lip stuck out as if she were pouting.

"I am sorry. I did not mean to suggest . . ." I stopped
talking. I did not know what it was I wanted to say,
anyway.

"I saw you at the church at Christmas Mass. You
were wearing a bright red shirt with yellow piping, and
you had a pair of new moccasins made of deer hide."

Suddenly I was embarrassed at my bare feet and the
old clothes I wore.

"You should dress up more often, and you should cut
your hair. You could be a very handsome man."

The girl leaned toward me, and I bent my head to
accept the kiss on my cheek. Then, as quickly as she had
appeared, she was gone out the door.

I was alone once again, and darkness fell in the room.
The excitement of what had happened stirred me
physically, and the pleasure brought my imagination to
life. The strong feelings I had the first day I laid eyes on
the girl were shared by her. Juana loves me, as I love her.

I lowered myself into the chair and situated myself at
the desk once again. I folded my arms on the desk, lay my
head down, and thought about Juana Cathalina.

Fr. Paiva came in quietly. He stepped around behind
his desk, placed his hands on my shoulders, and gave me
a comforting embrace.

"Bless you, my son," he said. "Come. Let us pray
together that this Godly man has now found his reward in
Heaven."

While Fr. Paiva lifted up his prayer for Bishop
Calderón, I began to weep once again. But it was not
because of grief at the loss. It was shame I felt for having
impure thoughts of the woman on such a terrible day.

Chapter 18

San Luis
February 18, 1676

Saturday is always a busy day in San Luis. It is
market day, and people come great distances to trade
their goods in the plaza. Not all are Apalachee. There are
Amacanos who bring shells and sharks teeth from the
coast, Apalachicoli who come with deer hides from the
north, and even Chacatos who carry fine baskets for a day
and a half from the west.

The Chacatos also have buffalo robes that would
come in handy on these cold nights. I will try to trade for
one today.

Fr. Paiva rings the church bell at noon, signaling the
beginning of the market. That is at least two hours away,
and since I arose early I have time to write about my
disappointing journey to Turkey Roost and Ocuya.

Bip Bentura and I arrived home late last night. We started out as friends on Tuesday. By yesterday we had nothing pleasant to say to each other.

I asked Bip to go with me on this journey, and after he said he would go, he was invited to a clan buffalo hunt by Chief Matheo Chuba. I think Bip was disappointed in his decision to go with me, and wished he had gone hunting with Chuba.

The reason I asked him to go was because some of the chiefs no longer answer my questions for the census, and none of them will tell the truth about why they play the ball game. Bip is respected everywhere in Apalachee, and I thought the leaders at Turkey Roost and Ocuya would trust me more if Bip were with me.

When we were done at Ocuya, we started home and made our camp on a lake that is part of the River San Marcos. I speared a bass in the shallows while Bip cut wood for the camp fire. After we ate, we sat by the fire and talked.

The chief at Turkey Roost had said to me that his people never played the game, so he knew of nothing he could say to help me understand it. I asked Bip if he thought the chief was telling the truth.

Bip laughed. "The people of Turkey Roost have a game every year before the spring planting. One year it is at Turkey Roost, and the next year at Aspalaga. I myself once played in that game."

"Then why did you not speak up when he lied to me?"

Bip lit his tobacco pipe before answering. "If a man lies to your face, it is shameful. If he knows you know it is a lie, he must have a good reason."

I did not understand the logic behind what Bip said, but I went on. "And Ocuya deceived me by saying there were only sixty people among his three villages, and by saying that Chuli had been abandoned completely. When you and I passed through that country it was obvious the people were hiding in the woods."

Bip continued to puff on his pipe, sending up thin, gray wisps of smoke. I asked him why he thought the principal men lied to me. Bip did not react well to the question. "Maybe it is your fancy clothes, and the shortness of your hair," he said.

That was a strange thing for Bip to say. He wears his hair cut short, and it was he who told me to ask the friar to use his scissors to cut my hair so it would look neater than if I used a knife.

"The clothes you are wearing now are more Indian than mine, but in San Luis you dress yourself just like a Spaniard, and none of the Apalachee seems to mind," I said.

"These people have known me all my life," Bip answered, "and I am Apalachee. They trust me. You are Timucua, a foreigner to some of these country people. When you walk in with short hair looking like a Spaniard, there is no wonder they do not trust you."

That is when I lost my temper and said some things that insulted Bip Bentura. We went to our beds and tried to sleep, but it was the night of the full moon and I was so full of anger I laid awake imagining all of the things I should have said to him.

Bip must have had the same problem, because he got up and went back to the fire. When I opened my eyes, he was sitting there smoking his pipe again. I rolled over and sat up.

"There is one more thing I need to say to you," he said. Again, I could not think of the right thing to say, so I just sat there waiting for him to skin my hide with his tongue once again.

"You need to understand the Spaniards and how they feel about their women. Among Apalachee, who an unmarried girl chooses to lie with is her business. But the

Spanish get upset, saying it is a sin. They deal harshly
with the man. Sometimes they will send the girl away to a
convent to protect her from her own passion."

"Why are you saying this to me?" I asked.

Bip got up and relieved himself on a bush, and then
he came over and squatted down next to my bed. "There
are no secrets in the mission or in the village," he said.
"Even Florencia knows about what is happening between
you and his niece. He warned Chief Matheo Chuba that if
it continues, he will put an end to it."

I stood up. "And the deputy governor is mistaken," I
said. "There is nothing improper going on between me
and Juana Cathalina."

Bentura chuckled. "Go back to sleep," he said. "You
are a bigger liar than Ocuya and Turkey Roost,
combined."

Maybe I should have grabbed my knife to answer the
insult, but I remained calm. I picked up my blanket and
started walking home. Bip followed me, but there was
nothing left for either of us to say. He is not the friend I
knew three days ago.

It is late in the afternoon, and looking out of the
doorway of the convento I watch the market vendors
packing what they did not sell. Some will go home today
if they live nearby. Most of them will stay in the village
with relatives or sleep in the council house so they can
attend Mass tomorrow.

Fr. Paiva is in the church, preparing for tomorrow.
He said I could use his desk if I wanted to write a letter. I
have no one to write to, so I will continue with this
journal I have been working on for so many years.

Juana Cathalina did not come to the market today. It
is the first time we have not seen each other on Saturday

The Last Timucuan

for over a month. Even when she is there, we cannot touch each other or even speak. Her mother always hovers nearby, along with Juana's four younger brothers.

There are always a large number of people at the market, and Juana and I play a game. I move around so I am always at a safe distance behind her chaperone. When Juana turns to speak to her mother, I am a face in the crowd, and our eyes meet. She always smiles when we do that. From what Bip Bentura said, perhaps we were not as clever as we thought.

Juana Cathalina's mother came to the market today with her husband Pedro de Florencia. She bought fruit that she put in a basket, and a dozen turkey eggs someone brought all the way from Turkey Roost. She must have spied me, because she was pointing her finger in my direction while her husband looked to where she was pointing. I came back to the convento.

I forgot to buy the buffalo robe.

My heart aches for not having seen my beloved, and I am worried that my own brashness and carelessness may have put her in danger.

And I am thinking more about Bip Bentura. Perhaps he is a better friend than I thought while I was angry. He gave up a buffalo hunt to go with me. He told me why some of the chiefs might not trust me, and I was too proud to listen to what he said.

He risked our friendship by explaining to me the danger we face, Juana Cathalina and I.

There is nothing her parents can do to destroy the love I feel for her, but I cannot stand the thought that they might send her away to a convent. The priest of Santa Fé told me of such places. There is one in Cuba. The women dedicate their lives to Christ, and are forbidden to marry or have children. That would not be a happy life for a woman with the passionate nature of Juana Cathalina.

Perhaps, with time, I can rise in stature in the eyes of the Florencia family. I can become a leader, and not just a scribe and a parish interpreter. I could join the militia, as the deputy governor suggested to me when I first came to San Luis.

Fr. Paiva has his disagreements with the Florencias, but he is respected and has powerful friends in San Augustín. Perhaps he can tell them I would be a suitable mate for Juana Cathalina. She is now 14 years old. If she were Timucuan, she would be almost too old for a good marriage.

Perhaps this is all a dream, this idea that I could someday become a member of the Florencia family.

Chapter 19

San Luis
February 24, 1676

I returned today from my final journey for the deputy governor and the priest. I have come from Ivitachuco, the second largest mission in all of Apalachee. There are four villages in addition to the large town where Misión San Lorenzo is located. With the friar's help, I calculated that there are 1,200 people living there.

The priest of San Lorenzo went with me to the villages and was present when I asked questions about the ball game. Ivitachuco has a ball field, and the chiefs were all willing to talk to me. Perhaps because they see so many Spaniards, my short hair did not offend them. I left my Spanish clothing at home in San Luis.

Seventy-five people from Ivitachuco moved across the river to Asile where there is a large Spanish farm and ranch. Asile is on the Timucuan side of the river, but only Apalachee live there. I counted the people in my Apalachee census. If that is a mistake, Florencia can just subtract 75 from my total.

The Apalachee people work there at the farm, and the Chief of Asile assigns them to tasks like raising corn and wheat, and tending the owner's pigs, cows, and chickens. When he is paid with grain and meat, the chief keeps his share and distributes the rest among the workers. The people are well fed, but poorly clothed. The chief said that sometimes the owner cheats him and does not pay for all of the work done.

Bip Bentura offered to go with me, but we do not travel well together and his friendship is worth more than his help. Of course, I did not say that to him. As it turned out, I did well without him.

Tomorrow I plan to see Deputy Governor Florencia and present my census report to him. I have my journal book, and it will not take much time for me to write down what I learned. Once that task is complete, I will write a full report on the ball game and present it to Fr. Paiva. It may take longer to write, although I have all of the information at hand.

───────

I went to Florencia's house this morning. A man I had never seen met me at the door. He introduced himself to me, and we shook hands. His name is Jacinto Roque Pérez, and he is the new lieutenant at the garrison. Pérez was polite, and treated me with respect. When he heard my business, he asked me to sit in a chair beside the door.

"The deputy governor is ill today. I will show him what you brought with you," he said. Pérez took my journal book and writings and went up the stairs to Florencia's room. The lieutenant is about my age, but considerably shorter than me. He has a trim physique, like a runner, unlike many of the Spaniards who have a stocky build. He also has a sense of dignity about him.

I could hear the muffled voices as he and Florencia spoke.

While I waited, I noticed a shadow at the top of the stairs. It was Juana Cathalina, and she was leaning over the banister looking at me. She put a finger to her lips and motioned to indicate she would come down the stairs. Just then, another door opened and I heard her mother calling her name. I did not see her again.

When Lt. Pérez came down the stairs, he said that Florencia would look over what I had written and that I should return in two days, when he might have time to ask me questions.

———

It has been the longest two days in my life, waiting for the next chance to see Juana Cathalina. I filled the hours writing the report to the priest, even staying up late at night using an oil lamp to see.

It is better to be completely honest with the priest, I decided, and to tell him that some of the chiefs, particularly those in the north, lied to me and denied knowledge of the ball game. I heard the same stories five or six times from other chiefs in other parts of Apalachee, and I believe there is nothing more to be learned.

When I am done with the deputy governor, I will tell Fr. Paiva that I am ready with my report to him.

———

A cold rain began last night and has continued throughout the day.

The deputy governor was sitting in a comfortable chair when I arrived at his house. Lt. Pérez was with him, and the three of us sat before the fire for an hour while I told what I had learned. It was another hour before Florencia ran out of questions.

He was unhappy that I counted only 7,580 Apalachee Indians in the province. He thought there were many more. When I said that 75 of those people actually lived in Timucua, his frown deepened. He did not believe my count of only 120 people living at Bacuqua was accurate.

"I know that more than 10,000 Indians died in the epidemic of 1659," he said. "Surely there must be more than 7,580 left alive."

Pérez spoke up for the first time. "Those 10,000 deaths were mostly Timucua, I believe. Perhaps there have never been as many as we thought."

That seemed to satisfy Florencia for the moment. The deputy governor had a copy of Bishop Calderón's mission report from the year before. He thumbed through the papers, holding each page so that the light of the fire reflected on it, making it easier to read in the dark room. "Comparing the two counts, they are somewhat similar," he admitted.

Neither Florencia nor Pérez asked me if people were hiding out, avoiding being counted. They were more interested in whether I covered the entire province, and visited every mission, village, and hamlet.

I could truthfully say that I had been almost everywhere. "There are Chiscas who have taken over a small community north of Escambe. I did not go there. The friar said they are warlike, and I would be risking my life going without soldiers."

"Check that, would you, Jacinto?" Florencia said. "Send some men to chase them out if they will not join themselves to the mission at Escambe."

"Yes, sir," said the lieutenant, and he made a note in his journal.

I said that no one had seen an Englishman, although they were known to be among the Chisca. Also, no one reported seeing a gun anywhere in Apalachee that was not in the hands of a Spanish soldier.

Neither man seemed concerned when I said that there were *cimarrones* from Yamassee, Tocobaga, and Chacato living in Apalachee villages. "There are even three Tocobagans right here in Talimali," I said.

When I said that, they had no more questions. We had discussed each mission and all of the villages they served, throughout Apalachee. Florencia said he would have Pérez rewrite my report and then submit it to Governor Salazar in San Augustín.

"I cannot write any better than Juan Mendoza has," Pérez said. "I suggest that I do a brief addendum, and submit it as written."

As I was preparing to leave, Florencia said he had something to discuss with Lt. Pérez, and he wanted me to walk around the parade ground and return in a little while.

It was still drizzling, so I did not walk far. I took cover under a shed where a Spanish blacksmith was hammering nails on an anvil. He was so intent in his work he had not seen or heard my approach, and I startled him.

"What do you want?" he said, still holding his hammer and looking me up and down.

"Just shelter from the rain," I said. "I am Juan Mendoza, the parish interpreter, and scribe to the deputy governor."

That seemed to satisfy him for the moment, and he went back to his hammering. When he was done, he looked up again.

"There will be 22 houses when the ones under construction are finished. More Spanish soldiers and artisans are expected to come to San Luis in the spring. I can scarcely keep up.

"We do not usually see Indians in this part of town," he said as he used his tongs to dip a hot nail into a bucket of water. "There is a sentry who comes around to challenge your kind, to see what business you have here."

I realized that the man was nearly deaf from years of hammering iron, so I introduced myself once more, in a louder voice, as the deputy governor's scribe, and the parish interpreter.

"The guard is watching out for thieves," the blacksmith said.

It was time for me to return to the house of the deputy governor, so I bid the blacksmith a good day.

Florencia was not yet ready to receive me, so I sat waiting on the chair inside the front door. Juana Cathalina's younger brothers were playing, running up and down the stairway. I do not remember their names, but one was about eight years old, and the other about five.

The older boy wore a soldier's hat and waved a wooden sword in the air. He chased his brother, who had feathers in his black, curly hair, and wore only a loin cloth. The older boy menaced me with the sword, and I waved my arms in the air as if I were frightened, which made both of them laugh.

A black servant girl came in and scooted them up the stairway. I watched for Juana Cathalina, but did not see her.

"We have decided that your duties should change," the deputy governor said when I was admitted into his study. "You did a good job – better than expected. It seems the bishop did not exaggerate your abilities.

"I want you to join the Apalachee Militia. I will make you a sergeant. You will train under Lt. Pérez, and you will serve as his scribe, as well as my own. In addition to being a militiaman, you will be writing our reports."

I was almost overcome with gratitude and excitement, but tried to hide my emotions. Can this be the opportunity I need to prove myself worthy of Juana Cathalina?

I thanked Florencia for the trust he had placed in me, and pledged to be the best scribe in La Florida.

Before I left, Florencia had one more thing to say. "With your new duties, there will be little time for you to work as parish interpreter. Maybe you know of someone you could suggest to the friar as your replacement."

I said I would give the matter some thought. When I walked out the door, I saw that it had quit raining. Juana Cathalina was sitting by her window upstairs. She was singing. I did not know the song. She has a beautiful voice.

Chapter 20

The information I collected on the ball games was voluminous, filling the two notebooks the friar had given me in the beginning. In one notebook I wrote down the rules of play, such as the number of men on each side, the scoring, the appointment of officials to make sure the game was fair, and the conduct that might have a player thrown out of the game.

Knowing of Fr. Paiva's interest in the legends of the game, I collected that information in the second notebook. This is how it began:

> In long ago days, there were two chiefs who lived in neighboring villages. One was named Ochuna Nicoguadca, signifying the lightning bolt. The other was Ytonanslac, a wise and elderly man who was allied with other Apalachee gods. Ytonanslac had an orphaned granddaughter, Nicotaijulo, whose name means "Woman of the Sun."
>
> The village leaders sent her to fetch water every day. In the course of her employment, she

became pregnant in an extraordinary way and gave birth to a son whom she hid among some bushes. There the panther, the bear, and the blue jay found him. They brought the child to his great grandfather, Ytonanslac, telling him how his granddaughter, Nicotaijulo, had given birth to the child. Ytonanslac ordered them not to tell anyone else about the child, whom he called Chita, and later he called him Oclafi, meaning, "Lord of Water." In his twentieth year, his name was Eslafiayupi.

As he grew to manhood, Eslafiayupi excelled in courage, in his skill with bow and arrow, and in "chunky," the game played since the beginning of time. Because of his renown, he attracted the attention of Ochuna Nicoguadca who thought that he might be the son of Nicotaijulo. This concerned Ochuna particularly because his shaman foretold that some day a son born to Nicotaijulo was destined to kill him.

So begins the ancient Apalachee legend of the origin of the ball game. It is a long story that takes a great deal of time and patience in the telling, and much more in the writing.

Baltazar, the Principal Chief of San Pedro de Patali, told it to me first, and I insisted he tell it slowly so I could write every word. The telling and the writing took from sun up to late in the day.

I wrote it again when the *Inija* of Aspalaga told it. When I compared the two manuscripts they were exactly the same, without even one word out of place. Two more times, I listened to the tale from other chiefs and compared what was said to what was already written two times in my notebook. There were no differences. That is why I was not too upset that some of the chiefs did not want to tell me the story. I already knew it.

The Timucuan storytellers of my youth in Laguna Oconee sometimes embellished their stories, adding things that occurred in their imaginations. Not so, these Apalachee storytellers. They do not tolerate even small revisions to a legend.

I wrote down the whole story for Fr. Paiva, along with descriptions of the ceremonies that are observed before and during the game. It should be interesting reading for a friar, and give him an understanding and respect for these people, much as they have earned my respect.

It was not necessary for me to dwell on the playing or scoring of the game. Fr. Paiva has witnessed three games here at San Luis, and he knows how they can become violent when the players get overly enthusiastic to win the point. Broken arms and gouged eyes are common.

After reading what I had written, the priest asked questions of me. He wanted to know about the skull or scalp that is buried in front of the pole before the game starts. That is the one question I could not truthfully answer. I do not know whose death it is to represent, and never thought to ask.

There was only one ceremony I deliberately left out of my description. It is what the chief says to the young women the night before the game. Fr. Paiva wanted to know what it was he said to them, but I did not want to tell him because I was afraid he would have bad feelings against the chief. Paiva was so persistent with his questions, I finally said that the chief was lifting the taboos for the night and encouraging the women to sleep with whoever asked them.

I told him of the lifting of the pole, with women and men on opposite sides, pulling on grape vines. No other kind of rope was allowed. The eagle in its nest at the top of the pole must always face to the east to honor the God of Thunder.

The priest asked many questions about the gambling and about the shaman's practice of preparing a sack of magical herbs that the players rub on their hands to make them play better. He wrote down my answers, and they seemed to satisfy him.

When we were done and the friar had no more questions, it was late at night and I wanted to go to my bed. He thanked me for all of my hard work and said he probably now knew more about Apalachee spirituality than any white man had ever known, and that his final report would be helpful to other priests and beneficial to the Indians.

"Florencia and I talked today," said Fr. Paiva. "He said that you also did a good job with the census, and that he has come to rely on you to such an extent that you will have no time to work as parish interpreter."

I felt bad when he said that. He also had come to rely on me.

"I would like to ask that you be available to help me finish this one project," he said. He was holding up the notebooks and loose papers about the ball game.

Before I slept last night, I wondered about what else there was for me to do. I thought my job was finished.

I have spent the last four days accompanying Jacinto Roque Pérez as he performs his duties around San Luis. There are thirty soldiers and four officers, if you count the adjutant and Juan Fernandez de Florencia, who is captain as well as Deputy Governor of Apalachee Province.

Roque is unmarried, but has been given his own house as if he has a wife and family. The other unmarried soldiers live together in the barracks in a compound behind the governor's house.

Much of Roque Pérez's morning is devoted to disciplining the young men who are rowdy and a long way from home. He settles arguments between them, and decides who should stand guard duty and who should clean the latrine.

What surprised me the most are the number of reports he writes. Every time he locks a man in the brig, there is a report to write. Whenever a trader comes to San Luis from the north, Pérez questions him about whether he has seen Englishmen, and how far to the south he has encountered Chiscas, and he writes all the answers in a report. In addition to all the reports, he writes requisitions for food and supplies, and receipts for whatever is delivered to the garrison.

Some of these papers have many copies, one of which is sent to San Augustín, another to the lieutenant in charge of soldiers at Santa Fé. He even sends a copy to the deputy governor, although his house is only a stone's throw from the garrison.

Two or three times a week, we receive reports from the sergeant major or the governor in the capital. Sometimes the exact same report is received from both of them, delivered by the same runner on the same day. Reports come to San Luis that have nothing to do with Apalachee. Every one must be read, initialed, and kept forever in a box.

Roque plans to read every report aloud, with me sitting at his side. He will then ask me how I think it should be handled. When I know enough and he trusts my judgment, it will be my responsibility to read everything that comes in, to bring important matters to his attention, or show them to the deputy governor if they are civil matters and not military.

Roque says to me that the Spanish are more prolific in their writing than they are efficient in their procedures.

———————

Today has been a very bad day – so bad that I told Roque Pérez I had taken ill and needed to go to my bed to rest. For two days I have been reading old reports and separating them into stacks of those that should be filed and those that should be acted upon by the adjutant. Roque looks at what I have done to see if I am making good judgments.

The third report I read today made my hands tremble. It came from the lieutenant at Santa Fé. It was a copy of a report addressed to the governor in San Augustín. It was of no concern to Apalachee, and was one that I ordinarily would set aside as unimportant. I folded it and tucked it in the sleeve of my tunic before I left he garrison.

The body of the report says:

"There has been an arrest in the murder of two Acuerans who were killed by *cimarrones* two months past. The Chief of Potano sent word that the murderer had been apprehended and was chained to a post in the main council house. The man is now in my custody, and, if it pleases Your Excellency, he will be sent to

San Augustín for trial. My sergeant is in the process of questioning witnesses and securing affidavits and other evidence of guilt.

The murderer is an Utinan, of western Timucua. We have been told he was born in Laguna Oconee, a village that no longer exists. He calls himself Calesa, but we do not believe that is his name. Calesa is said to be a vile curse word, and not a proper name."

Chapter 21

Yesterday was bad, being reminded of what my brother, Carlos, has done with his life, and wondering whether it would somehow involve me here in Apalachee. Today was worse. I got very little sleep, and was awakened early by the sound of Bip Bentura calling my name.

When I opened the door and looked outside, he was facing me with his hands on his hips. "We need you at the council house," he said, and then he turned and walked away before I could answer him.

I have been in the council house many times, and some mornings I sit with the men and drink cassina while they discuss what is to happen during the day. I have never been so rudely summoned, and I took my time getting there.

Before I ducked through the doorway, I could hear the men arguing among themselves. When they saw me, they stopped talking. The council house was half full. Almost all of the men in Talimali were there, and not just their leaders. Bip stood next to Chief Matheo Chuba in his place of honor.

"We are joined by the parish interpreter," Bip announced in a loud voice. "Perhaps he will use his talents to interpret for us."

There is a support post inside the door and to the right. It is used by the priest to nail up announcements of church events, and requests for work volunteers and singers for the chorus. I have never seen anyone read what he puts there. Now there was a crowd of men around the post.

"El Juego de Pelota esta Prohibido," appeared in large letters at the top of the paper. Bentura speaks and reads Spanish very well, as does Chuba and several others. They did not need me to translate.

I took my time and read every word. Fr. Paiva's order prohibited the ball game from being played at Misión San Luis, in the village of Talimali, and in any of the surrounding towns served by the mission.

"The game is based on idolatrous worship of pagan gods, and, as such, is the work of Satan," the order said. "The game should never again be played. Nor should the pole ever again be erected on the field that is circumscribed by the Stations of the Cross. As such, the field is Holy Ground, and the pole dedicated to the pagan god of thunder, a desecration of it."

Chief Chuba and his *inija* did not wait for my answer. When I turned around they were already gone. The rest of the men were following them outside. It was just as well. There was nothing I could think to say to them.

———

Fr. Paiva was expecting me. He was sitting at his desk clutching the crucifix, as if I had interrupted him in his prayers.

"You betrayed me," I said. They were the harshest words I had ever spoken to a priest, but there were many more, much worse, that stuck in my throat and fought to get out.

"You told me that you only wanted to improve on the questions you ask at Confession. You never said that you intended to rob them of their games and their ceremonies and their entertainments."

Fr. Paiva stood up slowly. He placed the crucifix in its case and closed the lid. When he looked at me, his face had turned red, and the veins in his neck stood out. "I confront Satan at every turn with these people. God requires of me that I expose the Devil's lies and free the people from the grip of his deceptions and save their souls. The game that is played is idolatrous devil worship, and can no longer be tolerated."

I tried to control my passions and form an answer.

"And," he said, "I will require of you that you speak to me with respect."

When I answered him by saying that my duty was now to the deputy governor and not to him, Fr. Paiva reminded me that everyone's first duty is to God. Then he said that since I now serve the deputy governor, he should provide for my needs in the future.

He took his seat, bowed his head for a moment, then addressed me again. "I am leaving in two days for Cupaica. I will show the priest the notebook, and encourage him to stand with me and forbid the playing of the game in his precinct. From there, I will ask him to carry it to Aspalaga, and so forth, until it has been considered by all the priests of Apalachee."

He reached his hand across the desk. I did not take it. "I want to thank you for your work in exposing this evil," he said. "I know that you do not believe it now, but perhaps with time the people will accept what I have done . . ."

I started to leave. As I reached the door he said that when he returns from Cupaica he will have other uses for the storage room in which I sleep. "Perhaps the deputy governor can find a place for you in the barracks."

————————

Jacinto Roque Pérez and I were called to Florencia's house this morning to discuss a shipment of corn to San Augustín. The deputy governor was sipping a cup of tea and eating a sweet cake as he spoke to us.

"Chuba has given me the names of 17 men who can be spared from the planting," the deputy governor said. "They are not the strongest, but they should each be able to carry two arrobas of grain."

He told us the men who carried the grain would stay for two months and would work on the construction of the new fort before coming home. "Some are single, but four of them are married men with wives and children. It cannot be helped."

Roque Pérez said that so many of his men were ill, he hoped it would not be necessary for them to go as guards.

The deputy governor answered that there had been no trouble on the Camino Real for many months, and that he decided to send Bip Bentura with them. "He has made the journey many times and can provide the discipline to keep slackers moving at a good pace."

"Bip has no family, other than his wife," Roque Pérez said. "Chuba can do without his enforcer for two months."

Both of the Spaniards laughed.

We were interrupted when a servant entered the room and said that the priest was outside, demanding to see Florencia.

When Fr. Paiva came in he was red-faced with anger. He clutched in his hand two of his orders, which he threw down on Florencia's desk. One was the order banning the games, the one he had posted in the council house.

Someone had smeared paint on it and written insulting words.

Fearing that such might happen, the friar had posted the second order at the council house the night before. It said, "No one should make so bold as to deface or spill paint on any orders displayed here."

On this second order, some artist had drawn a picture of a priest choking an Indian.

Florencia laughed out loud. "Bring this man to me." He flipped the poster across the table to his adjutant. "I could use a talented artist."

It was funny, what he said. Even I laughed along with him and Roque Pérez. And the artwork was excellent – as good as any I have ever seen.

Fr. Paiva saw no humor in it and demanded of the deputy governor that he provide a sentry to patrol the council house at nighttime to prevent a reoccurrence, and to apprehend the culprit.

"Fr. Paiva, I have no jurisdiction in the council house. As you have reminded me from time to time, the council house belongs to the Apalachee. It affords them a place where they should be respected and not intruded upon by outsiders. I believe I have in my desk a letter with your signature, reminding me to enter only with the consent of the chief."

The priest snatched the papers from the table and walked out. I have never seen such an ugly display of temper between two Spaniards. They usually hide their disagreements from Indians. I am not happy with Fr. Paiva for what he did with my report, but I felt shame for the way he was disrespected by Florencia.

———————

The priest was gone to Cupaica, and I used his desk and writing materials yesterday afternoon to write down all that happened these last two days. I worked late and burned a whole candle. So much that has happened is disturbing to me, but nothing could have prepared me for what happened last night.

I had not been asleep long when I was suddenly awakened. Someone was at the door of my room, tapping on the wood. The moon was almost full, but it was darkened by a cloud. Still, looking through the crack in the door I could see that my visitor was Juana Cathalina.

This was only the second time she had come to me at nighttime. She knew the friar was away and that we would not be caught together unless a sentry saw her coming or going from her house. I was glad to see her.

Later, just before she left, I chastised her for taking such a risk and cautioned her to be careful going home and to stay in the shadows.

When I had closed the door behind her, I crawled back into bed and enjoyed the smell of her skin on my bedclothes. After a moment I rolled over and closed my eyes, but then I heard loud voices from across the ball field. I slipped outside and made my way from tree to tree until I could see what was happening. A sentry had Juana Cathalina by the arm and was tying to force her to go with him to the house of the deputy governor. She called him filthy names and threatened him if he did not let go of her arm.

I thought of running to help her, but before I made my move she stopped resisting him and led the way home, with him keeping step beside her.

Only moments after they had entered the house, the windows, both downstairs and upstairs, began to glow with lamplight. I could hear voices. Juana Cathalina's father Pedro is a rancher and was not there, but her mother was crying loudly. She demanded to know where her daughter had gone so late at night.

"Tell me, have you been with some one?" she cried out. The shutters were open, and anyone awake in the Spanish village could have heard every word.

I moved from shadow to shadow back to the convento storage room and got back in my bed. I heard the deep voice of the deputy governor, pleading with the women to lower their voices and to stay calm. I also heard Juana Cathalina. She cursed so vilely that her mother was finally shamed into silence.

Later, there was again movement at my door. I pretended to be asleep. The sentry came in and looked down at me, then, apparently satisfied of my innocence, he returned to the Florencia house.

Chapter 22

A messenger came for me while I was reading military dispatches at the barracks. He said I was needed at the deputy governor's house.

As I sat on the chair inside the front door waiting to be admitted into the office, another door cracked open. I could see enough out of the corner of my eye to know that the mother of Juana Cathalina was spying on me. I pretended not to notice her.

When Roque Pérez opened the door and invited me into the office, Florencia was sitting at his desk. He was blotting dry something he had been writing. Roque Pérez slumped slightly in his chair beside the desk.

The deputy governor placed the writing in a heavy envelope and used two wax seals to secure it. Then he looked up at me. "We have decided that Bentura may need help on the journey to San Augustín. We are sending you with him to escort the men. We expect no trouble, but it will be good to have a man with military training to go with them."

I wondered whether he was being honest with me, and decided to test him. "Would you like me to carry a musket? I am also good with a shotgun."

The two men exchanged glances. They always do that when they are lying and need time to think of an answer.

"As I say, we do not expect trouble," Florencia said. "This is just a precaution. You will wear a military tunic, and it will be obvious to everyone that you are under my command. Your native weapons should suffice."

He handed me the letter and told me it was an official communication for the sergeant major in San Augustín, and that I should deliver it to the presidio upon my arrival. Roque Pérez said nothing at all while I was there. He shook my hand as I walked out.

I decided to go to the convento to pack my things instead of returning to the barracks. As I walked around the west side of the Florencia house, I heard the sound of weeping from an upstairs window. It was Juana Cathalina. Her mother was with her, and her voice was harsh. Some day she may be the matriarch of the family to which I belong, so I need to be kind to her.

We leave tomorrow. It should take 12 days to get to San Augustín. I hope to return to San Luis by Easter.

———

We were delayed for half a day when two of the men suddenly took ill the night before our departure. Fr. Paiva looked at them and told Roque Pérez that they were not faking, but that they were very ill and not fit to travel. Two replacements were summoned. They are both married men with families. They were angry, and their wives and their village chief were there to say how badly they were needed at home. Bentura told them the truth. He said they would be needed to work on the fort for two months before they would be allowed to come home.

We got to the Aucilla River last night. Where the trail meets the river it is swollen with spring rains. Bentura sent men upstream and downstream looking for a safe place to cross. Bip knows of a place three leagues to the north where the river disappears underground, only to bubble to the surface again farther on. It is hard to get to because of swamps and dense woods and would delay us even further. He chose a place for the crossing that was swift but shallow.

We crossed the river at first light. One of the new men got his feet tangled in eel grass. Bentura and I went to help him, but the current dragged him under and the weight of the bundle on his back held him down until he drowned. One arroba of grain floated down stream while the other was saved.

Bentura chose four men to carry the dead man, and he led them back to San Luis. The rest of us will wait here for their return. These people are superstitious about a foreigner leading them. That is how they think of me, as a foreigner. They also blame me for the banning of the games. Even Bip treats me coldly since Fr. Paiva posted the order.

One man said he was going fishing down stream. It is now close to dark and he has not returned. If he goes back to Talimali, Florencia will have him arrested and whipped. The others are afraid to leave.

I carried my papers with me. They would not be safe at the barracks, and I no longer trust the friar enough to leave them at the convento. I found a plank of wood from where a Spanish house is being built at San Luis. It is flat, and makes a good lap table for my writing.

While I was trying to save the drowning man, my leather case went under the water. The papers were wrapped securely, but some of the pages got wet. It has been a sunny day, and I laid them out to dry on the ground and on a log. The men show no interest in them. Nobody here can read.

Fredric M. Hitt

Just now, darkness is falling, and it is time to put away my writings and go to sleep. But I want to write one more thing, so I will remember it forever. Somewhere to the north, a man is blowing on his reed flute. The tones echo from a high limestone cliff and float down the dark river to where we make our camp. It is as beautiful as anything I have ever heard, and makes me sad. I wish Juana Cathalina were with me to hear it.

Chapter 23

San Augustín
August 4, 1677

San Augustín is as the bishop described it the night we had dinner with the deputy governor at San Luis three years ago. It is a poor town, full of shabby people. Even the Apalachee people of Talimali are better fed than some of the Spaniards here.

The slaves are the worst off. Their clothes are in tatters, and their black skin wraps only muscle and bone. They have no fat to protect them in the winter. For all that, however, it is the dullness of their eyes that betrays their true state.

I saw only one black man with a soul still shining in his eyes. He was chained to a post in a market for slaves. Spaniards were inspecting his physique and bidding to buy him. One man who was inspecting him, dressed as a rancher, seized him by the upper lip when the slave refused the command to open his mouth so he could see his teeth. The black swung his head about and spit in the rancher's face.

The owner rushed forward to apologize for the slave's actions, and took a whip to him, bloodying him about the neck and shoulders.

"He's trouble!" the rancher said.

No one would pay enough money for him, so the owner dragged him away into an alley.

There are many more Spaniards here than at San Luis. I have seen some wearing regal clothing with shirts of silk and satin, and fancy stitched collars, but there are many others who dress as poorly as the Indians. There are artisans, such as stone masons, carpenters, and coopers who dress decently.

The town is full of Indians. On the first morning I saw Guale, Surruque, Mayacans, and Yamassee. Bip had never before seen a Guale or a Mayacan, and I told him who they were. There are more Apalachee here than Timucuans, which surprises me since this is the homeland of the Eastern Timucua. There is a common village where many of them live together. They have no chief, but only a village governor.

We are housed in the decrepit old council house in that village, just north of San Augustín. It is full of fleas. It will be home for the Apalachee men Bip and I brought from San Luis. He and I plan to start for home in two days, after we attend Mass at Nombre de Diós.

I have been to San Augustín twice before. I was seven years old when we were brought here from Oconee by the soldiers. That was when my father, Coya, was locked away in the old wooden fort. The second time was when Big Bow and I came to collect my father and take him home to die.

The place is not the same as I remember it. My memory is of forests of trees stretching from the river to the town. There are no trees left, only stumps where they have been cut down to build houses.

———————

I delivered the sealed letter from Deputy Governor Florencia to the office of the sergeant major. His clerk took it to him and then came outside and told me that I should return with Bip Bentura early tomorrow morning to talk to his boss. I don't care enough about seeing a sergeant major to walk all the way into town, but it will give me a chance to visit the Saturday morning market. Perhaps I will find a gift there to take home to Juana Cathalina.

Before I returned to the council house, I walked to where the new fort is being built on the waterfront. It is larger than any council house, so massive that when you get close it blocks out the sky. Three stone walls are standing, each twelve feet above the ground. There are parapets with gun emplacements where the walls meet. Where the west wall will be built, Yamassee workers are digging a foundation trench deeper than the height of a tall man.

Spanish soldiers sit in the shade of a tree, laughing and telling stories.

Betrayed!

I have been lied to by Florencia and Roque Pérez. Bip Bentura and I almost came to blows when we left the office of the sergeant major. Now that I have had time to reason, I believe Bip is innocent. He could not have known that my journey was a cleverly laid trap to keep me away from Juana Cathalina.

Like the slave I saw yesterday, I do not intend to submit.

This morning the sergeant major disclosed to me the content of the order I carried to him from the deputy governor of Apalachee. While Bip and I sat in chairs before his desk, he said that I was required to stay with the workers from San Luis, to provide for their sustenance and to administer any discipline required to keep them in line.

"You will be entrusted to collect the money owed to them for their labors and give them only what is needed for their necessities. What is left over in the pay account, you will carry with you and give to the chief of Talimali when you return with the workers upon their release."

The sergeant major expressed his displeasure that only 15 men came from San Luis to work. Bip explained about the man who drowned and the one who ran away, but that did not satisfy the soldier.

"The 15 men you have brought will do the work of the 17 who will be going home on Monday," said the sergeant major. "They will work 13 hours each day, instead of just 12. And it only makes matters worse that you are so late in arriving. The men who are leaving have worked three months, instead of just two, waiting for you people to relieve them. If the men who come to take their place are likewise tardy, we will have no compunction about holding them beyond their time."

He said that Bip Bentura would leave with the workers going home on Monday.

Then the sergeant major turned to me. He was now smiling. He had before him the letter I had carried from San Luis. "You come highly recommended by the deputy governor," he said. "I see you are both a scribe and an interpreter."

When I did not comment, he went on. "We do not expect manual labor from literate people such as you. You will be dividing your time between supervising the workers of San Luis and doing something much more interesting and challenging."

The sergeant major stood up and went to a table. He picked up a sheaf of papers and carried them back to his desk. "You do read Spanish and Timucuan, I assume?"

Again, I made no reply.

"And have you ever served as a scribe to record testimony in an official proceeding?"

I shifted in my chair. "No," I said. "I have never done such a thing."

He glanced at the letter, then nodded. "But you do write both clearly and quickly. At least, that is what Florencia tells us."

Again, I made no reply, and he went on. "A trial is scheduled to begin soon. It is a murder trial, and it will be of great interest. One of our two scribes has died, and you will take his place."

The sergeant major patted the stack of papers he had place on his desk and told me I should spend my spare time studying them to familiarize myself with what would be said at the trial and the names of the people and places that would occur in the testimony.

"And you have time to practice your writing. You will work with the other scribe, testing each other on speed and accuracy. Governor Pedro Hita de Salazar is a brilliant judge, but I am afraid he is not a patient man with incompetence."

I sat across the desk from the sergeant major, so the writing on the papers was upside down to me. I stared at the cover long enough to decipher part of what was written there. I could not read it all, but one word was in big letters and stood out from the rest. It said, "Calesa."

I have no more intention of participating in the trial of my own brother than I have of remaining in this filthy town for three months, wet-nursing fifteen Apalachee workers.

———

Bip Bentura and I were taken by boat to a place called Anastasia. It is an island across the bay from San

Augustín, covered with palmetto bushes and wind-beaten scrub oak trees. There is a watch tower there where soldiers are on the lookout for boats that might approach the bar. But it was not the watch tower we came to see.

Below the surface, under the trees, bushes, and dirt there is a rock the Spanish call coquina. It is from this rock that they build the walls of their fortress. The soldier said that the best coquina will withstand a cannon shot without shattering.

Fifty men come here each day to dig out the rock and haul it by hand and by oxen wagon to a boat on which it is taken to San Augustín. The Spanish call it quarrying, and it is very hot and tiresome work. The men use picks and axes to cut deep grooves in the stone, and then they break it into pieces, using wedges, hammers, and pry bars.

Smaller pieces can be handled by one man, using a handbarrow or by carrying it on his back. Larger hunks of coquina require four or more men to load on the wagon.

On our way back to San Augustín the soldier took us to the mouth of the river where men were collecting oyster shells and loading them on boats. They are hauled to a kiln next to the fortress. There they are burned until they turn white with heat. The Spaniards use it in making mortar to strengthen the walls of the fort.

There were Apalachee men from Cupaica digging out the oyster bed. They all had bloody hands and feet. I asked the soldier why Guale were not used for this job, since they have harvested oysters all their lives and know how to do it without bloodying themselves. He had no good answer.

When we returned to San Augustín, he showed us the work being done on the fort. He took us to the place I saw yesterday where they were digging to lay a foundation for the west wall. There was trouble today. A man was at the deepest part of the trench when the sandy walls fell in on him and crushed him to death.

One of the other Yamassee refused to go back into the hole, saying he was frightened by close spaces. He was whipped until he finally gave up and went back.

Bip watched me for two hours this afternoon, here in the council house, as I wrote down all that has happened today. I can tell he feels bad about how I have been deceived. I laid the quill aside to rest my hand for a moment, and our eyes met. I walked over to the bench where he was sitting and sat next to him.

"I am going with you," I said. "By the time you get to the river crossing at Tocoi, I will be waiting for you. Indians flee from San Augustín all the time. There are not enough soldiers to chase them all."

Bip Bentura put his arm around my shoulder and looked me in the face. "Juan, you are not just another Indian to the Spanish. They know who you are, and what Florencia has ordered. You are a prisoner here. If you leave, they will come after you."

"They have no right to demand I stay," I said.

Bip put his lips near my ear so no one else could hear. "Do you remember? Have you forgotten that you have been sworn as a soldier? That even now you wear the tunic of a militiaman? If you leave, they will call you a deserter. You will be shot. If they do not want to waste a bullet, they will find some other interesting way to kill you. Then you will no longer be a problem for the Florencias."

There was a dance later that same night in the council house. Spanish soldiers were here to make sure the

Yamassee did not fight with the Guale, and that the Apalachee were not knifed to death by the Timucua.

I know that what Bip said to me was right. I will have to stay here, at least for awhile, until they forget about me.

That may be why I went into San Augustín while the soldiers were busy keeping the peace late into the night. It was not hard to find the man I was looking for. They keep him in a cage behind his owner's house.

"What would you do if you were free?" I asked. He told me he would go south to the land of the Surruque. "They welcome my kind," he said.

That was a good enough answer. I had brought along a hand axe used by the stone cutters. With one swing, I knocked down the chain that held the door shut. I cut the leather bonds around his hands, then handed him the knife.

His skin was so black I could barely make him out as he ran down the alley and turned right toward the trail that led south from the town.

Chapter 24

O nce again I have been betrayed. First it was the priest, who lied to me about his intent and involved me in banning the people's game. Then it was the deputy governor, who tricked me into leaving San Luis. And now the man I thought of as my best friend has done likewise.

Bip Bentura left San Augustín this morning on his way home. He refused to carry with him a letter I have written to Juana Cathalina, a single folded piece of paper that could be hidden in his clothing and handed to her in private.

His words were so harsh they stung my ears. "You are a drowning man, Juan," he said, "grasping to drag another man with you to his death. You will never be respected by the Spaniards, much less accepted into one of their families. You are a savage to them, and not even Apalachee, at that."

It was then that I slapped the *inija* across the face. Others in the council house were looking on, and they grabbed me and pinned my arms behind my back. A man from our village handed his knife to Bip Bentura, but the *inija* gave it back.

"I have no time for a love-starved fool," he said. Bip walked out of the council house and was gone.

It is a grave matter among Apalachee to give offence to an *inija*, as it would be among my people. They hate me anyway because the ball game was banned. Now that I have publicly humiliated Bentura, I doubt I could last a week without falling on my knife or having some other fatal accident.

The sergeant major agreed with me that my duties in preparing for the trial were more urgent than watching the men in the council house. He consented that I should share a room with the other scribe, in the garrison, where I would be close to my work.

Convento de Santo Domingo

My dear Monseñor Morell,

By your leave, a bit of parenthetical observation:

An undated and unsigned letter, written on parchment,

has been discovered among the papers, and I have chosen

to insert it at this point. You will note that in the context of what went before, the writer, the Indian Juan Mendoza, referred to a letter written to the woman, Juana Cathalina de Florencia. I believe this to be that selfsame letter.

Whereas many of the original materials are written in the Timucuan tongue, and have required the services of aninterpreter, this letter is composed in Spanish. Accordingly, you have the original document. The penmanship is so extraordinarily precise that there was no reason to duplicate it.

Yours in Christ
Fr. Manuel de Soto

My love,

By now you must know that we have been deceived and betrayed, and that I will not be returning to you as we had hoped. My heart accepted our separation and eagerly anticipated the coming of Easter, the celebration of the resurrection of our Savior, when I would see you once again in the church. In my mind's eye, you are wearing the new yellow silk dress you described to me when last we were together.

It is the anticipation of that day that has sustained me. Now I know it is a painful delusion, and my heart has been torn from my chest, leaving a cruel void. The pain rips me like a knife. I cannot sleep. I cannot think clearly.

And yet I feel most acutely the anguish that you are suffering. I remember the sound of your cries at the time of our separation, and the recollection of it haunts me. I dedicate my life to drying your tears. If we cannot live together where we have lived before, we will find another place to live where we will be free to create our own family.

There is a place I want you to see. It is not far, only two days away from you, yet so remote that we would not easily be discovered. It is a magical place of beauty, a river not of water, but of music, as charming and comforting as Heaven itself. We could be together there for awhile, for a day or two or three. From there, we could go to another place described to me by my father. Your people do not even know of this village, and could not find it even if they searched for us a thousand years. We would be free, my love.

Until we meet, my love.

Chapter 25

*I*t came to me last night in a dream of my father. I went to visit him at Oconee and stood before him, but because he was blind he did not know I was there. Coya asked Big Bow if there were reports of my approach to the village. When I spoke, he knew me by the sound of my voice, and he embraced me.

Above all, I must remember not to speak. Carlos has not set his eyes on me in eight years. He would not recognize me now. My hair is cut short and I am dressed as a Spaniard, in trunk hose, a colorful silk blouse, and deerskin shoes. My skin is no darker than a soldier who spends his time out of doors. If he looks at me he will see a Spaniard, or perhaps a mestizo.

But the sound of my voice would betray me. Even if I speak Spanish, he will know me.

———

It is Monday, the first day of the trial, and all is in readiness. Alfonso Garza is the chief scribe, and a good one. I am to be his assistant. Sr. Garza transcribed the

Residencia proceedings when Governor Pablo de Hita Salazar investigated the affairs of his predecessor, Governor Nicolas Ponce de León. He also accompanied Bishop Calderón on the visit to Guale, after the bishop left me in Apalachee.

Sr. Garza has worked with me to improve my writing speed. "Remember, Juan," he told me, "only speed and accuracy are important. Nobody cares if the writing lacks beautiful flourishes. If some of it is illegible, you can always do it over at your leisure and embellish it to your heart's content."

He also taught me what he calls "tricks of the trade." He said that some words can be abbreviated, such as "Tim" for Timucua, "SA" for San Augustín, "G" for governor, "SM" for sergeant major, and "CX" for Calesa the defendant.

When I asked Garza why he added the X, he laughed and said there are many names that start with C, but that Calesa is the only one who is doomed. Sr. Garza likes to make jokes, but I do not think he would laugh if he knew that I am Calesa's brother.

The trial begins at noon, and I am writing this now to get my fingers limber. Garza has not yet come outside of the presidio into the courtyard where all is in readiness for the event. The governor has provided both his scribes with small tables that face each other, so we can signal back and forth when we are tired and need to rest our fingers or take a drink of water. When I write, Garza will rest, and when I rest, he will work.

To my right, a platform has been erected, and on it sits the governor's large desk and a tall chair. He will be high enough to be seen by everyone who comes to watch the trial, and yet be shaded by the limbs of a live oak tree. Garza and I will sit in the sun, but it is a cool day and we should be comfortable.

There is a bench for the sergeant major to sit on when he is not presenting his evidence or his arguments. Another, smaller, bench will be occupied by the defender who will speak for Calesa. (It is interesting that I no longer think of him as Carlos).

Calesa is chained to a post. He injured two soldiers yesterday when they were taking him to the river to wash the stink off of him for his trial. The sergeant major has 10 armed guards to watch him and to keep order during the trial.

All the townspeople will be here, and many came early and are choosing places to sit where they can see and hear everything. Some have black slaves or Indian servants to carry their comfortable chairs. A few sit on three-legged stools, while children and servants sit on the ground.

Governor Hita Salazar has ordered that no one be required to work on the first day of trial so that the Indians might attend and learn a lesson of Spanish justice. They will sit apart from the Spaniards on the hillside to the west. They will be able to see, but I doubt they will be close enough to hear what is said.

A woman has appeared with a suckling child. She is allowed by the guards to sit in the dirt, inside the roped-off area where Calesa is restrained. I do not know who she is. Perhaps she is Calesa's woman.

Garza is now at his table. I will set aside my personal writing, take a drink of water and prepare myself for what is to come.

The first day of trial was brief, and lasted barely two hours. The sergeant major summarized the charges against Calesa. He is accused of killing up to six people, at different times and places.

Calesa went alligator hunting with a Christian Yustagan named Lorenzo two years ago, and struck him in the head with an axe. He scalped him and robbed him of his possessions, and left him for dead. Lorenzo woke up, and crawled to La Chua ranch. He told a member of the Menéndez family what Calesa had done to him, and then he died.

Another man, a Christian Acueran named Alonso, was living in the woods near Santa Fé with a *cimarrona* named Maria Jacoba. They were accosted by Calesa and the *inija* of a Timucuan chief named Jabohica.

The sergeant major said Calesa murdered Alonso to take his woman, and that when he tired of her he planned to kill her also, but he was persuaded by the *inija* to return her to her people at Potano, because the *inija* read a bad omen in the clouds.

Fearing for her life, Maria Jacoba told the Chief of Potano what Calesa had done to Alonso. The chief then seized Calesa and delivered him to the soldiers.

The woman, Maria Jacoba, was also brought for trial, charged with breaking the law by being a *cimarrona*, and fleeing a mission village to live a sinful life in the woods. Her crimes were not as serious as those of Calesa, but they were being tried together for the convenience of witnesses, and because their crimes were related.

"The man who calls himself Calesa freely admits to killing four Christians and one heathen," the sergeant major said in his opening statement. "We believe the true number of people he has murdered is six."

I could have stood up and said that Calesa was also responsible for the heartless killing of 12 people at Laguna Oconee, including his own father and his uncle. But it was not my place to speak, so I kept my head down and continued to transcribe what was said.

My eyes met those of my brother. Carlos was studying my face. Maybe I looked familiar to him. I do not think he recognized me.

The defender stood up and said that Calesa should be found innocent because he was ordered to kill by his chief, and because what he might have done was proper under pagan beliefs, when killing one's enemies was sanctioned. It was not a strong argument, but the governor listened as carefully as if it made sense to him.

Garza and I sat together in the garrison after everyone went home, and he looked at what I had written down. He thought it was good, but that I still tried too hard to write in the classic way.

"Speed and accuracy, Juan, speed and accuracy," he said. I looked at Garza's writing, and he explained to me again his use of abbreviations. What he had written down was almost exactly the same as my memory of what had been said.

Sr. Garza has a wife and daughter in Cuba. He misses his family and writes to them every week. Now, with the trial, he has something interesting to tell them.

———

Governor Hita Salazar insisted on starting the second day of trial one hour after sunup, and he worked straight through to darkness with only three short recesses.

It was his intention to finish this business in only two days. "Other matters of state are more important than the trial of a murderer," he announced early in the day.

Thomas Menéndez told his story first, about what Lorenzo, the man who had been attacked with an ax, said to him before he died of his wounds at La Chua Hacienda. Menéndez is related to the governor by marriage, and Hita Salazar paid careful heed to what he had to say.

The woman, Maria Jacoba, gave her statement next, about how Calesa killed Alonso in the woods near Santa Fé. When she was done she asked to be taken back to her room because she feared Calesa's evil and did not want to be in his presence.

The Chief of Potano was there, dressed in his formal attire of a turkey feather match coat and leather leggings. He had his hair arranged on the top of his head in the old fashion, decorated with mistletoe, and shiny with bear grease. He had standing with him all the other chiefs and principal men of Potano.

He told the story of how he learned of Alonso's murder from the woman, and what Calesa said to him when he was arrested. "He felt no remorse at all," Potano said. "Calesa was proud of the deeds, and he bragged to me that he had killed five people, not just the three he admits to today."

A Spanish officer read statements he had taken from witnesses in all of the deaths, and spoke of digging up the body of a pagan Indian killed by Calesa. There were so many people killed, the governor had trouble keeping them straight in his mind.

Only once did the governor ask either Garza or me to read to him what we had written down. Hita Salazar got frustrated when the defender and the sergeant major got into an argument about something Maria Jacoba had said, and he ordered me to read back a part of her testimony. Without thinking of the consequences, I found the paper where I had written what she had said and read it aloud. When I looked up from my reading, Calesa was smiling broadly at me. He knew who I was. He recognized my voice.

Despite the governor's intentions, we did not complete the trial today. The testimony was finished and the evidence was complete, but tomorrow morning the sergeant major and the defender must present their arguments and recommendations on what to do with Calesa, and then the governor will announce his decision.

Most of the Indians were back at work on the fort today, but it appeared that every Spaniard in San Augustín attended the trial. Sr. Garza said to me that there were more than 500 people present.

Gamblers, both Spaniards and Indians, made wagers on the outcome. Most of them thought the governor would have Calesa hanged for his crimes.

The scribe work went well, although it was exhausting to both me and Sr. Garza. We work well together.

I intended tonight to write for myself everything that happened today, but I am so tired not even the cassina will keep me awake.

Governor Salazar appeared well rested and relaxed this morning. He came late, well after the others were there.

The sergeant major spoke first. He went through each murder and reminded the governor of what the witnesses had said. He also made much of Calesa's admission that he had murdered at least three people.

"He is the essence of pagan savagery," the sergeant major said, and he told the governor that Calesa should die for his sins and crimes.

The defender, a young priest, argued that Calesa was innocent by virtue of his lack of knowledge of the sinful nature of his deeds. He spoke of the state of the Indians before God came to La Florida and of the honors that were bestowed on young men who killed their enemies in battle. The killing of Alonso was on the order of his chief, the friar argued.

"He wanted to be *Noroco*, a hero to his people for slaying three of the enemy. Are we to judge him harshly for living in conformity with his nature?" he asked.

It was not a persuasive argument. The governor was polite and listened patiently, but his mind was made up. When the priest sat down, Pedro de Hita Salazar picked up the paper he wrote last night and read his decision aloud.

He found Calesa to be guilty of five of the six murders. He could find no persuasive evidence of his direct involvement in the sixth murder, for which he found him not culpable. Hita Salazar sentenced Calesa to death by garroting.

He found Maria Jacoba guilty of leaving her village without permission and living in sin. He sentenced her to 100 lashes. This drew gasps from the women who were present, and the sergeant major shouted for silence, restoring order.

The defender complained that it was the harshest sentence ever imposed on an Indian woman, and that because of her small stature, it might kill her. He further pointed out that the woman had informed against Calesa. Otherwise, he might have gone on to kill many more people.

The Governor granted the priest's request that he delay imposition of the sentences for two days, and that he take the time to pray that he be just.

———————

Friday, November 16, 1677

Governor Pablo de Hita Salazar called me to come to his office in the presidio.

He asked that I copy his final judgments, which he had written out in his tight scrawl. He said that Sr. Garza had bragged on my skill as a scribe and said that I have the most beautiful writing in the province.

I spent the morning writing the orders, and making two additional copies of each one. One would be kept in the official records in the Provincial Archive. One would be posted in the council house, and the other nailed to the door of the church.

I was surprised to find that he had changed his mind about killing Calesa. Instead, his order sentenced him to 100 lashes and a lifetime of hard labor at the prison called Castillo de Morro, in Havana.

Maria Jacoba was, indeed, sentenced to 100 lashes.

——— ——— ———

The whippings took place in the plaza on Saturday morning. They were well attended, as there were many people there for the market. I did not go, but watched from the doorway at the presidio. Maria Jacoba was strong, and survived the beating.

Calesa took his beating as a man, stood tall and never cried out even as the whip master flayed the skin from his back.

As far as I know, Carlos never told anyone about me before his boat left for Cuba, and I never told anyone in San Augustín that he was my brother.

Sr. Garza was on the same boat that carried Carlos to Cuba. He was excited about seeing his wife and child after more than a year of separation. It made me think of Juana Cathalina.

Chapter 26

December 20, 1677

I have inherited Sr. Garza's work. Since he left, there is no one else in Governor Hita Salazar's employ who can translate his orders into Timucuan and Apalachee. I have no understanding of the Guale tongue, but there are very few of them left alive. Their territory is now populated by Yamassee.

My duties to the men of Apalachee continue, although I spend very little time with them because of the hostility they have shown me. Their condition and treatment is intolerable, so I decided to speak to the governor on their behalf.

I asked to see Governor Hita Salazar on Tuesday, but he was too busy to see me. Today I was given some of his time. I told him about the problems I have with the paymaster, who gives me only a small portion of the men's pay to distribute to them. Lately, instead of reale coins, he hands me cheap beads and small copper bells for the men to trade in the market.

"These men have worked hard," I told him, "and they are paid only a pittance. Unskilled Spaniards are paid four reales a day. Skilled workers such as carpenters get much more, up to eight reales. Apalachee workmen, who do the most dangerous work, receive only one reale, plus a ration of three pounds of maize a day."

The governor listened politely for a moment, but then stood up and walked to the window while I continued to speak.

"To hand them trinkets in payment for their sweat and blood is unjust," I said, "and we have been here almost four months, and no one comes from Apalachee to relieve them and let them return to their families."

Governor Hita Salazar turned back from the window to face me. I noticed, for the first time, weariness in his face, and that his hair was turning gray where it hangs down over his ears. "This will be good news for you, I think, but bad news for the people of San Augustín." He walked back to his desk and sat in his chair. "We are not a profitable colony, as I am sure you know. We consume much more than we produce, and are dependent upon receiving a yearly subsidy, a shipment of money and supplies, from New Spain to sustain us."

I knew of the subsidy, but said nothing. I was waiting for the good news he had promised.

"Two years ago the shipment was hijacked by French pirates, causing us great hardship. Now, just a week ago, the subsidy shipment went to the bottom of the ocean, within sight of the bar at San Augustín.

"In short," he said, "we have no more money, and although it is of no consequence to you, building a stone fort is a great expense. The paymaster hands you beads and trinkets because that is all we have left.

"I will soon be issuing an order, and I want you to write it for me. It will announce that work on the fortress will cease until such time as we have money to pay the workers."

There was not even enough money in reserve to compensate Matheo Chuba and the other chiefs for the work performed by their men.

"We will have a nice Christmas festival for the Indians," he said. "After that is over, everyone can go home."

———————

I went to the council house on Christmas Eve to collect the men from San Luis, and to go with them to Christmas Mass. They were gone home, every one of them. They did not even wait to collect the maize that they could carry on their backs so they could eat on the long journey.

The governor had work for me to do, and I promised to remain in San Augustín until the New Year. But my mind was not on my work. I daydreamed about going home and being reunited with Juana Cathalina. How would I be received? Surely, now that I am scribe to the governor, I would be accepted by the Florencias. Could we be together in San Luis, Juana Cathalina and me, or would she be willing to go away with me?

I joined with a band of Apalachee who had come to San Augustín carrying a shipment of corn, but who were returning to their home at Cupaica. Nowadays it is not safe to travel alone, even in Timucua. Not that these men were ready for a fight. They had all been beaten down by the work of toting three arrobas of corn for such a distance, and many were ill or crippled. They were barely able to carry the corn that they were given to sustain them on the journey.

We passed through what remained of Urica and Arapaja. When we got to Ayacouta, it was so overgrown that the men I was with did not even recognize it as an old town. San Francisco de Potano still held people, as did

Santa Fé and Potohiriba. Six mission villages had ceased to exist.

At the Aucilla River I separated from the others, who took a trail north toward Cupaica. The last two days I traveled alone. At night I prayed for a good homecoming, and that Juana Cathalina would run to my arms. Then I remembered that it was her uncle who had sent me away, and I had to laugh at my own stupidity.

———————

I have been home for three days now, if you can call this Apalachee place a home for a foreigner, a Timucuan. No one flew into my arms when I entered Talimali. Only Bip Bentura looked for me, and he took me to his house to rest and to eat a good meal. I was anxious to climb the hill to Misión San Luis, to offer my prayers at the altar and perhaps get a glimpse of my beloved.

I did not climb the hill that first night, and may never again go to San Luis. The news that Bip had for me has crushed my heart. He said that in my absence, Juana Cathalina was married to Jacinto Roque Pérez. Even now, she carries his child in her belly.

I should go away from here, forever.

Chapter 27

Talimali
September 1678

I have not written for a very long time. My hands are now hardened and callused, and feel clumsy holding the quill. My penmanship has suffered. Nine months have passed since my return from San Augustín, and I have yet to attend Mass, visit the market, or even climb the hill to San Luis.

Fr. Paiva, upon hearing of my return, came to see me. He asked me to come back to San Luis. He said he cannot work effectively without a parish interpreter, and that my old job and room await me at the convento. He was very kind. Neither of us spoke of the woman, Juana Cathalina.

I told him I would think about his offer, but I never do. He betrayed me once before, and as much as I want to trust him, I cannot. He is a holy man, and God speaks through him, but he is a Spaniard and no more trustworthy than the rest. Nor do I feel kinship with the Apalachee, for that matter. Only Bip Bentura has proved to be a good friend, and sometimes he and I have our differences.

I live in the house of the *inija* and tend to his crops. I cleared a second field for Bip Bentura during the heat of the summer. It is not a big farm, but large enough for a respectable planting of maize and melons. I just harvested the corn, more than 60 arrobas.

It is the first time I have produced such a crop by myself, through my own sweat and muscle. It has kept my mind occupied and given me an idea for the future. When it is time to go, I will cross the river into Timucua and never come back to Apalachee. I will find an abandoned village away from the Spanish road, and plant my crops. God willing, I may find a sweet smelling Timucuan girl to marry. I would even consider a widow, unless she has grown too fat or has a sharp tongue.

———————

Bip Bentura returned from the council house early this morning and awakened me from a sound sleep. He was heating chert in the fire and preparing his tools to knap arrow points. I rolled over to my side and leaned on my elbow watching him as he worked.

"Matheo Chuba and I have convinced the council that the time has come to strike back at the Chiscas," he said.

For more than a year, now, the Chiscas have come from the southwest, burning remote Apalachee villages and farmsteads, and taking people as slaves to sell to the English.

"Now that harvest is done, it is time to teach them a lesson they will not forget," Bip said.

He said that Deputy Governor Juan Fernandez de Florencia had sanctioned an attack on the Chiscas and had offered six muskets with shot and powder if men could be found who knew how to use them. This was to be a war by the Apalachee militia, without the soldiers of San Luis.

"You know how to shoot," Bentura said. "I want you to teach the others about the musket and to lead them against the Chiscas."

I said I would be happy to teach the men to load, aim, and fire the musket. "But this is an Apalachee problem," I said, "not a Timucuan problem."

Bip had an antler tool in his right hand, and pressed the tip of it against the heated chert he held in a piece of leather in his left hand. A sliver of rock flaked away, and Bip ran his thumb over the edge, admiring the sharpness.

"There will be one soldier who will accompany us," Bip said, looking at me from the corner of his eye. "The lieutenant, Jacinto Roque Pérez, will be an observer and will give us advice."

By noon I had changed my mind. I will go to war against the Chiscas. If I die, at least I may gain the respect of the Apalachee. I have no wife or children. Most of the others are family men. Even Roque Pérez is a family man. It is possible one of us may not return alive.

Talimali
January 14, 1679

Part of what I am about to write down, I remember. Some of it I have been told by others.

I remember when we departed San Luis and met up with the men from Cupaica who were to accompany us. There were 188 Apalachee warriors with their faces smeared red with clay, one Spanish soldier, and one Timucuan. I did not wear any sort of battle paint, since I thought it would look foolish on the face of a Timucuan.

We walked for seven days from Cupaica. We diverted from the main trail, on which we would surely have been discovered, and went southwest until we came across a northbound path. It was the idea of Roque Pérez, who spends a lot of time studying maps and asking directions.

We approached the village of the Chiscas at night and were inside it before they were aware of our presence. The men in the first rank carried a banner from the church at San Luis, with a crucifix painted on one side and Our Lady of the Rosary on the other. Matheo Chuba, as chief, led the charge with Bip Bentura at his side.

The last thing I remember proved to all of us that God was with us. There was a tall green tree in the center of the village. When the muskets began to shoot, the fire from the muzzles ignited the green leaves. They blazed like dry tinder and floated on the breeze, torching the houses with the people caught inside. I know that green leaves do not ordinarily burst into flame, but I saw it happen.

———

Bentura told me first, but I have heard the account from no less than 20 men who were there. This is not my story; it is theirs.

Roque Pérez had stayed out of the fight, observing from the edge of the village. He was discovered by three Chisca warriors and knocked to the ground. They held a knife to his throat and shouted that he would be killed if we did not put down our weapons.

Bip said that I did not hesitate, that I shot and killed the man with the knife, and, having no time to reload my musket, I knocked another man to the ground with it and stepped on his face, snapping his neck. I carried Pérez to safety, although I had arrows sticking from my back and my shoulder and my hip. Depending on who tells the tale, I may have killed as many as four other Chiscas before I lay down.

The Chiscas fled the village, and many of them jumped into the river gorge where they drowned. Only five Apalachee were killed and forty wounded, but more than a hundred Chiscas died that night.

My first memory beyond that of the flaming green leaves was 10 days later, when the victory procession entered San Luis. I was on a litter, carried on the shoulders of four strong men. Above my head, the holy banner flapped in the breeze. I had returned a hero to the Apalachee people.

Chapter 28

Misión San Luis de Talimali
February 22, 1686

A great catastrophe has befallen San Luis and its people. Ten nights ago a fire burned eleven houses, two where Spanish families lived, and nine built by Apalachees. The Spaniards and Apalachees worked side by side in a heroic attempt to save the town, carrying buckets of water from the spring at the bottom of the hill.

The church was protected from the flames by men climbing ladders and throwing water on the roof. There was no time to save the convento, and it burned like a torch. The council house and Chief Matheo Chuba's house were upwind of the flames, and were not harmed.

Deputy Governor Antonio Matheos investigated the cause of the fire and blamed it on the cooks for letting their fires burn too hot, allowing sparks to float about on the air. That was a ridiculous accusation, since the fire occurred at nighttime when the women had gone home and the fire pits were cold.

A Spanish sentry said that he saw lightning strike the convento. I was attending a dance at the council house, and did not see how the fire started. But we all heard a loud clap of thunder just before the church bell was sounded. Matheos could not find a witness who would blame the Apalachees, so he gave up.

My personal loss was great. I lived at the convento because I am once again working for the friar as parish interpreter. My clothing and other possessions were burned, but they can be replaced. Already, the Apalachee seamstress has provided me with a new tunic and work pants. The people of Talimali have been generous with their gifts, to the point that I want for nothing.

The only things they cannot replace are my writings. Since I returned to live in the convento eight years ago I have kept a journal on happenings in San Luis and Talimali. Fortunately, my earlier writings remained at Bip Bentura's house, and despite his urgings that I take them to the convento, I never did.

Now, if I want to continue what I began so many years ago, I must try to recreate eight years of history. Impossible! At the age of thirty-eight, sometimes I believe my memory is slipping, along with my speed and physical strength.

Ah, Well! Where do I begin? The last papers that exist concern the war against the Chiscas, in which I got hurt, saved the life of Jacinto Roque Pérez, and became a hero to the people. That is a good enough place to start.

My aching hip cries out to be mentioned here. I still carry the Chisca arrowhead, and there is no way to get it out. Walking downhill is the most painful thing I do, so I spend my time at the mission and not in the village at the bottom of the hill. The *isucu* provides willow powder, and it makes the hurt go away for a little while.

Fr. Paiva begged me to come back as parish interpreter. He promised he would never again ask me to tell him about the old ways of the Indians such as the ball game that he attempted to ban. I say "attempted," because most of the chiefs of Apalachee ignored his order and the deputy governor refused to enforce it. The game is still played, even right here at San Luis under the friar's nose.

Juan Fernandez de Florencia is no longer deputy governor of Apalachee. He took some good land that lays three leagues to the east of San Luis and built a cattle ranch, where he has been for six years. Jacinto Roque Pérez was deputy governor for four years. Now we have Antonio Matheos to lead us. The best thing you can say about Matheos is that he is not a Florencia.

Juana Cathalina has four children, and carries a fifth. I see her from time to time at church and in the market, but we never speak. Some people have long memories. Bip says it is good that we have let our feelings for each other die.

Juana's youngest brother Francisco has come to Apalachee. He was schooled at San Augustín, but his temper was so terrible he was exiled by the governor and forbidden to return to San Augustín. Juan Fernandez keeps him at the ranch so he cannot stir up trouble in San Luis.

Her brother, Claudio, came back from Havana, where he was taught to be a priest. He works with Fr. Paiva. Juana Cathalina's mother is the hen in the chicken yard, clucking around and keeping Juana's children from harm. Whenever I see the doña in the marketplace, she watches me with an evil eye.

Pedro Florencia, the father of Juana Cathalina, has his own farm and does not often come to the mission. There are as many Florencias as robins in the springtime, and even two Menéndez families who live and do business here.

Matheo Chuba, the Chief of Talimali, made me his counselor eight years ago. I sit beside him in the council house, and sometimes he asks me what I think he should do. Bip Bentura is still *inija*, and enforces his orders.

Everyone here has forgotten that I am Timucuan. Because I am counselor and parish interpreter, I am exempt from working my own fields, and spend my time giving advice to Big Matt, as I call him in private, and working with the priest.

"Chuba" means "big" in the Apalachee language, so that is why I call him Big Matt. Even Bip calls him that now, when the three of us are alone together, and Chuba seems to like the informality. The three of us are like brothers.

Big Matt says to me that I should marry his widowed sister before she is too old to have babies. He wants me to father the child who will some day become chief of Talimali. I have told him many times that I do not want to marry her, but he keeps asking.

I decided never again to trust the deputy governor, and refused his offer to come back to work as his scribe. Now it is my responsibility to confront him on problems where Indians are being cheated or abused by the Spaniards. That way, Matheo Chuba does not have to argue face-to-face with the deputy governor, and they can remain cordial. This is a hard job, and keeps me very busy. When Roque Pérez was deputy governor it was easier, because he sometimes showed a good heart for the Indians.

<hr>

Antonio Matheos, the deputy governor, has committed an outrage. He posted an order in the council house that the work stop on rebuilding the burned Apalachee houses in San Luis.

Work had already progressed to the point that fire debris had been removed and the ground covered over with red clay mined in the hills to the north. Cedar and pine saplings had been cut for the walls of the houses. One of the houses was within two days of completion. The deputy governor said he had studied the mission plan documents, and that the land upon which the burned houses had stood was reserved for the houses of Spaniards.

One family has lived there for four generations, since even before there was a mission on this hill. Antonio Matheos said that the burned-out people should move to the slope on the west side, far away from the spring. There is also no breeze or shade on that side and it gets very hot. Or they can find room at the bottom of the hill, in Talimali.

Big Matt agreed with me that the mission plan is a matter for the priest to interpret, so we went to the friars with our complaint. Fr. Paiva felt sorry for us and wanted to help. Fr. Claudio said that because he is a Florencia, perhaps he could reason with the deputy governor. Claudio came back with his head hanging down.

"It is the law," he said. "I have seen the plans. The bishop designated that land for the Spaniards many years ago, before the church was ever built. The parchment upon which the mission was laid out also contains the mark of the Paramount Chief of Apalachee, Don Patricio Hinachuba."

The Chief of Talimali had a good question. "What other laws do the Spaniards have on their side to benefit themselves at our expense?"

Fr. Paiva said he also wanted an answer to that question, so he arranged a meeting with the deputy governor to smooth over the hard feelings. I was there, along with Matheo Chuba, Bip Bentura, and the two friars.

We all saw the plans for the first time, with our own eyes. Only the land around the council house and the chief's house belonged to the Apalachee. The rest of the hilltop was set aside for the church, the soldiers, and the other Spaniards.

"We make no claim to the village of Talimali," the deputy governor said, "and I have no jurisdiction around your council house, Matheo Chuba's house, or the area of the gully where we throw our trash."

None of us were happy, but I had to agree with the priest that the bishop and the Paramount Chief Don Patricio Hinachuba had made an agreement called a contract, and we were bound by it. That is what I said to Big Matt when we were alone.

Some of the people who lost their houses have gone down the hill to Talimali. One man built a house next to the garbage dump, but his wife complained about the smell and the rats. Three families were so angry they moved west to live among the Apalachicoli on the other side of the river.

Chapter 29

Misión San Luis de Talimali
May 17, 1686

It was Bip Bentura who suggested last week at the council house that we take Deputy Governor Antonio Matheos at his word. "He says the council house is ours. He has no authority here."

Everyone in the house stopped talking and listened. Usually, when the *inija* spoke in the council meetings he was relaying the words of the chief. Whenever Bip spoke for himself, it was worth hearing.

"If he has no rights here, perhaps we should erect a sign to remind him," Bip said.

Everyone laughed.

The sign painting fell to me because my Spanish is better than that of the others and because I am trained as a scribe. Matheo Chuba told me what he wanted the sign to say:

Notice! No Spaniards allowed inside the council house without the permission of Chief Matheo Chuba or his *inija* Bip Bentura. This does not prohibit the friar from coming in to post notices of Mass or other church meetings that concern the Indians, but does prohibit entry by soldiers, as well as the deputy governor, and anyone else who is not first granted permission. On the order of Chief Matheo Chuba.

I thought it was too wordy and could have been said more succinctly, but it was what Big Matt wanted to say, and I wrote all of it in Spanish on a wooden board, and as soon as the paint was dry, I nailed it to a post at the entrance to the council house.

That was four days ago. Today, at our early morning meeting, the order was finally tested.

The men were enjoying some very good cassina and talking about clearing another field for the fall planting when the guard we posted at the door came inside. He said that the deputy governor was outside and respectfully requested that he be allowed inside, as he had a matter of official business to discuss with Chief Chuba.

We wiped the smiles from our faces and tried to look serious. Chuba invited the deputy governor to enter.

The Spaniard entered the council house, and a soldier entered directly behind him. The soldier was holding two ropes that were tied around the necks of a woman and a man. The hands of the man and woman were tied behind them, as if they were common criminals who might run away.

We knew the people. The woman lives in Talimali and is a cook who works at the mission. She is married to a man who has been gone for four months to San Augustín, working as a carpenter on the fort. The man with her is a fisherman from San Marcos who sometimes brings smoked fish to the Saturday market.

"These two were discovered lying together behind the council house last night," Antonio Matheos said. "It was after everyone else had gone home from the dance. They were making so much noise that a sentry heard them and arrested them for their indecency."

The deputy governor carries an elaborately carved hickory cudgel. At about a meter, it is too short for a good walking stick, but useful as a club. He pointed it toward the woman. "She freely admits that she is married, and that this man is not her husband."

The woman was shaking like a leaf in a windstorm, and her eyes were red from crying. Her companion was proud and stoic.

"The environs around the council house are yours to police," the deputy governor said, "and I turn these people over to you for your justice." He nodded to the soldier. The soldier offered the rope ends to Bip Bentura who took them in his hand and looked around, uncertain of what he should do.

The deputy governor and the soldier sat down on a bench to watch what would occur next. Nothing happened at all, other than a conversation between Big Matt, Bip Bentura, and me. We spoke quietly so that no one could hear what we said.

Finally, Bip stood up and addressed the rest of the Apalachee men. "Do any of you wish to be heard? Do you want to speak for or against this man or this woman?"

I do not know who said it, but a voice from the west side of the house was clear and distinct for all to hear. "Let he who is without sin cast the first stone."

Laughter echoed through the council house. Even Big Matt, who is practiced in keeping his emotions hidden, could not suppress a smile. Bip Bentura had a coughing fit and could say nothing.

The deputy governor leapt to his feet and swung his club in the air. He slammed it down on the bench with a crack that sounded like a pistol shot. "I demand that you deal seriously with this crime," he shouted.

Everything became quiet, as if breathing and even heartbeats had stopped. The Chief of Talimali stood up slowly. Bip Bentura was there to speak for him, but Big

Matt wanted to speak for himself and he motioned for his *inija* to sit down.

"This is our council house, and these are Indians. It is for me to decide what to do, and our guest, the deputy governor, has acknowledged our authority by bringing these people here."

The chief's reasonable tone seemed to calm Antonio Matheos. But as he listened to what the chief said next, the deputy governor's face grew red.

"These people should be more discreet," said Big Matt, "but it was the middle of the night and would have gone unnoticed if it were not for a nosey guard patrolling in an area where he should not have been. I cannot find that anyone has been harmed. If her husband hears about it when he returns, he can ask her about it. I have more important business to conduct here."

The deputy governor was on his feet again. "Cuckolds!" he said, as he headed for the door. "You are all cuckolds."

"What did he say?" the chief asked me after the Spaniard was gone.

"He said 'Cuckolds', I answered. "It is a Spanish word that means a husband who is deceived by his wife."

Big Matt looked up at the smoke hole in the roof, and stroked his chin as he sometimes does when he is deep in thought. "I must be a cuckold, then. My woman has been fooling me for 20 years."

October 30, 1686

Today we learned more about the deputy governor. We already knew he had a vile temper and that he lacked respect for other people. We now know that he has a long memory and a violent nature.

A boy came for me at the convento and said I should come quickly to the garrison where the soldiers live. I had never been in that building before, and I found it cramped inside, with little light because there are few windows.

Bip Bentura was there, sitting on a stool. His head was bloody and one eye was swollen shut. An ear was also hurt. A soldier was bandaging his wounds, using alcohol to wipe the cuts. Bip sat stoically, as if it were just another day.

When the bandaging was done, Bip thanked the soldier, but continued to sit on the stool. He said he was still dizzy and wanted to rest awhile to regain his senses. He would answer none of my questions until later, when we were at his house and there were no Spaniards to hear.

Chief Matheo Chuba had been summoned from a nearby village where he had gone for a visit, and was waiting at Bip's house. When the three of us were alone, Bip told us what had happened.

He was called to the deputy governor's house and went there by himself since the chief was not in the village.

"He had papers in his hands which he said were accountings of the maize harvest. He compared this year's crop with what we produced last year. I reminded him that now that work has begun again on the fortress, we have not nearly as many men available to work in the fields."

Big Matt sat in front of his *inija,* inspecting the eye which was now purple. He tried to lift the eyelid, looking to see the white of the eye. "He beat you with a hickory club over a few arrobas of maize?"

Bip winced as the chief applied pressure with his thumb above the eye. "He keeps records of what each field produces. He says that I cheated him from my personal harvest."

"I told you two years ago, Bip, that those old fields of yours are worn out, and that you should plant your farm on the other side of the creek."

"Ooh!" Bip said, drawing away from Big Matt's touch. "The old folks who work my fields are worn out, also. They would drown, trying to cross that creek to chase crows from the fields."

The chief opened his pouch and sorted through his medicines and tools. He pulled out a porcupine quill and touched it to his thumb to test its sharpness.

"He called me a thief, a rogue, and a liar. He said I was robbing him of his part of the harvest." Bip eyed the porcupine quill. "What are you doing with that thing?"

I grabbed Bip from behind, pinned his arms to his sides, and dragged him down on his bed. He resisted, but he is not a strong man. Big Matt straddled him. He grabbed Bip's hair to hold his head still, and with his free hand he stuck the quill above the eye where the swelling was the worst.

Later, I wiped up the blood that rushed out. Bip's face was white, and he was sweating and breathing heavily. In time, he felt better and sat up. Already, the swelling had gone down and the eye was beginning to open.

"I hate to be stuck," he said.

Big Matt winked at me, and then said, "We need to be rid of Antonio Matheos. He is the worst deputy governor I have ever seen. I do not believe the friar has the courage to confront him. Perhaps we need to appeal to the governor in San Augustín."

I reminded the chief that it was Governor Juan Márquez Cabrera who appointed Matheos as his deputy in the first place. "I do not think he would admit making a mistake. That is something a Spaniard is incapable of doing."

Bip's color had returned to his face, and he was ready to stand up. He had a small mirror hanging on the wall, and he stood before it and inspected his eye. "Matheos ordered a soldier to go to my storehouse and seize what remained of my corn. I told him I only had enough to eat during the winter, and some left over for planting. But he wanted it all."

The *inija* turned away from the mirror and faced us. He smiled. "That soldier was the same one who bandaged my wounds at the garrison. His name is Federico. He said to me that he will tell the deputy governor that he did as he was told, but that when he got there the storage house was empty."

Big Matt turned to me. "Have someone move Bip's grain to my storage house in case Matheos doesn't believe Federico and sends another man to check."

Chapter 30

November 3, 1686

D on Patricio Hinachuba is Paramount Chief of Apalachee. He makes his home at Ivitachuco, two days east of Misión San Luis. Without Hinachuba's influence in San Augustín, we have no hope of ridding ourselves of the deputy governor.

Bip Bentura still suffers dizziness and a loss of hearing in his right ear from being struck by the club. He is not well enough to travel. The Spanish watch Chief Matheo Chuba like a hawk watches a rabbit. Thus, it was I who was sent to Ivitachuco to talk to Hinachuba.

Big Matt told me to carry paper and ink with me to write down whatever transpires at Ivitachuco and whatever Don Patricio has to say on the subject of ridding us of the curse of Antonio Matheos.

We, of course, know each other, Don Patricio and I. We have been together many times at meetings in his council house and ours. When I said to him that my visit concerned the deputy governor, he said we should speak privately. The two of us, along with his *inija*, went into Don Patricio's house.

He had already heard of Matheos's treatment of Bip Bentura. It always surprises me that no matter how fast I travel, the news I carry always seems to be there waiting for me when I arrive.

"Shameful! Shameful!" Don Patricio said, shaking his head. "And I could tell you other terrible things Antonio Matheos has done here in Ivitachuco. But beating an *inija* is an insult beyond forgiveness. It shows how little respect he has for us. He could as well have struck Chief Matheo Chuba, or me, for that matter."

Don Patricio's *inija* had a smug look about him. It was his father who led the revolt against the Spaniards 40 years ago, and he had been heard to say privately that if the revolt had succeeded and all the Spaniards had been killed, Apalachee would be much better off today. He is well known for his resentment at having a deputy governor in Apalachee territory.

"Now do you see the need for war?" he asked Don Patricio. He said it softly, and respectfully, so as not to anger his chief.

Don Patricio did not directly answer the question, but said that our problems could only be solved in one of two ways: either by intercession by the governor, or action on the part of the people of Apalachee. He was not specific about what he meant by action on our part, and I did not ask. I did not want to know.

We decided to go to San Augustín to complain to Governor Juan Márquez de Cabrera, and we left the next morning. It took us 10 days to get there and 10 days to get home. My aching hip complained to me with each step.

I had never before met Governor Juan Márquez de Cabrera. He gave gifts to Don Patricio befitting his position as Paramount Chief of Apalachee, and promised food provisions for our return journey. When the chief said he wished to discuss the deputy governor of Apalachee, Cabrera said he did not have time to talk business with us. Instead, he sent us to speak to another Spaniard, Diego de Quiroga.

The new man is an overseer, sent by the Council of the Indies to help Cabrera perform his duties. Quiroga was a good listener and he took notes as Don Patricio spoke, but he was ignorant of the problems and people of Apalachee. He knew the Florencia family, but had never met Antonio Matheos, the Deputy Governor for Apalachee Province. In the end, all Sr. Quiroga said was, "I will look into it."

It was a useless trip. Neither Don Patricio nor I feel encouraged in any way. I have written everything on paper concerning the trip to San Augustín, so I can report accurately what occurred.

San Luis
November 25, 1686

I arrived home in San Luis only to discover that Chief Matheo Chuba and Bip Bentura have been imprisoned by the deputy governor and are being held in irons in the garrison jail. The only reason they were given for their arrest was that the deputy governor was dissatisfied with the harvest.

When I was allowed to enter, they were sitting on the dirt floor tossing bones and gambling. Big Matt stopped the game and listened carefully while I told him of my time with Don Patricio and the treatment we had received in the capitol.

He did not seem surprised by anything I had to say. "Don Patricio is a cautious man and a devout Christian. In dealing with the Spaniards, he would rather negotiate to divide a deer carcass. His *inija* would fight to possess it all."

Bip picked up the bones and handed them to Big Matt. "Your play," he said.

"By now he has heard about this," Big Matt said, shaking the chains on his wrists. "I want you to go back to Ivitachuco. Don Patricio will be waiting for you. He will want to know if I am prepared to go to war."

I did not have to ask what Big Matt was thinking. I left them there, sitting in the dirt throwing the bones.

I wrote down this account of the condition of Big Matt and Bip Bentura, and have collected some more food and willow powder for my second visit to Ivitachuco. This old hip has carried me from San Luis to Ivitachuco, to San Augustín and home again. I guess it can get me to Ivitachuco one last time.

———

The Ivitachuco council house was not full, but present were twenty chiefs from the eastern part of Apalachee, and their principal men, and three men who lead the Indian militia. They were formerly *paracousi,* or war chiefs, and they were sitting in a place of honor. Don Patricio had waited half a day to begin the council. He wanted to know what advice I carried from Chief Matheo Chuba, before making a decision.

Now there was no need to speak privately. Everyone was in agreement as to what had to be done. The planning took a full day. There were 14 soldiers throughout Apalachee and twice as many farmers and ranchers who would have to be dealt with, in addition to the people who lived in the Spanish village at San Luis. No one had a taste for burning churches or harming the friars.

"When our men come back from working on the fort, they tell us the condition of the presidio," one of the *paracousi* said. "They have only 130 soldiers and 7 officers, with another 6 men at Santa Fé." I had not known before that the workers are sometimes employed as spies.

"We also know that the Spaniards are preoccupied with the English in Charles Town who harass the missions on the coast," the *paracousi* said. "And with the French and English pirates who are a constant threat to San Augustín."

Don Patricio's *inija* leaned forward. "If we strike swiftly and decisively, it is my judgment that the Spaniards will be in no position to retaliate."

"Not immediately," one of the elders said. "But the Spaniards have a long memory."

I was instructed to go back and convey the message to Chief Matheo Chuba. If he had no objection, the date was set for midnight, December 14.

There was a runner waiting for me on the trail approaching Talimali. He took me directly to Bip Bentura's house. There I found Bip and Big Matt, sipping cassina and continuing their game.

Two days after I left for Ivitachuco the second time, they were turned loose and allowed to go home. Bip told me how it happened.

"The woman who cooks for the deputy governor is a good friend of mine," he said. "Matheos could not go to the toilet without me finding out."

Big Matt laughed. "I am concerned that you take so much interest in his toilet habits."

Bip ignored the comment and went on with the story. "The night after you left here, the Florencia family went to see the deputy governor. Even the old man, Juan de Florencia, came in from his ranch. Pedro de Florencia was there, along with Juana Cathlina and her husband Jacinto Roque Pérez."

At no time during the telling did the game stop, but Bip would always pause when it was his time to throw the bones.

"It was a heated argument, and a lot of cursing was heard by the cook who was hiding behind a door. In the end, the Florencias convinced Matheos that what he was doing was very dangerous, locking up a chief and his *inija*. They said that the Spaniards were outnumbered 100 to 1 by the Apalachee. They even mentioned the revolt 40 years ago, when all the Spaniards died."

"And so Matheos turned you loose?" I asked.

It was Bip's time to play, so Big Matt answered for him. "Not exactly then. It was when Juan de Florencia walked into the room and said he was going to write to the king and have him prosecute Matheos for stupidity that Matheos decided to turn us loose."

I began to worry about the war starting. All over Apalachee, men were arming themselves and moving into position. If someone did not know what had happened, it might be too late to stop.

I stood up and massaged my leg. "I will go back to Ivitachuco with the news." I said.

"Do not bother," Big Matt said. "I sent a runner to Ivitachuco two days ago. You passed him on the trail."

When I think of how close we came to war, my hands shake and sweat breaks out on my forehead.

There are those among the Apalachee who agree with Don Patricio's *inija* that Indian and Spaniard were never meant to live together. At the war council in Ivitachuco the question was asked about women, children, and priests.

"They should not be harmed, but allowed to return to San Augustín," Don Patricio answered.

After the meeting I heard a *paracousi* say that during the first revolt 40 years earlier, the worst mistake the Apalachee made was to allow witnesses to live. He said that the men under his command would not make the same mistake twice.

If only the Spaniards knew how close they came to provoking a war that might have killed all the priests, all the women, Juana Cathalina and her children, and all the other innocent people, perhaps they would change their ways and treat us better. Even some of the Spaniard men, like Juan de Florencia and the soldier, Federico, do not deserve to die, in my opinion. But opinions differ, and once a war had begun, some of the Apalachee would not be stopped. They would kill everyone.

Chapter 31

Misión San Luis de Talimali
December 20, 1686

A pall has fallen over Misión San Luis and the village of Talimali. The death of a good man at any time is a tragedy. When it occurs while we are preparing to celebrate the birth of Our Lord and Savior, all the joy of the season vanishes like fog at sun up.

Juan de Florencia, the patriarch of the Florencia clan, has died. We buried him today in the church floor, near to the altar.

It has been unseasonably warm, so the friars could not delay the burial for more than three days. Fr. Paiva and I studied the interment book and measured the floor carefully. We did not want to disturb the resting place of those people who had gone before. At the same time, space could not be wasted. I dug his hole next to where Juan de Florencia's father, mother, and sisters are buried. They were murdered 40 years ago.

Fr. Claudio de Florencia, Juana Cathalina's brother, sent runners throughout Apalachee and western Timucua to spread the sad news. People came immediately. By the time of the service, all 11 friars in Apalachee were here, as well as many of the important chiefs and principal men.

More surprising to me were the number of family members and friends who came. We see Florencias at San Luis all the time. Many of them live here. We do not often see the ranchers and farmers who only occasionally come to San Luis for supplies or visits, and certainly not all at the same time. At the service, I counted 40 Florencias and their relatives, not including the children, who crowded the front of the sanctuary. Behind them stood other Spaniards who were not members of the Florencia family.

There was not room in the church for all the Indians who came to pay their respects, and everyone below chief and *inija* rank stayed outside in the churchyard. As a church officer, I had a good place to stand so I could see and hear the Mass that was sung by Fr. Paiva and a senior priest from Misión San Lorenzo de Ivitachuco. Fr. Claudio was too distraught at the loss of his uncle to participate in the Mass, but stood weeping with the rest of the family.

From where I stood I could see the back of Juana Cathalina's head. She is taller than her husband Jacinto Roque Pérez. When she turned toward him I saw her face from the side. In her grief, she had a hardness about her. She looks like her mother.

After the Funeral Mass the Spaniards congregated in the house of the deputy governor to share their memories of Juan de Florencia. They invited Chief Chuba, Bip, and me to come to the house, and we did so, expressing our grief to members of the family. The women cried together while the men sat around getting drunk on rum.

The three of us Indians stayed for awhile, and then went together to Big Matt's house where it was quieter and we could talk.

"I have mixed feelings," I said. "On the one hand, the old man sometimes showed a good heart for the Indians. If he had been born an Apalachee, he would be the kind of man who would make a good chief. On the other hand, he was a Spaniard."

"And being a Spaniard, his death is good for us in the sense that there is one less of them to make our lives miserable," Chief Chuba said. Big Matt loves a good argument, and he never uses his authority to silence an interesting discussion.

"But the old man, he was a protector of the Indians," I argued. "It was Juan de Florencia who ordered Antonio Matheos to release you and Bip from the jail."

"It was also Juan de Florencia who tricked you into going to San Agustín to keep you out of the bed of his niece," Big Matt said.

Over the years, I have reflected on that painful time in my life. "It was her mother who made the decision to send me away. Florencia just did it to keep peace in his family," I said.

Bip Bentura was listening to Big Matt and me as we argued. "He turned us loose to save his own skin," said Bip. "As for Juana Cathalina, he did only what any one of us would do to protect our niece from a bad marriage."

I might have taken offense to what Bip said, but I saw the twinkle in his eye and knew he was just trying to keep the argument going.

"Florencia was smart enough to figure out that locking us up meant war," Bip said, "but we should not forget that Florencia also kept his drunken nephew at the ranch so he could not come here and cause trouble." As usual, Bip Bentura could see both sides.

Big Matt was just now warming up to the argument. "If you loved Florencia so much, why have you not cut off all of your hair, as Juan and I have done?" In following old custom of both the Apalachee and the Timucua, Big Matt and I had both shorn off all our hair before the funeral.

Bip was quick with his answer. "Look at the Florencias," he said. "Their own kin has died, and they do not cut their hair. Why should we show more respect than they do?"

Big Matt had the answer. "It is because we are Apalachee, and civilized, and not Spaniards. When a snake loses its mate, it does not lie around grieving, but goes looking for its next meal. The higher animals are capable of feeling the loss. Even a mother squirrel cries sorrowfully for the rest of the day when a hawk snatches away one of her young."

———————

January 4. 1687

When a chief dies, the whole village mourns for a year. With Juan de Florencia barely cold in the ground, his relatives had a party to celebrate the New Year, and got drunk on Cuban rum.

The nephew, Francisco de Florencia, battered an Apalachee woman who was a servant in the Jacinto Roque Pérez household. This is the same Florencia who was banished from San Augustín and kept at the Florencia ranch so he could not cause trouble.

When I went with Big Matt to ask that he be punished, Deputy Governor Antonio Matheos laughed at us and said the woman was asking for a beating.

———————

March 5, 1687

Since the death of Juan de Florencia, the treatment we receive from the deputy governor has gone from bad to worse. Antonio Matheos fears no one, neither the Indians nor the Florencias, nor God. He wields his cudgel like a swatter for flies, and every day he batters or threatens someone with it. Even soldiers have been beaten.

On Saturday morning he was in the market and took after a woman he claimed had cheated him when he bought dishes. He struck her above the ear and raised the club to hit her again. I was standing right there, and without giving it a thought I snatched the club from his hand. When he turned to look at me, his eyes were wide with fear, but they quickly narrowed in hatred.

I was saved by the priests. Both Fr. Paiva and Fr. Claudio Florencia were there and argued for me, saying I did the Christian thing by protecting her. Matheos knew there were too many witnesses, and after awhile he took his club and went back to his house without apologizing to the woman, who was still bleeding from the head.

This morning a new order was posted outside the council house. It said that because of poor harvests it was necessary to close some old unproductive fields and clear new land for planting. My two fields were the only ones to be abandoned. The new fields will be community fields to provide corn for the citizens of San Luis.

I am not worried. The friars, the chief, and his *inija* will not let me starve.

Chapter 32

Misión San Luis de Talimali
July 11, 1687

Today is a good day for the people of Apalachee. Tomorrow will be even better. We will be rid of the despised Deputy Governor Antonio Matheos, and perhaps even the Florencias will be gone.

A runner arrived from Ivitachuco in the middle of the night. He carried an urgent letter from Don Patricio Hinachuba, the Paramount Chief of Apalachee. Bip came and awakened me at the convento, and we went together to the house of Chief Matheo Chuba, where a pot of cassina was already steaming on the fire. The messenger remained outside, waiting for instructions.

"Sit down and read this aloud," Big Matt said as he handed me the paper. "Bip and I think we understand it, but we want to hear it from you."

By the light of the fire I recognized the bold strokes and fine penmanship of Hinachuba. The letter was addressed to Matheo Chuba.

"You will have a visitor," I read. "He is Sr. Diego Quiroga. Your man Juan Mendoza will remember him as the Spaniard who listened to our complaints in San Augustín last fall. You will now address Quiroga as

'Governor'. He has taken the place of Juan Márquez Cabrera who has been arrested for his crimes."

I looked up in amazement at the news. Big Matt and Bip were sitting there watching me, and smiling broadly. "Read on, read on" Matheo Chuba said, waving his hand toward the letter. "There is more to be learned."

I turned to the side so the light of the fire would shine directly on the page, and to keep the smoke from my eyes.

"He comes to investigate what we told him, but he is already convinced that Antonio Matheos should be removed as deputy governor of Apalachee province. He will take him back to San Augustín. Others will decide if Matheos should be imprisoned for his crimes.

"I have spoken to Governor Quiroga about the many outrages practiced by the Florencia people. I encourage you to share your stories with him also. Perhaps this good man will relieve us of our suffering at the hands of the Spanish settlers."

When I was done reading, the *inija* took the letter from me and folded it and put it in the trunk which holds all of the important documents of Talimali. Big Matt's wife handed me a cup of hot cassina. The three of us sat there talking until sunup.

It will be at least midday before the Quiroga party arrives at San Luis. Until then, only the three of us know what is to occur. Not even Antonio Matheos knows that this may be the last day for him to terrorize Indians.

Big Matt said that I should record the events of the day carefully, so that some day we could tell the story to our grandchildren. That is why I have come back to the convento and written all of this history.

———————

Fredric M. Hitt

July 14, 1687

Governor Diego de Quiroga has now departed San Luis. He plans to go to Ayubale and Cupaica before crossing the river once again on his way home to San Augustín. Big Matt invited him to return to Apalachee in the future, when he has time to visit the other towns.

Quiroga was with us for only two days and three nights. He arrived at midday. A soldier had been sent ahead to announce his coming, but the deputy governor and the Florencias had no idea of the purpose of his surprise visit. Only Big Matt, Bip Bentura, and I knew what was to occur.

The governor and his escort of six soldiers feasted on a meal of roasted beef, corn, and garden vegetables at the house of the deputy governor. After the meal, Quiroga spoke to Antonio Matheos and the members of the Florencia family who were present. I was not there, but I have been told what happened by two servants who were in the house.

Quiroga spoke of recent events that had occurred in San Augustín. He said that the Council of the Indies believed Governor Juan Márquez Cabrera's judgment to be severely impaired, and had sent Quiroga as an overseer, since Quiroga had already been chosen to succeed Cabrera as the next governor at the end of his term.

Cabrera fell out of favor with the leading families of San Augustín because he spent too much money building the fort, and not enough on developing trade for the merchants in the town. He was also criticized for his neglect of the Timucua Indians, and his failure to control them so they would remain in the villages along the royal road and help in the transport of corn and vegetables to the capital.

Even so, Cabrera might have survived until the end of his term had he not gotten into a dispute with the bishop of Cuba, who wanted more money spent on the churches and less on the fortress. Cabrera left San Augustín without permission and went to Havana where he argued with the bishop face to face.

It was then that Quiroga decided that Cabrera had abandoned his post. When Cabrera returned from Cuba, he was arrested. He was put on a boat bound for Spain where he would answer for his crimes.

An Indian girl was serving tea when Governor Quiroga announced the purpose of his visit to Apalachee. He said that Antonio Matheos was relieved of his duties as deputy governor of Apalachee Province and would return with him to San Augustín to face discipline.

Matheos immediately started a fuss and grabbed his cudgel, as if to strike Governor Quiroga, but he was restrained by two soldiers and placed in the garrison jail cell.

On the second morning of Governor Quiroga's visit, he addressed the chiefs and principal men of Talimali and neighboring towns. The visit of a governor to the council house was a great event, and the Apalachee all wore their formal, ceremonial attire.

By the time Quiroga spoke, everyone had heard that Matheos was locked up in the jail where he had sent so many people. One Apalachee was caught with a rock in his hand, approaching the barred window of Matheos's cell. The rock was taken away from him by a soldier, and he was told to stay away from the garrison.

"The King of Spain sends his greetings to the people of Apalachee," Governor Quiroga said, after Bip banged a stick on the cabana rail to silence the talk and bring the meeting to order. "He has heard your cries and has sent me to bind your wounds and to do justice."

Sitting next to me, Bip Bentura spoke softly. "Smooth talker," he said. Big Matt and I struggled not to smile.

The governor went on with his prepared speech. He had it all written down on paper, and he read it to us as if it were a letter.

He told of the first time he had heard of the complaints from Apalachee, when Don Patricio Hinachuba and I met with him in San Augustín a year earlier. He admitted that in the beginning he thought we were telling fanciful tales. In time, and with more investigation, he realized that what Hinachuba and I had told him was the truth.

Until Governor Cabrera made the mistake of abandoning his duties and going to Cuba, Quiroga's hands were tied, and he could do nothing. But once Cabrera was arrested, Quiroga vowed to bring relief to the Apalachee by removing the evil Antonio Matheos from his position.

It was a nice speech, as far as it went. When Quiroga folded his papers and sat down, Bip Bentura stood up to speak for Chief Matheo Chuba. I knew what he was going to say, as we had gone over it the night before.

"The people of Apalachee thank you and bless you for what you have done for us in ridding us of the oppression we have suffered. The crimes inflicted on us are worse than even you know. There are limits to how much Christian men should have to endure, and Antonio Matheos has gone far beyond that mark."

We had argued among ourselves that what was said about limits of endurance might be interpreted as a threat against authority. Big Matt decided that it was what he meant to say, so it was not changed. Governor Quiroga listened carefully and showed no signs that he was offended by the *inija's* words.

"But there is more that you could do to ease our suffering," Bip said. "We are infested with Spanish settlers who come to Apalachee and dishonestly take our land to build their ranches and farms. They order our chiefs to supply workers for clearing the land and planting and harvesting the crops. They say it is owed by us as service to the king." Bip put his hand above his eyes and peered around the house, as if he were looking far and wide.

"But we do not see the king. He never comes here to enjoy his lands, and we ask each other if we are being deceived. We wonder if service to the king is no more than service to the Florencia family."

That was another thing we argued about the night before – mentioning the Florencias by name. Again Big Matt favored straight talk, so it was said.

Bip Bentura told Quiroga that there would be no justice until the Spanish settlers and soldiers were removed from Apalachee. It was a strong statement. The tension was so high that I do not think anyone took a breath until the governor stood up and replied to what Bip had said.

"There are those in San Augustín who would not argue that it was a mistake to allow settlers to come to Apalachee. It is a complicated issue, and it is one in which we welcome your views. I dedicate myself to restoring justice to you people, and if it requires the removal of settlers, so be it."

"Smooth talker," Bip repeated under his breath. This time I could not hide my joy. Neither could Big Matt. We both smiled broadly.

"I have appointed an experienced man as my deputy for Apalachee," Governor Quiroga said. "You know him, and I know you respect him. Jacinto Roque Pérez will be deputy governor."

———————

It is a disappointing ending to a joyful day. Half of our problems are solved. We no longer have to fear the blows from Antonio Matheos's hickory club, but the Florencias and their puppet, Roque Pérez, still have authority over us. If Governor Quiroga believes his own words about removing the settlers from Apalachee, he is the only believer. We know that they will never leave unless there is a war to drive them out.

Chapter 33

*T*he new deputy governor, Jacinto Roque Pérez, has offered to meet with us to, "Discuss misunderstandings that may have developed regarding the rights of the Indians and the proper role and authority of the Spanish government in Apalachee Province."

That is exactly how he phrased it in a letter delivered to Chief Matheo Chuba on the morning after Governor Diego de Quiroga departed San Luis for his home in San Augustín. It is the first time in memory that any member of the Florencia family has offered to talk about our differences. Usually they post their orders and ignore our petitions.

Don Patricio Hinachuba, the Paramount Chief of Apalachee, received the same letter and came to Misión San Luis to speak on behalf of all Apalachee. We met together in Matheo Chuba's house the day before the meeting with the Spaniards. Hinachuba had with him three of his closest advisors and the Chief of Cupaica. I was there, along with Big Matt, and his *inija* Bip Bentura.

It was Don Patricio's idea that we fix upon a few simple problems and see if the Spaniards would enter into a treaty or written agreement to correct them to our satisfaction. Later we could talk about more serious abuses, such as the way Spanish settlers cheat the Indians by taking their stock without fair payment.

We agreed that the easiest problem to fix was the keeping of Indian women at the haciendas and farms, which is clearly against the rules laid down by the governor and the bishop. When I was a scribe for the lieutenant governor, I saw those regulations with my own eyes. Chief Hinachuba was also familiar with the rules.

"It is beyond dispute," Hinachuba said. "The Spaniards are forbidden to keep our women over night. We all know why they do it, but up to now they have ignored our complaints."

Big Matt agreed. "The priest will be at the meeting. I think he will support us on the point." Nobody mentioned that Chuba's own daughter went to the Florencia ranch four months before and has not returned.

The Chief of Cupaica, who suffers with two Spanish farms near his village, complained of the inability of men to obtain religious instruction from the friars. "They keep the men away from Mass and require that they work even on the Sabbath." Again, we expected strong support from the priest on this issue.

Big Matt complained of the increasing demands on him for Indian servants in the Spanish households of San Luis, including that of the deputy governor. "Juana Cathalina is the worst of the lot," he said. He looked at me from the corner of his eye, as if he expected I might say something. "She does not even pay the women who grind corn for her, but expects me to do it."

Chief Hinachuba thought it was a problem unique to San Luis, since there are no Spanish settlers living in other towns. "And since Juana Cathlina is the wife of the deputy governor, I doubt that he will agree."

The Paramount Chief had one other idea. "The parish interpreter is entitled to his fields. He has the same rights as a chief or an *inija* in that regard. I have always thought it was illegal that Juan Mendoza was deprived of them by the former deputy governor."

All eyes turned to me. "Chief Chuba and Bip provide for my needs," I said. "And I have no family to feed. But I have seen the standing orders from San Augustín. I am entitled to the fields and to the labor to produce my crops."

Those were the only problems we could think of that might easily be solved.

———

I have a writing desk I use at the convento. It was made for me by a carpenter who comes and goes from San Augustín where he works on the fortress. He had seen such a desk at the presidio and was clever enough to build one for me. It has a hinged top that can be lifted to reveal a compartment in which I can store papers, quills, and other supplies.

The desk is too heavy for one man to carry, especially if he has a bad hip. I had two altar boys haul it to the council house. I carried the three-legged stool.

I was there at the request of Don Patricio to record what was said, and later to prepare an agreement to be signed by the deputy governor and the paramount chief.

It is amazing how word spreads in this country. The council house was filled with people from Apalachee. Even a delegation of Chacato Indians came from Ayubale, and a few peaceful Yamassee who have settled to the north to work the Spanish farms.

People love to gamble and were taking bets on whether the Spaniards would agree to our demands. Someone at the meeting last night must have spoken to others, because the gamblers knew exactly what we would be asking. I placed a small bet on the outcome.

Don Patricio Hinachuba sat in the place of honor because he outranked Big Matt. Bip Bentura spoke for him as his *inija,* since Hinachuba's own *inija* was sick and unable to travel. Big Matt took the second highest cabana, where he could turn around and talk privately with Don Patricio.

Only three Spaniards came to the council house. Deputy Governor Jacinto Roque Pérez looked splendid in his soldier's uniform with all of its decorations. He had with him his lieutenant. Fr. Claudio de Florencia sat on a bench on the front row. He is the only priest we have since Fr. Paiva moved away to serve the people at Aspalaga.

Nothing worthwhile was accomplished, so I will not waste my time recording all of it here.

Roque Pérez started with a nice speech. He said that he was delighted to be serving again as Deputy Governor of Apalachee, and that he looked forward to showing us Spanish justice by listening to us and solving our problems.

"A new day is dawning for peaceful cooperation and mutual respect between our peoples," he said.

Some groaned out loud, but were silenced when Big Matt rapped his attention stick on the boards of his cabana.

When Roque Pérez was done, Bip Bentura stood up and congratulated the new deputy governor, and said that the leaders of Apalachee looked forward to improving relations with the Spaniards.

"First, we would like to correct the practices of some of the ranchers and farmers who keep our women on their farms over night, when they belong at home with their families."

The deputy governor became red in the face. "I have heard that complaint before," Roque Pérez said, "and it is a lie. No woman has been kept against her will. They are free to leave when their chores are done for the day."

Bip looked toward me, and I nodded, indicating that I had with me the friar's copy of the regulations concerning how workers were to be treated by the settlers.

"If you would like to see it, the parish interpreter has with him the regulations issued in San Augustín," Bip said. "It is expressly forbidden to keep a woman over night, even if the she wishes to stay."

"Those regulations no longer apply, and are subject to different interpretations," the deputy governor said. "And I resent the implications that we somehow take advantage of these women. If we are to make a success of these discussions you should refrain from questioning our good motives."

The friar of San Luis Claudio de Florencia had his eyes fixed on the floor and did not speak up.

When Bip Bentura objected to Christian men being required to work on the Sabbath, the deputy governor said that the Yamassee and Chiscas had become so unruly that it was necessary that the farms and ranches be defended every day, including Sunday. Again, Fr. Claudio de Florencia did not object to the outrage.

On the question of my fields, Roque Pérez sounded thoughtful and reasonable. He promised he would take the matter under consideration and let us know his answer in a few days.

When the meeting was over I chased after the gambler with whom I had made my wager and collected my winnings.

The chiefs met together in Big Matt's house. They said I should not waste my time trying to write a document for the Spaniards to sign. Bip Bentura had the most interesting thing to say. "The Spaniards have a saying: 'Blood is thicker than water.' Where the Florencia puppet priest is concerned, they should say 'Blood is thicker than Holy Water.'"

A week later, Big Matt's 12-year-old daughter came home from the Spanish hacienda. Either they have been feeding her well, or she is three months pregnant.

I am still waiting for my fields to be restored to me. Perhaps Roque Pérez has forgotten his promise. I have given up. No agreements have been reached on even the simplest questions, so there are no treaties to prepare.

Chapter 34

Misión San Luis
February 11, 1697

Two calamities have occurred on the same day. The first brings great sadness and anger to the people of San Luis and Talimali. To make matters worse, I have had to write the story twice. It was my own stupidity and carelessness that caused the second calamity.

The first involves the woman who now prefers to be addressed as Doña Juana Cathalina. No longer will she accept the title Señora, as befits the other Spanish women of San Luis. She punishes servants for forgetting the proper respect by assigning them other duties when it is time for them to go home to their families.

It is the saddest thing I have ever witnessed, and one that will be difficult to write down. But I shall try, for the second time.

Juana Cathalina has required for a long time that Chief Matheo Chuba provide her with six servant women to clean her house, mind her children, grind corn, and prepare meals for her family. She has another woman who carries a jug of milk from the country each morning. She even requires Big Matt to bring her fish every Friday.

Yesterday she told Big Matt that she needed yet another woman to go to the forest to gather chestnuts. Big Matt answered that he had no other woman to do the work unless he called one in from the planting fields.

Juana Cathalina pointed to a pagan woman, a widow who was nursing her simple-minded and crippled five-year-old child. "She will do. Send her."

When told what was required of her, the woman said that she could not leave her child because she needed constant attention and could neither walk nor feed herself, but Juana Cathalina promised that if the woman would go for chestnuts, she would watch the child and provide for her needs until the woman returned. Big Matt ordered the widow to go. He told her that Juana Cathalina could be trusted to care for the child.

When the mother of the crippled child came back before dark with her bag full of chestnuts, the child was nowhere to be found in the yard outside the house.

I was in the convento when I heard the Indian woman banging on the front door of Juana Cathalina's house and asking in a loud voice where her child had gone. Juana Cathalina would not come outside or give her an answer.

The child was discovered in the creek at the bottom of the hill. She must have rolled into the water when no one was watching, and drowned. Juana Cathalina said that it was an accident, and no one was to blame.

We are used to death in Apalachee. Men are killed in battle against the Chiscas, or die on the trail between San Luis and the presidio at San Augustín. Old people die in the winter from the cold, and from illnesses that spread quickly. But so few children are born here nowadays, and they are not supposed to die before their parents. That poor, pathetic little girl was all the widow had left in her life to love, and now she has been taken away without even an apology. The guilty person calls it an accident and goes about her life.

Fr. Claudio de Florencia said the child was not baptized and could not be buried beneath the floor of the church, but would be laid in the pagan field. This so angered the people of Talimali that Chief Chuba went to Jacinto Roque Pérez and warned him that a revenge killing might happen. After Fr. Claudio met with the deputy governor he changed his mind and agreed to conduct a Funeral Mass and lay the child beneath the floor, but far from the altar.

————

The second accident, which occurred last night, is one for which I accept complete responsibility. Fortunately, I am the only one harmed by my carelessness.

I began writing the sad story of the death of the widow's child the night it happened, and used an oil lamp to see by. The lamp rested on a corner of my desk in the convento. As I wrote, I was moved to tears. I stood up to go outside and clear my head, and I must have jostled the table. Outside, I said a prayer to God in Heaven for the child's salvation.

I smelled smoke, and ran inside. The lamp had fallen over and the flaming oil covered the desk and spilled onto the mat on the floor. The flames were moving up the wall toward the thatched roof. I dragged the desk outside so that the entire convento would not be lost, and ran to the outdoor kitchen next to the convento to grab two buckets of water the cooks keep there to put out fires.

A sentry heard my shouts, as did Fr. Claudio. They both rushed to help. We saved the convento from fire. The only losses were the mat on the floor, part of the wall that will need to be patched, and the writing desk and all of its contents. Inside the desk were my personal writings for the past seven years.

Fredric M. Hitt

The earlier papers were still in the leather case in which I store them under my bed, safe from my stupid carelessness. Fortunately, the writings I do for Fr. Claudio are kept in his apartment.

It is almost time for the Funeral Mass for the child. I promised the priest that I would assist him. When I return, I will try to remember what was written on the burned manuscripts. If I am feeling too sad to work, I will wait until tomorrow.

I met with Bip Bentura and Chief Matheo Chuba after the church services for the child. We went to Big Matt's house and talked about the events of the last few years. Our chief has never understood why I write things down, and chides me for it, since he sees me as a scribe with no purpose. I told him what Palacios said to me about recording the history of the bishop's visit, but Big Matt thinks it is foolishness. Bip Bentura sees what I do as important, and he worked hard to help me remember the past.

The stone Castillo de San Marcos at San Augustín was completed two years ago after twenty-five years of labor, and we no longer send our young men there to work. Here in San Luis, we are building a wooden blockhouse which should be completed by summer.

Neither of these fortresses will make anyone safe. English pirates attacked San Augustín four years ago. While the soldiers and many of the people cowered in the fortress, the pirates burned the town and took blacks and Indians as slaves to be sold in Charles Town.

French pirates from the Gulf of Mexico now control the San Martín River and threatened to burn the hacienda at La Chua, where I used to go to sell horses, as they did once before in 1682. Yamassee and Englishmen with shotguns and pistols attacked Misión Catalina in Timucua three years ago, burned it to the ground, and killed twenty people.

Traveling the royal road to San Augustín is dangerous, with so many of the missions destroyed by Creek and Yamassee and Chisca Indians armed with English weapons.

Bip's memory of the wars was accurate, and he reminded me of details that I had forgotten. Big Matt had nothing to say about the battles, but wanted me to remember how the Spaniards have prospered and grown fat while the Apalachee have suffered.

Some Apalachee are allowed to raise pigs and cattle for their own use, but only animals owned by the Spaniards are loaded on the Cuban boats that come to the gulf port of San Marcos. Our people are forced to sell to the Florencias and are sometimes paid with what the Spaniards call "promissory notes." But we have never been able to redeem the papers for money or trade items, so what good are they?

Even the friars raise hogs and cows and sell them to raise money for the churches, since the situado payments from the governor sometimes do not come. The priests ship their animals to San Augustín, but prefer to deal with the Cubans, who pay a higher price in gold and can also trade sugar, rum, and wine for the Lord's Table.

Two times the rum has been stolen from the parish store house, and Indians got drunk on it and caused trouble.

With all of the boats coming in and out, only corn is still carried on the backs of the men along the royal road to San Augustín, but even they must go with soldiers for protection.

Talimali is greatly diminished. Big Matt says there are now fewer than 800 people in the town and the farming hamlets, compared to 1,200 just a few years ago.

It is the same throughout Apalachee with many people leaving the province to get away from the Spaniards. Some have gone to Charles Town to live with the English who treat them better. Ten of those people have been seen among the Chiscas and Yamassee who raid remote Apalachee villages looking for slaves. Three of the eleven Apalachee missions have been burned, or closed their doors.

Maybe it was not a good idea to remember how far we have fallen. I am sorry I involved Big Matt in the discussion because it made him very sad and angry at the same time. Bip looks on the bright side and says that some day soon he may move his family out of Apalachee and go to live among the Pensacola people, or maybe further west to Mobil Town where the French live.

The thought of Bib moving away bothers Big Matt, who depends on him as his *inija*. When Bip left to go to his own house, I told Big Matt not to worry about his *inija* going away, because Bip is just a dreamer.

None of the three of us are the men we were ten years ago. I am more crippled than ever with my bad hip. Bip is a dreamer, and Big Matt is getting to old for his responsibilities.

Only Don Patricio Hinachuba, the Paramount Chief of Apalachee, is still a strong leader. But even Don Patricio is sometimes said to be too close to the Spaniards, and not close enough to his own people.

Chapter 35

Misión San Luis
April 24, 1698

Work on the San Luis blockhouse came to a halt because of a scarcity of iron nails to secure the plank walls. While we waited for more nails to arrive from San Augustín, Big Matt ordered the men to make good use of their time by cutting additional planks with which to replace the thatched roof of the church.

We have lost the convento once because of fire, and almost a second time. The burning of the church would be a much larger calamity, Fr. Claudio said, and a plank roof is less likely to burn than dry thatch. Within five days the woodworkers felled enough pine trees and cut a sufficient number of planks. It was Big Matt's plan that the work on the church roof be started as soon as the blockhouse is finished.

Today, however, we have suffered yet another abuse by Deputy Governor Jacinto Roque Pérez. He had a soldier post a notice saying that the lumber set aside for the church roof was being commandeered to build a new house. Bip and I went to see the deputy governor to complain, but Roque Pérez was too busy to receive us. Instead, he sent an aide outside who said that Roque Pérez was working on the plans for the new house, and as soon as he was done he wanted the construction to begin.

Bip and I went to the convento to tell the priest. After all, it was Fr. Claudio who suggested the thatched roof be replaced with wood. We were surprised when the friar defended the action of Roque Pérez.

"He has his responsibilities, and providing sufficient housing is one of them. It is my nephew and his family who are coming from San Augustín, and they will need a house to live in," he said.

When Bip continued to argue, Fr. Claudio quoted scripture. "Render unto Caesar that which is Caesar's, and unto God that which is God's," he said.

Bip Bentura answered that the planks belonged to God, and not to Caesar, which made the friar very angry. Fr. Claudio said that ignorant Indians should not distort God's word to prove a point.

———

April 25, 1698

The subject of the commandeered lumber, and what to do about it, was discussed at length at the council house meeting this morning. I made the point that without the support of the friar, it was unlikely we could win the argument with Roque Pérez.

Bip said we should refuse to work on the new house, and leave it to the Spaniards. "If they want to steal God's lumber, it will be their sin and not our own."

No one disagreed, and Big Matt forbade anyone to help build the new house.

When we came out of the council house we were confronted by a very angry man whose house stands next to where the deputy governor proposes to build the new house. We went with him and saw the sign that had been posted on his door.

"This house is to be removed no later than April 29 to make room for new construction." It was signed by the deputy governor. Two other houses, one on each side, had identical signs posted

There is no room in San Luis for more houses, and the east slope of the hill is too steep for building. It was tried once, but the summer rains and the soft ground caused the new house to collapse.

Big Matt is angrier than I have ever seen him. He and Bip left for Ivitachuco to talk to Paramount Chief Don Patricio Hinachuba and seek his advice.

San Augustín
May 17, 1698

I have come to San Augustín on official business for Misión San Luis. The Custos of Missions here has a horse to send to Apalachee to carry supplies back and forth. Because I was once a caballero, Fr. Claudio asked me to go and fetch the animal.

It was a coincidence, but a convenient one. Big Matt was trying to decide how to deliver a letter Don Patricio has written to Governor Laureano de Torres y Ayala. The Florencias no longer allow our leaders to travel outside Apalachee, fearing we might tell others of the treatment we receive. That is exactly what I am doing. I carried Don Patricio's letter in the sleeve of my tunic.

Upon my arrival I went to the office of the governor and told the clerk there that I carried a petition from the

Paramount Chief of Apalachee. The clerk wanted me to leave the letter for the governor to read, but my instructions from Don Patricio and Big Matt were that I was not to part with the letter unless I handed it directly to Governor Laureano.

After a day of waiting outside the Governor's house, I was approached by a soldier who said that the governor had no time for me, but that I would be taken to his notary who would listen to what I had to say.

I met with the notary Manuel Quiñones at his house. He is taller than most Spaniards, and thin, with angular features, brooding eyes, and bushy eyebrows. During our meeting, his eyes never moved from my face, except when he looked down to write notes on a paper before him.

Sr. Quiñones seemed inclined to listen, so I showed him the letter from Don Patricio and talked freely to him of all the abuses being suffered by the Apalachee at the hands of the deputy governor and the Florencias.

When I told him that women were kept on the ranches, and came home pregnant, he showed the first sign of emotion, frowning and shaking his head disapprovingly. From the questions he asked, I believe Quiñones was shocked at my stories.

Yesterday, Quiñones met with Governor Laureano, and when he was done he came looking for me at the council house where I was working with the old mare I had been given by the priest at the monastery.

"Governor Laureano has agreed to send an official visitor to Apalachee to investigate the charges you have made," said Quiñones. "He has not decided who to send or when he will go."

I am a poor judge of Spaniards. At one time I loved a woman who turned out to be evil of the worst kind. I risked my life to save Jacinto Roque Pérez, who, next to Antonio Matheos, is the cruelest tyrant I have ever known. But to me, Manuel Quiñones is a good Christian and an honorable man.

If Governor Laureano is as honorable and as Christian, we will have our visitor to investigate what happens at Apalachee. The mare and I are now used to each other. I will load her with supplies and be on my way home by daybreak.

———

Misión San Luis
July 11, 1698

The visitor came to San Luis in June. He introduced himself to the leading men at the council house and said that he is the Royal Treasurer of La Florida and that he came at the request of Governor Laureano de Torres y Ayala to see how the Indians were treated and to address any complaints.

In the days that followed, we waited for him to ask us questions, but he never did. He spent his time socializing with the Florencias and visiting the farms and ranches. The last night he was here, the whole Florencia clan was in town, and they drank wine and laughed and danced into the night.

The visitor's name is Joaquín de Florencia. They are all cousins of each other. We expect nothing to come of his being here, other than retribution from the Florencias.

———

I lost my room in the convento and have moved into an empty house next to Bip Bentura in the village at the bottom of the hill. Fr. Claudio said he needed my space at the convento for storage, but it was an excuse to cover the punishment I received for seeking a visitor.

The house where I am staying is small, but large enough for one person. Bip and his wife enjoy having someone nearby to talk to. Many of the people of Talimali have moved further away from San Luis.

The priest still expects me to work for him, and to walk up and down the hill to the mission each day. It is sometimes painful, but good exercise for old bones. It is still my habit to meet with Big Matt and the other men at the council house each morning.

————————

Talimali
November 30, 1698

Before I could finish writing about living in Talimali, word came of a terrible happening. In the beginning I thought it was just a wild story, like we sometimes hear, but when I heard it from a Chacato from Ayubale, a village seven leagues to the northwest, I knew it was true.

Francisco de Florencia, the youngest brother of Juana Cathalina, has committed a terrible crime. In his younger years he was banished from San Augustín for his unruliness, and when he came to Apalachee he was controlled by his uncle, Juan de Florencia, until his death. No one ever knew he was capable of murder.

The Chacato of Ayubale are hunters, unlike the Apalachee who live outside the mission villages and raise corn.

Each summer, the Chacato men go on a buffalo hunt in the hills. Nowadays, most of the buffalo are gone, but it is a tradition they still honor. Some Chacatos work on the Florencia farm, and when they asked their boss if they could go on the hunt, he wanted to go with them.

The Chacato hunt master could not refuse him, so they took Francisco de Florencia on the buffalo hunt.

Florencia carried a keg of rum with him, and shared it with the men at night. He also had three shotguns, and he taught some of the Chacato how to shoot. It was a bad hunt, and after three hot days, and no meat or buffalo hides to show for it, they started home.

On Friday they encountered a band of 24 Tasquiqui Indians who were on their way to San Luis to trade at the Saturday market, as they have for many years. The Tasquiqui are peaceful people who have good relations with Apalachee and Chacato alike.

The Tasquiqui made their camp a little distance from where the Chacato bedded down for the night. Florencia was in a foul mood and drunk on rum. He shouted insults at the Tasquiqui and when they answered him rudely he chased after them, shooting his gun. Florencia hollered for the Chacato to grab their weapons and follow him, and some of them did.

The Tasquiqui had no weapons to speak of, other than small bows suitable for bringing down rabbits and birds. When the sun came up, 16 of the Tasquiqui traders were dead or dying, and the others had run away. Some of the Chacato were sickened by the butchery and refused to fight.

The leaders of Talimali went to the house of Jacinto Roque Pérez to demand justice for the Tasquiqui, and that Francisco de Florencia and the Chacato who participated in the killings be arrested and sent to San Augustín for trial.

Chief Matheo Chuba, *Inija* Bip Bentura, and I were admitted into the house. The others remained in the yard outside. The deputy governor listened to what we had to say, but he was not sympathetic to our position.

"I have already looked into what happened," he said. "It was the Tasquiqui who started the fight by shooting their guns at the Chacato. As magistrate of Apalachee, I have decided it was in self-defense that the Chacato retaliated."

The immensity of the lie almost took our breath away.

Big Matt stood up. He is old, but still a powerful man, and he leaned over Roque Pérez's desk. "Tasquiqui have no guns. They were coming to market, as they have for 20 years of Saturdays. They carry fruits and nuts and beaver hides, and snares for small animals, but no guns."

Roque Pérez stood, signaling that the meeting was over, but Big Matt was not through. "I will tell you something else about the Tasquiqui. They are not Christians, but they are usually peaceable people until they are provoked. And when that happens their revenge will not be denied forever."

"You have said quite enough," Roque Pérez said in a loud voice.

Chief Chuba walked to the door. He stopped and turned once again to the deputy governor. "You have not heard the last of this from the Tasquiqui. None of us have."

Chapter 36

Talimali
September 3, 1700

C hief Matheo Chuba, his *inija*, and I have returned from Ivitachuco where we listened to Don Patricio Hinachuba's account of his visit to San Augustín. I must admit that my pride was hurt when I learned that the paramount chief had taken it upon himself to go to the presidio to accomplish that which I had failed to do. My efforts led only to a brief visitation from Joaquín de Florencia, and produced no improvement in the way we are treated by the Spaniards.

From now on I will defer to Chief Hinachuba in such matters. He is a man who knows how to solve problems and who to go to with our complaints. Perhaps that is why he is Paramount Chief of Apalachee, and I am a lowly parish interpreter.

Instead of appealing to the governor, Hinachuba went to see his friend, Alonso de Leturiondo, the priest of the cathedral in San Augustín. Fr. Leturiondo has

championed the cause of fair treatment for the Indians of
La Florida for many years.

Leturiondo listened to Hinachuba and learned of the
abuses the Apalachee have suffered at the hands of the
Spaniards. He stood up in the pulpit of the San Augustín
Church for three Sundays in a row and preached against
the evil treatment, and shamed the people with his stories.

Chief Hinachuba was there for each Mass, and he
said that the brave priest even spoke the names of the
guilty people, some of whom were there in the church,
listening. He told of the way we are treated by the
Florencia family, about the crimes of Antonio Matheos,
and of the governors who have turned a deaf ear to our
cries against the injustice.

Fr. Leturiondo reminded the people of how hungry
they were 30 years ago before the Apalachee decided to
save them from starving by growing more corn. He spoke
of how the Apalachee and Timucua labored and sacrifice
by carrying the food on their backs to San Augustín. The
priest made the people lower their heads while he prayed
to God for the souls of those Indians who died on the trail
and at the river crossings.

He told them that the Apalachee now raise pigs to
provide bacon and lard, and cattle for beef, and how we
gather nuts and fruits and deer meat and carry it to San
Augustín.

"And he told the truth of what happened when the
Spaniards came to Apalachee," Chief Hinachuba said.
"He told those assembled in the church how the ranchers
and farmers forced the Indians to cut down the trees and
clear the fields for their ranches and farms. He thundered
when he said, 'We Spaniards told the Indians that it was
their duty to the King of Spain, but it was only the
Florencias and corrupt governors who benefited.'"

The priest told of Spaniards who control trade
through threats and violence, and how they cheat the

Indians by giving them useless paper instead of real money for our labor and for the cattle and swine we raise. He said that the Apalachee are treated no better than common slaves, and that we should be respected and treated as human beings and children of God. They must have been powerful sermons, the way Hinachuba describes them. On the last of the three Sundays, the priest said that the only solution was for the settlers to get out of Apalachee, leaving only a few soldiers behind to keep the peace, and priests to teach the Gospel, and that soldiers should be forbidden to engage in trade.

"The most powerful families were there listening to Fr. Leturiondo," Don Patricio said. "The merchants of San Augustín, the treasurer of the colony, the leaders of the clergy, and even the governor himself."

I asked Don Patricio what Fr. Leturiondo said about the priests who sometimes use the port of San Marcos to ship cattle and pigs to Cuba to make a profit. Don Patricio did not remember the priests of Apalachee having been criticized in the sermons.

We asked Don Patricio what would come of it all. He said that he did not know, but that Fr. Leturiondo promised to continue to speak out until another official visitor would be sent, and not one who was a member of the Florencia family.

We returned to San Luis today after listening to Don Patricio, and we are all much more hopeful about the future.

Friday, September 6

The good will Big Matt felt in his heart after hearing of the success of Don Patricio's journey to San Augustín was short lived.

This morning we were together, working on repairs to the roof of the church. Despite his age and size, Big Matt likes to climb the highest ladder, and he was toting a load of palm fronds on his shoulder when Juana Cathalina Florencia came running up, screaming profanities. Big Matt came down the ladder to see what had her so disturbed.

"Where are my fish?" she demanded to know.

Big Matt laid down the fronds and said to the woman that there had been a bad storm at San Marcos, and it was too dangerous for the fishermen to go out in their boats. He spoke in a soft tone.

"You get me my fish!" she shouted, and then she continued cursing and saying she had nothing to feed her guests for dinner. Then she slapped the Chief of Talimali across the face, bloodying his nose. Everyone was there to see it. The workmen, the cooks, and passersby turned their faces away. The friar was there also, but he said nothing at all. He just turned his back and walked inside the church.

When she had gone back to her house, Bip and I took Big Matt home and packed his nose with cobwebs and moss to stop the bleeding. Bip was red in the face, and swearing in Spanish, but he is unaccustomed to foul language and unskillful in making sense with it.

Despite the humiliation he had suffered, Big Matt started laughing. "You should never swear if you do not know how to do it properly," he said.

Bip was not humored. He said that he would go to the deputy governor and demand that he tell his wife to apologize to the chief for slapping him.

"How long have you been married, Bip?" Big Matt asked. "Would you say something like that to your own wife?" He put both hands on his *inija's* shoulders and looked down into his eyes. "This, too, shall pass, Bip. This, too, shall pass."

Misión San Luis
March 14, 1701

The official visitor arrived today in San Luis. He went first to Ivitachuco where he met with Don Patricio for three days. We have known he was coming for more than a week. Unfortunately, the Florencias also knew he would be here.

His name is Juan de Ayala Escobar. We are told he is not related to the Florencia family, and is a treasury officer in San Augustín. As such, he reports to the Council of the Indies and to the king. The governor has no authority over him.

I was happy to see my old friend, the notary Manuel Quiñones, who is assisting Ayala. Sr. Quiñones is the man who was so kind to me when I went to San Augustín seeking the help of the governor. He said to me today that he was very sorry the last visitor who came to Apalachee was a member of the Florencia family, but that the decision had been made by the governor.

Ayala Escobar was determined to investigate our complaints, and he scheduled a meeting in the council house for anyone who wanted to be heard. Big Matt sent a runner throughout the territory, inviting people to come and tell their stories of abuse.

The council house was almost full, with more than 2,000 people attending. Sr. Quiñones transcribed what was said, leaving me with nothing to do but listen.

The day of questioning by the visitor has been a failure. Seven people stood up to testify as to conditions in San Luis, and the treatment we receive from the Spaniards. Everyone was willing to talk about the abuses of the former deputy governor, Antonio Matheos, but no one would speak against the Florencia family or any other farmer or rancher.

All during the day, at least one member of the Florencia family, or a senior military man, was present in the council house. Even Pedro de Florencia, who almost never comes from his farm, was here in the afternoon.

Big Matt had predicted what would happen. Over the past week, there have been many rumors of people being threatened for speaking against the Florencias. When the day finally arrived, everyone was afraid to tell the truth.

Quiñones acted as scribe for Sr. Ayala, who asked the questions. After the visitor was finished and had left the council house, Quiñones remained to sort though his papers.

"They are lying," I said. "The witnesses, they are afraid to tell the truth."

Quiñones looked up from the manuscript he had been studying. "Yes. I thought so, too" he said. "They are intimidated. Perhaps it is because of the formality of the occasion. Maybe it is because I write down what they say, or because Ayala wears a uniform."

"Or maybe they do not want to speak with a Florencia watching them," I said. "You have come a long way to listen to lies, my friend."

Quiñones put his papers in a wooden box with his pens and ink, and closed the lid. He did not stand up to leave, but sighed heavily and leaned back on the bench. He said nothing for a long time.

Finally, he looked about. We were the only ones left in the council house. "Would it be possible for me to speak privately to some of these people?" he asked.

The third night of the visit of Sr. Ayala and his party to San Luis, a dance was held in the council house for their entertainment. Quiñones told Sr. Ayala that he had an indigestion problem and needed to stay in bed. All of the Florencias were there, including their children. Every soldier in San Luis was inside the house keeping the peace or patrolling outside to make sure there was no trouble.

Bip Bentura had arranged the entertainment. Every dancer within four leagues of San Luis was there to perform, with every musician, and every storyteller, and every clown.

"Unless Ayala falls asleep, or Roque Pérez realizes what is happening and walks out, they will be there to sunup," Bip said.

While the Spaniards marveled at the talent of Apalachee, some of us were in Bip's house at the bottom of the hill in Talimali. We posted Indian guards to make sure we were not interrupted.

More than 50 people came to talk to Quiñones, some from as far away as Cupaica. We had Indian farmers, and pig people, and laborers from the farms and ranches. I told my story, as did Bip Bentura. Even Big Matt slipped out of the dance long enough to be heard.

No one spoke of Antonio Matheos, whose crimes were many years ago. We talked about the Florencias and the other settlers and the soldiers and even the priest who no longer protected us from the worst of the Spaniards.

Farmers told of being cheated of their cattle and pigs and corn. They showed Quiñones the worthless pieces of paper they received as payment, which represented more than 3,000 pesos. Some of the papers were 10 years old. An average pig brings the owner one peso when it is loaded on the boat.

When I spoke of the drowning of the crippled child, Quiñones wiped the tears from his eyes with his kerchief. When Bip Bentura told of the murder of 16 Tasquiqui traders, Quiñones laid down his pen.

"Surely not!" he exclaimed. "Every violent death is required to be reported to the presidio. I have seen no such report."

"And who writes these reports?" Bip asked.

The first rooster had crowed by the time Quiñones gathered the 72 pages he had written down. He bid us buenos noches and went to his bed.

Chapter 37

Misión San Luis
June 10, 1702

Twenty-one days ago a cowardly band of Apalachicoli and Yamassee, and their master, the devil Englishman Governor Moore of Charles Town, slaughtered men, women, children, and the friars of Santa Fé. My mind can scarcely comprehend it. The village of my youth is destroyed, the church in which I was baptized is burned to the ground, and the people I knew are either dead or carried away to slavery.

We knew some of it within four days, as a few people escaped to Potohiriba. From there, a soldier crossed the river into Apalachee and delivered the news to Ivitachuco and San Luis. Our new deputy governor, Manuel Solana, sent soldiers to Santa Fé, and they returned today with an account of what happened.

The Apalachicoli struck at dawn on May 20. We had heard rumors of a planned attack by the English, but no one believed they would strike where there was a garrison of Spanish soldiers.

Western Timucua's Deputy Governor Juan Ruíz de Canizares fought bravely from behind a stockade fence in the convento garden and drove the enemy out of the burning village. He chased after them as they fled, with only 10 men still alive and able to fight.

Perhaps Ruíz was braver than he was clever. The Apalachicoli set a trap for him a day later, six leagues to the north. The soldiers were weary and most of their powder had been expended. They stumbled into an ambush. Everyone died, including Lt. Ruíz and his horse.

The story was told by a woman who was taken from Santa Fé as a slave, but later escaped the Apalachicoli and was found wandering in the woods.

———————

October 7, 1702

The Apalachee Paramount Chief Don Patricio Hinachuba addressed those assembled in the council house at Ivitachuco. I was designated as the official representative of Chief Matheo Chuba of Talimali.

"If they will attack Santa Fé, they no longer fear the Spanish soldiers. Who is to say that Ivitachuco or San Luis or Cupaica or Ayubale are any safer than Santa Fé?"

He said only what many others had said privately, and what all of us had been thinking. Unless Santa Fé was avenged and the Apalachicoli and English were punished, no one was safe.

I was with Don Patricio when he went to the deputy governor in San Luis three days after the meeting in Ivitachuco. He asked me to write down what was said so there would be no argument later as to what happened.

"If you go, do not expect help from San Augustín," Solana said after he listened to Don Patricio's plan for a surprise attack on Achito, where the Apalachicoli and

Yammassee meet for their war councils. "They have worries enough at the presidio. I can spare only three men from here, but if you are intent on going, I will provide muskets and powder and a sergeant to lead you."

A council house is a busy place before a war. Chert for spear points and arrow heads was being heated at the edge of the fire, and the best knappers of Apalachee were busy at their trade. New, powerful bows were being fashioned from maple saplings and arrows were being fletched with feathers by the men who knew how to do it properly.

So much activity was going on that the *paracousi* and chiefs who were planning the attack on the Apalachicoli camp at Achito had trouble hearing each other, so I spoke loudly when I stood up to address them.

"I am the best marksman in the Apalachee militia," I said. "No one has the steady arm and keen eye to hit the target as often as I do."

"And no one doubts your courage," Big Matt said. "After what you showed us against the Chisca 25 years ago, no one will call you a coward for staying behind."

It was useless to argue. No one wanted to say it to my face, but I heard their whispers and saw how they watched me as I walked around in the council house. To them, I am a cripple. They needed younger, more agile men for the 20-league march to Achito, and for the escape back to the south.

I would slow them down and endanger my own men. I knew it in my mind, but in my heart I wanted to go and, if God willed it, to die in the act of punishing the Apalachicoli and Yamassee. It was Don Patricio's decision that I stay behind, and in war his word is law.

I watched as the artisans of Talimali prepared the weapons of war. Some practiced with the muskets, but there was little powder to spare so they did not actually fire them. On the morning they left Talimali, they festooned their hair with colorful feathers and painted their faces red.

They will meet with the others at Bacuqua. A company of 170 Timucua from Yustaga will be there also. Together they will constitute an army of 800 warriors if all the chiefs keep their promises.

If it be God's will, Santa Fé will be avenged and the Apalachicoli and Yamassee are doomed. When the warriors were gone, I went into the church, and Fr. Claudio Florencia and I kneeled before the altar and prayed for their safe return. There is no lonelier feeling than staying behind with the women when the men march off to war.

October 21, 1702

I scarcely have the heart to take quill in hand and place it onto the paper. I use no ink to write, although I have plenty of it. I write with my own blood, in memory of my countrymen who shed their blood, in the same way our Beloved Savior shed his blood upon the cross.

We were betrayed by a spy, and the Yamassee knew our men were coming to Achito. They set a trap at a river crossing, and a band of Apalachicoli attacked from the south at the same time.

Five hundred men died or were taken prisoner. Three hundred escaped, most of them dropping their weapons and fleeing for their lives. The platoon led by Big Matt was almost wiped out, although he escaped with only an arrow in his shoulder. Bip Bentura was with the soldiers who carried muskets. They found cover in a patch of woods and escaped the arrows that rained down on the men in the open, and the gun fire from the English weapons.

With most of our men dead or carried away into slavery, Apalachee and Western Timucua are vulnerable to attack from every quarter.

God have mercy on us and deliver us from our enemies. Hear our prayer, Oh Lord!

Chapter 38

Office of the Fiscal
Protector of the King's Revenue and
Properties
San Augustín de La Florida

November 30, 1702

Juan Mendoza, my friend,

I pray that this finds you in good health and safety, and may God bless you with a full and happy life and many more productive years in His service.

My sincere apologies for not writing to you upon my return to San Augustín, as I promised I would when I departed your beautiful mission and village.

You have, no doubt, surmised from military dispatches the reasons for my delay. In the unlikely event you have not heard of the difficulties here at the presidio, or that your understanding is imperfect, I shall relate to you our true condition.

San Augustín is under siege by our enemies. Perhaps I should say it is the Castillo de San Marcos that is under siege, and that the town is fully occupied by the English and their pagan Indian allies. Fifteen hundred Spaniards and Indians who belong to Misión Nombre de Diós are huddled here together in the fortress which has kept us safe from arrows, musket shot and cannon balls for twenty-seven days.

Only the careful planning of the governor has saved us from violent death outside the walls or starvation within. Grain is stored here in great quantities, and we have cattle and pigs inside the walls, sufficient to sustain us for a short time. It is water that is the problem. We are cut off from the river, and the well within the walls produces a salty, metallic fluid unsuitable for drinking. God has blessed us with rain. We rejoiced at a hurricane that struck us last week, rendering our barrels full to capacity.

The coquina walls of the fort swallow whole the cannon balls from the English ship that sits off the bar, and after the first week of bombardment, with no visible damage to the Castillo, the English seamen decided to save their powder. If they knew the terror experienced by those of us inside, they might have continued the fusillade until we surrendered.

Sometimes at night, bands of Indians approach the fortress with ladders, intent on scaling the walls. The soldiers are alert and accurate in their shooting from the parapets, and take a heavy toll on the enemy. The moat has deterred them, also.

The doors of the fort are kept closed even in the heat of the day, and the stench of human death and excrement and unwashed bodies is disgusting. The Indians congregate to the east side of the yard, and we Spaniards to the west. When the sun is the hottest, we have shade.

We pray for rescue, and search the horizon each day for a glimpse of sails of a Spanish man-of-war come from Cuba to save us. Governor José de Zúñiga y Cerda dispatched two fleet-footed soldiers to Surruque where there is a bark sufficiently seaworthy to reach Cuba. Zúñiga assured us that the men would escape detection by the English Colonel, Daniels, who approached the town from the west. From the vantage point of Governor Moore on the English warship, he could not have seen the men as they ran through the town on their way to the south.

Fredric M. Hitt

Nothing could have saved the northern missions. Colonel Daniels came ashore on the island of Guale and moved south, burning villages and mission churches indiscriminately. The docrinas at San Pedro and San Juan del Puerto are destroyed, and the Indians taken as slaves or scattered into the woods. The friars had warning of the invasion, and made their way to San Augustín and the safety of the Castillo.

In the town, the friars' library was burned on the first day. Moore's men destroyed the collected works of the Greek and Latin fathers, along with the Holy Bible. God shall surely have his justice, and cast the English into the hottest climes of Hell.

Fr. Leturiondo of the Church at San Augustín reminds us constantly to be joyful, even in our distressful situation, and to count our blessing. I count mine, and one of them is that I now have the time to write to my good friend Juan Mendoza and fulfill my earlier promise to communicate the results of the visitation to Apalachee.

On the subject foremost in your thoughts, I have both good news and bad. As you know, I was subservient to the official visitor, Juan de Ayala y Escobar. I was his notary, and not authorized to conduct my own investigation. That is, of course, exactly what I did when I became convinced that the people were fearful to speak out.

I remained silent about what I had learned until we reached the river crossing at Solomototo and were a day from reaching San Augustín. I told Sr. Ayala what I had done and showed him the statements I had collected and the report I had written. He demanded that I either destroy the papers immediately, or return to Apalachee and show them to the deputy governor so I could hear his response to what Ayala characterized as, "scandalous and absurd accusations."

Of course, I refused to do as he ordered, but presented them to Governor Zúñiga y Cerda at the same time Ayala presented his own report.

The governor shared Ayala's scorn at my having exceeded my limited authority, and was particularly distressed that my judgment and evidence painted such a damning view of the performance of the deputy governor and the abuses of the Florencia family.

But he read my report, and every statement I had collected. He also read Ayala's bland writings, and in the end he did not know who to believe. He said to me, "If your report is accurate, and the statements to be believed, the entire Spanish population of Apalachee should be removed to jails and punished as criminals. On the other hand, if there is no substance to your charges, it is you who should be sent to the darkest prison for such slanderous lies."

When he had time to consider, the governor said that he would send yet another visitor to

Apalachee to find the truth. He could not decide who to send. There are so few educated men here, and fewer yet who have no blood relationship or business connection with the Florencia family.

Before he could make up his mind, this business began with the English. If we are rescued, I will be here to remind Governor Zúñiga y Cerda of his promise to send an honest man to report on your true condition.

My conscience has bothered me on yet another point. You asked me if Ayala y Escobar was of the Florencia family, and I said he was not. I was new to San Augustín at the time, and did not know all of the family relationships. I have learned since that he is related to the Florencias by marriage.

Addendum, written December 19, 1702

My dear Juan Mendoza,

The day of our salvation came five days ago, and the English ran from the guns of two

Spanish ships that appeared off the coast, but Governor Moore was trapped and could not escape by sea. Moore burned his ship, and fled overland, trying to catch up with Colonel Daniels and his band of criminals who were fleeing toward Charles Town.

San Augustín was devastated. It will take years to rebuild. Only 20 houses remain. Some of them, the ones occupied by the English soldiers, were so full of fleas that we burned them ourselves to destroy the vermin.

At the proper time, I will remind Governor Zúñiga y Cerda of his promise. That day will come when his house is rebuilt, and he has had a comfortable night's sleep.

God bless you and the people of Apalachee.

Your friend,

Manuel Quiñones.

Chapter 39

Misión San Luis
April 25, 1703

The governor's official visitor has come and gone
from Apalachee. I should write a letter to my good
friend, Manuel Quiñones, to tell him what a venal and
corrupt man the governor sent to us. Whatever hopes we
had of fairness in our dealings with the Spaniards have
been dashed.

Bernardo Nieto Caravajal carried written instructions
from Governor José de Zúñiga y Cerda on how he was to
conduct his visitation. He spoke sweetly to us in the
council house the morning after he arrived, and said that
he and the governor shared a dedication to justice for the
Apalachee and for all the Indians of La Florida.

Only twenty Indians were there to hear what he had
to say. Many others thought it was a waste of time. Chief
Matheo Chuba, Bip Bentura and I were there because it
was our duty, and perhaps because we still had hope. The
deputy governor was there, and the Florencias and other
Spaniards who live in San Luis.

"Governor Zúñiga y Cerda requires that everyone
have his say in this public gathering so we can listen to
each other's complaints and understand each other's
points of view," he said. "It is best to have a public airing

of grievances so that solutions can be considered openly and resentments lanced before they fester."

Neither the governor nor Sr. Caravajal understands what it is like to be subject to the powerful Florencias, and how they punish those who oppose them.

Chief Matheo Chuba answered Caravajal by saying that only a crazy person would risk punishment by speaking the truth of how we are treated, if the Florencias were there to hear.

I stood up to support what Big Matt had said. "If the visitor has come to Apalachee to protect us, perhaps he should stay with us to protect us from the vengeance that would surely follow if we speak our minds."

Caravajal's answer was to read aloud the orders he carried from the governor, and to say that he was prepared to hear the truth and rule justly. He called upon any Apalachee who wished to testify to step forward. No one at all stood up to speak.

Chief Chuba whispered to me and asked if I thought he should walk out.

"It is your council house. You can stay or go. You can also demand that the Spaniards be the ones to walk out."

Big Matt stepped down from his cabana and walked out of the council house. Bip Bentura followed him. I followed Bip, and all of the other Apalachee followed me.

———

Bernardo Nieto Caravajal stayed in San Luis for three days. I said that he was corrupt, and that is not a word I use very often. But what else can I say?

On the morning of the fourth day, before the sun came up, I watched from the door of the convento as a soldier brought two Florencia pack horses to the deputy governor's house. He loaded them with smoked hams, dried beef, tallow, and lard.

The visitor and the governor came out of the house and shook hands. When he left for San Augustín, Bernardo Nieto Caravajal had two soldiers with him for protection and two new horses weighted down with gifts.

Misión San Luis
October 12, 1703

A plague came to San Luis and Talimali, causing sores, fevers, and death. Most people who got sick died within three days, although the young ones lingered for a week or longer.

One hundred and forty people died, most of them Apalachee, but also a few Spaniards. Instead of burying them singly, Fr. Claudio Florencia decided to dig one large hole at the back of the sanctuary and put all of the Indians who were Christians in it, piled on top of each other. The three dead Spaniards each had his own burial hole.

Misión San Luis
December 1, 1703

With the coming of cold weather, it is time to make repairs to the church and council house. There are so few strong men that Bip could not find enough of them to do all the work, so all we did was fix the roof leaks of the church and repair the cracks in the walls so worshipers would be warm and dry for the Christmas celebration.

We also made one repair in the council house. It is in sad shape from the summer hurricane. Two support poles are leaning badly and need to be reset. Rats have dug under the walls and gotten into the corn crib, and there are roof leaks all over, including one directly above Big Matt's cabana. We fixed the leak to keep the chief dry. The rest of the leaks, the poles and the corn crib can wait for spring.

Chapter 40

*T*he prophetic words of Matheo Chuba have come back to haunt the Spaniards. Five years ago, Big Matt warned Roque Pérez that the killings of the Tasquiqui Indians by the Chacato buffalo hunters and the drunken Spaniard Francisco de Florencia would not go unpunished.

His exact words were these: "I will tell you something else about the Tasquiqui. They are not Christians, but they are usually peaceable people until they are provoked. And when that happens, their revenge will not be denied forever. You have not heard the last of this from the Tasquiqui. None of us have."

I wrote his words the day they were spoken on May 2, 1699, and that is how I remember.

Most of the people who lived at Ayubale were Chacato. That may be the reason the English governor, James Moore, chose Ayubale as the first Apalachee village to be destroyed, and why he carried with him a band of vengeful Tasquiqui Indians.

One thousand two hundred people lived there. Misión Conception de Ayubale served them. Now the people are all dead or taken as slaves, and the church is destroyed.

When news of the attack on Ayubale came to San Luis, our new deputy governor, Juan Ruíz de Mejía, called us together at the block house. He said we must go to the aid of Ayubale, and that we would be met by reinforcements from Timucua Province and from San Augustín.

There are fewer than 400 Apalachee men and boys left to fight in San Luis, and 40 Spanish soldiers. Half the soldiers stayed at San Luis under the command of Roque Pérez, in case the English were coming here next. The others, along with all of the Indians in the militia, set out for Ayubale with Ruíz de Mejía leading the way.

This time, because there are so few fighting men, I was allowed to go, but I carried medicines and bandages to treat the wounded at the rear of the column. I did not carry a weapon.

The Tasquiqui warriors and British soldiers were laying in wait for us beside the trail this side of Ayubale. It was a terrible fight that lasted an hour or more. We were badly outnumbered and outflanked. No reinforcements came to rescue us. It ended when the Spaniards ran low on powder, and Deputy Governor Ruiz de Mejía was wounded and captured. Two other soldiers were captured with him.

I counted the dead and wounded. Twenty Apalachee died, as well as seven soldiers. Two of the brave soldiers gave their lives protecting the rest of us as we fled to the south. Twelve soldiers were wounded, and nineteen Apalachee. Among the Indians who were hurt was Chief Matheo Chuba. Big Matt was shot in the side by a musket, but he took it away from the man who shot him and clubbed him to death.

Bip Bentura and I carried our chief home to Talimali. He lost a lot of blood, but his heart is strong.

———————

February 12, 1704

The English have withdrawn from what is left of Ayubale, but no one knows where they went or where they plan to attack next. A squad of men went there and came back. They told us that of the three priests who served at Misión Conception de Ayubale, one, Fr. Parga, was beheaded by the Tasquiqui. Another, Fr. Mendoza, was found burned to death, with the crucifix melted into his chest. The third friar, Fr. Angel Miranda, was not found. Two soldiers were burned at the stake. There was no sign of Juan Ruíz de Mejía.

The horror of the story has afflicted all of us, both Indian and Spaniard. The Spaniards are loud in their condemnations of the deputy governor of Timucua Province for not sending soldiers to save us. The Indians are quieter, but secretly blame the Spaniards here.

We also worry that someone among us spies for the English and reports to them our every move. This recent ambush by the English and Tasquiqui outside of Ayubale seems to echo the trap we fell into when we went to punish the Apalachicoli Indians for their attack on Santa Fé.

Someone posted a notice in the Talimali council house while we were attending Mass. It was not an official paper of the priest or the deputy governor, but a message from the English Governor James Moore. It invited the people of Apalachee to leave San Luis and go to Charles Town. Moore promised that the Indians would be treated respectfully, and that those who came voluntarily would not be considered slaves, but free men.

The notice could only have been posted by someone who comes and goes in the council house. No stranger would have been allowed inside, which makes us think it was a spy.

Bip Bentura received a report that a similar message was posted at Ivitachuco, and Don Patricio Hinachuba sent word that more than 500 of his people have fled to Charles Town. At least 100 people who live in Talimali have deserted the village since Sunday.

Meanwhile, Big Matt still lies in his house. He was hurt worse than we thought. He has a hot fever and he sleeps too much and cries out day and night. Fr. Claudio prays over him each morning and an *isucu* packs the wound with moss, but nothing seems to help him. Either Bip or I are with him at all times, along with his poor wife.

The missing Ayubale priest Fr. Angel Miranda came to San Luis today carrying a letter from the Englishman, James Moore. It was addressed to both the deputy governor and the people of Talimali. When Roque Pérez demanded to know what Moore had to say, the friar refused to answer him until the leaders of Talimali were there to hear.

Bip Bentura and I were summoned to the deputy governor's house, since Big Matt is sick in bed. All of the most important Spaniards were there, including the lieutenant in charge of the soldiers, Francisco de Florencia and his brother, Pedro, and even Doña Juana Catalina de Florencia. She did not look at me or even seem to know I was there.

The priest read the letter. It said that Governor Moore held the Spanish Deputy Governor Juan Ruíz de Mejía as a prisoner, but that he would return him alive if certain conditions were met.

First, Governor Moore said, Roque Pérez was to surrender all of the remaining Chacato Indians in the province to Moore, so they could be rendered justice by the Tasquiqui. Roque Pérez interrupted the reading by saying that it was out of the question, and that the Chacato people were the subjects of Spain's king and entitled to protection.

Secondly, Moore demanded the payment of 400 pesos in gold as reparations.

Jacinto Roque Pérez reacted angrily. "If Governor Moore will come to San Luis, I will feed him his ransom from my cannon."

The friar spoke softly, saying he was just a messenger following his instructions. He asked Roque Pérez to think it over, and give him his decision in the morning. Roque Pérez said his answer was final.

When Fr. Miranda rose to leave, Roque Pérez asked him why he was going back to see Governor Moore, who had killed so many priests and innocent Indians. "He will surely kill you, also," Roque said.

The friar stopped in the doorway, and turned back to answer Roque Pérez. "My people are with him. His camps are full of Christian Indians in need of their friar."

Roque Pérez did not stand, but turned his head dismissively and looked out the window as he offered his reply. "Go with God."

Chapter 41

Misión San Luis de Talimali
July 14, 1704

On the morning of the 10th of July, word came of an attack on the mission at Cupaica by hundreds of Creek Indians and English soldiers. The messenger had run all night to spread the alarm and to beg for help.

Jacinto Roque Pérez gathered together the Spanish troops and the Indian militia at the San Luis fortress. He sent soldiers to surrounding villages looking for volunteers, and conscripting men who did not want to come. By midday, 120 of us milled around inside the palisade walls awaiting our orders.

While we waited, another man arrived on horseback, shouting and hollering. It was the friar of Misión San Pedro y San Pablo de Patale. That village had also been attacked in the nighttime and had been overrun by Creek, who murdered another priest and set fire to the church.

Patale is four leagues east of San Luis. Cupaica is more than three leagues to the west.

Before Roque Pérez could decide what to do, we got word of the ambush of three soldiers who were bringing a shipment of guns, lead, and powder from the port of San Marcos. Two of the soldiers were killed. The third man ran into the woods and escaped.

"There is nothing we can do to relieve the people of Cupaica or Patale," said Roque when he and his officers came out of the block house to talk to us in the afternoon. "We seem to be surrounded. We must prepare for a siege."

July 18, 1704

Don Patricio Hinachuba, the Paramount Chief of Apalachee, arrived in San Luis today along with 60 warriors. He came at the bidding of Roque Pérez to help plan a defense and counterattack against the English and their Creek allies.

We met in the council house. Don Patricio sat in the cabana reserved for the highest ranking visiting chief. The bench belonging to Matheo Chuba, the Chief of Talimali was unoccupied. I had draped it in black cloth and laid a wooden cross there in his memory, to mark his passing during the night.

When we were all gathered, Roque Pérez and his Spanish officers entered the council house. Those of us who serve in the militia sat together wearing our green tunics. When I looked around the cavernous house, I felt we were swallowed up by empty space. In a house that could hold 3,000 or more people, there were fewer than 300. There were only the people of Talimali, plus a few from Cupaica who came here when their town was burned, and the men with Don Patricio from Ivitachuco.

Three years ago there were 11 villages with missions in Apalachee. Now there are two.

I did not make note of everything Roque Pérez had to say, as I usually do. We have heard it all before. Some things I do remember.

He said that it was time to rally together to defeat the hated Englishmen and their murderous Creek allies, and that he and his lieutenants had hit upon a military tactic that was sure to catch the English while they are overconfident and unaware. Because he feared there were spies lurking about, he could not announce the plan in the council house, but would meet later, privately, with the leaders of the militia.

He was looking for commitment on the part of the Apalachee. He wanted to know how many men could be counted upon to leave in two or three days to fight the enemy.

Don Patricio Hinachuba remained seated and listened carefully to what Roque had to say. When he finally did speak, his words were no surprise to me or to Bip Bentura, as we had consulted with the paramount chief upon his arrival in San Luis and knew what was in his heart.

"How many soldiers are coming from Timucua Province to support us?" he asked. "And how many are on the road from San Augustín?"

Roque Pérez glanced nervously at his lieutenants and then looked down at the papers he held in his hand before answering. "We have communicated with the deputy governor at Santa Fé. He knows our predicament. I would expect a response later today or tomorrow morning at the latest. As for the soldiers from the presidio . . ."

"Is this the same soldier from Santa Fé whose men got lost coming to our rescue at Ayubale?" Don Patricio asked. It was unlike Don Patricio to interrupt a speaker or to speak disrespectfully to a Spaniard. He had more on his mind, and he stood up so that everyone could hear what he had to say.

"We are tired of this war we cannot win," he said "and weary of false promises of help from Spaniards who live too far away or have problems of their own."

Roque Pérez seemed stunned by Don Patricio's tone, but he listened quietly while the paramount spoke his mind.

"We will no longer fight the Spaniards' war against the English," Don Patricio said. "The great nation of Apalachee has been destroyed by it. Thousands of our people have already gone to Charles Town to be with the English, or moved west to live among the French, or have disappeared into the woods with no intention of ever returning to their homes."

Roque Pérez's face had turned red and he was sweating, although it was a comfortable time of day in the council house. "Apalachee could do with a stronger chief," he said. "Is this how you repay us for all we have done for you Indians?"

Roque looked around as if he were searching for a friend, someone to agree with him, anyone who would challenge what Don Patricio said. His eyes met mine, and then he looked at Bip, then the other leaders of Talimali. He shook his head. "Your ingratitude is abysmal."

Patricio raised his hand. "Hear me out. If the English and the Creek come to Ivitachuco, we will not resist them. We will make peace and some of us may go with them to Charles Town."

"Then I say the men of Ivitachuco are no better than women," Roque answered. "But we have warriors at San Luis, valorous men who are worthy of the name Apalachee."

Some of the men, even militia fighters, laughed out loud at the Spaniard's feeble attempt to divide us. At first, no one noticed that Bip Bentura had stood up. When the laughing stopped, he spoke his piece.

"We have no chief today to speak for Talimali," he said. "As you all know, Chief Matheo Chuba died last night. He died a Christian with his soul saved by the grace of Jesus Christ. But let no man forget that Big Matt was Apalachee, and not Spanish."

It was the first time I had heard anyone call him "Big Matt" publicly, but it was not said disrespectfully by the *inija,* but lovingly. I looked around and saw smiles on some faces, and tears rolling down others.

"As his *inija,* I know what was in his heart. If he were here, Big Matt would tell us to make peace if we can, and defend our families if no peace is to be had. He would say that the Spaniards have betrayed us time and time again, and disrespected us and are deserving of no further sacrifice of Apalachee blood."

Bip had been looking directly at the Indians as he spoke, and not the Spaniards. Finally, he turned back toward Roque Pérez and his officers.

"We are not well organized now, and we are entering a time of mourning. You should not expect help from the men of Talimali. It may even be that some of us have such a bad heart toward you Spaniards that we would fight along side the English. The time has come for you Spaniards to leave Apalachee."

Chief Matheo Chuba, the *cacique* of the largest town in Apalachee, has died, and few people take note of the loss.

In olden days, before the friars came, the death of a great leader was observed properly and with dignity. Mourning lasted for a year, and burial of the bones was sometimes delayed for half a year, depending on the stature of the man or woman, and the beliefs of the clan, and the season of the year.

My father told me stories of widows and clansmen who, in their grief, cut off all their hair; of relatives who took knives or shells and cut their own flesh to show the pain in their hearts; of how the corpse would be as lovingly attended in death as it was in life, placed in a charnel house where the bones would be cleaned until they were shiny white, and before burial carried about in satchels on the backs of kinsmen.

Chiefs were laid to rest in mounds of sand and ochre, surrounded with their jewelry, knives, tools, and things they loved in life that would accompany them to the Village of the Dead.

To my shame I did not write it down as it was taught to me, and many of the old customs are lost to memory. As a writer of history, I have failed to record some things that were important.

Today, the old ways are condemned by the friars as pagan and un-Christian. But who is to say they were evil? The old customs must have been satisfying to the ones who practiced them, otherwise they would have done something else with their dead.

When we lay Big Matt to rest in the floor of the church in two days, who will be satisfied? Who will remember, or care that he is gone?

When I speak to the friar in the morning I will ask that Big Matt be eulogized at the Funeral Mass and honored as a great man and leader of the Apalachee people.

Chapter 42

Fr. Claudio de Florencia asked me to work with him today to inventory and pack in barrels the church furnishings and implements. Roque Pérez has announced that he has received orders from the governor in San Augustín to abandon Apalachee Province.

There is one last service to be performed at San Luis. It is the Funeral Mass for Chief Matheo Chuba tomorrow morning. The friar said he will wait until after the interment to crate up the items necessary for a proper Funeral Mass.

I wrote down everything on a ledger. Fr. Claudio would name or describe the item, and in which barrel or crate it could be found. Some of the things were too large to pack, such as the processional cross and some of the statues of the saints.

"When the time comes, the church property will be taken to San Marcos where it will be loaded on a ship bound for San Augustín," Fr. Claudio said before we began. "The ledger will tell us what we have and where it can be found."

Not even Fr. Claudio was prepared for the number and variety of items we found behind the altar, in the sacristy, and in the storage rooms. It was a 50-year accumulation of valuable church items, and things that should have been thrown away long ago.

Even with three young boys to help, it took us all day to finish the counting and packing. The friar trusted no one to handle the fragile items, such as the little containers that held the viaticum for the Eucharist for dying persons. He wrapped each one carefully in cloth and layered them in the crates and barrels with palmetto fronds so they would not be jostled or broken.

The valuable items, such as the silver patens that hold the bread at Eucharist, and the small crosses imbedded with precious stones, and the glass containers of chrism oil used at baptisms, were touched only by the friar. The boys folded the canopies and altar clothes, damatics, and other vestments and robes that could not be broken and were not worth stealing.

When the boys were gone, Fr. Claudio said a prayer that nothing would be broken, and that God would bless the voyage with calm seas. Claudio was emotional, and tears rolled down his face as we looked around at the bare walls of the sanctuary and the naked altar. Light from the setting sun filtered through cracks in the old walls.

"There is something I would like to ask," I said. "I would like to dig the hole for Matheo Chuba on the row nearest the altar, where he will be properly honored for his service to the church and to the people of Talimali."

Fr. Claudio wiped the tears from his eyes. He put on his eye glasses, opened the burial book and ran his finger over the diagram of the floor that showed where people had been laid to rest.

"The front row is reserved for the clergy, for officers, and for soldiers of the crown who have died in service to the king," the friar said. "There is an unused place on the second row, where chiefs and important Indians are honored. Big Matt will rest comfortably among his own kind."

I felt sudden anger, not because Matheo Chuba would lie among other chiefs instead of with Spaniards, where he would probably feel uncomfortable, but because the priest had called him by his secret name, Big Matt. From the lips of a Spaniard, it was disrespectful.

———————

An order was posted on the door of the church, another at the council house, and one in Talimali. It was signed by Roque Pérez, and in the preamble it said that after 57 years the Spaniards were leaving Apalachee Province and retiring to San Augustín.

"All inhabitants of Misión San Luis are ordered to prepare for a 10-day journey to San Augustín beginning at daybreak on Saturday, August 14, 1704. Soldiers will afford protection, but each family should provide its own food.

"The Deputy Governor can provide no assistance or protection to laggards, or those who disobey this order or choose a destination other than San Augustín. No one will be allowed to remain in San Luis or the village of Talimali. I have instructed my sergeant to burn all structures to deny them to our enemies."

While the Apalachee honored Chief Matheo Chuba in death, the Spaniards went about the business of packing their household goods to be taken to San Marcos for shipment on the boat. From inside the church, we could hear how they argued and cursed among themselves in the plaza where the ox carts were being loaded.

Roque Pérez ordered that only women and children and those who were infirm would be allowed on the boat.

The other Spaniards, including the soldiers, would walk to San Augustín.

———————

August 13, 1704

Fr. Claudio has given permission to use his desk on this last night in San Luis. When I am done writing, it will take only a short time for me to pack my possessions for the journey. I have only my clothing, my aged, unused weapons, and my writings.

Bip Bentura has decided to go west, to a new French colony called Mobil. A Frenchman he knows says the people will be welcomed and allowed to settle there. Bip is so much respected that almost everyone in Talimali wants to go with him.

The Spanish ranchers have come to San Luis to join the people bound for San Augustín. They abandoned their cattle, thinking they would all die on the trail. Bip's people have rounded up 400 cows and bulls and plan to drive them to Mobil. Pigs are not good herd animals, so the large ones will be left behind.

"Come with us, Juan," Bip said to me. "You have no home, other than with us."

There is truth in what Bip said. I have few friends in this life, and no kinsmen. It has been more than a year since I have spoken Timucuan. I wonder if anyone still lives in Santa Fé, in Potano, in Oconee, or any of the other villages where I grew to manhood.

Perhaps I still have family, somewhere. I doubt that I would recognize anyone after so many years, or that they would know my face. Maybe Bip is right, and I should go with him.

When the Spaniards reach Ivitachuco, Don Patricio Hinachuba will join them for the journey east toward San

Augustín. However, he has no intention of going that far. He fears that he may be charged as a traitor once he reaches the presidio.

"The Spaniards will need someone to blame for their defeat in Apalachee," Don Patricio said to Bip and me after the Funeral Mass for Matheo Chuba. "They could say I caused it by refusing to fight against the English. I may go as far as Potano Province, and find some empty village with a good fishing stream and fertile land to grow corn. If the Spaniards want me, they can come and get me."

Don Patricio is feeling his age, and asked me to come with him and help him keep the Apalachee people together. I do not know many of the people from Ivitachuco. The few friends I have live in Talimali. Still, it is a great honor to be asked to rule along side a chief of Don Patricio's stature. It is something to consider.

Some people are going to join the English, and others are going in every direction, other than with the Spaniards.

There is one other person in this life I call a friend. It is the notary, Manuel Quiñones, who told the truth about how we were abused by the Florencia family. He is one of the few honest Spaniards I have ever known, but he lives in San Augustín.

Tonight I think it would be best to go with Bip Bentura to Mobil, but I am not sure of what to do. As with all important decisions, I will pray on it and leave it to God. By the time the sun comes up, he will tell me what to do.

Chapter 43

San Augustín
November 12, 1708

My good friend and mentor, Manuel Quiñones, has urged me to write down the events that occurred before and since the fall of the missions of Apalachee and Western Timucua. While Spanish governors and priests have told their versions, with long letters and manifestos in which they point their fingers of blame at each other, there are so few literate Indians that not one of us has stepped forward to tell the truth of what occurred.

Today at Mass I heard scripture that encourages me:

But I say unto you, Love your enemies, bless them that curse you,

do good to them that hate you, and pray for them which despitefully

use you and persecute you

That ye may be the children of your Father which is in heaven:

for he maketh the sun to rise on the evil and on the good,

and sendeth rain on the just and on the unjust.

Gospel according to St. Matthew, Ch 5, v. 4-5

Sr. Quiñones is a rare creature among Spaniards, a just man. Fr. Alonso de Leturiondo, San Augustín's pastor who bears the title "Protector of the Indians" is another. Both of these men have read my extensive journal collection of writings, including those written by my father. My trust in them is such that I allowed them to see even those passages critical of Spaniards.

Where shall I start in recounting these past four years and the manner in which God has sent rain on each of us, saint and sinner alike?

———————

When I departed Misión San Luis on the morning of August 14, 1704, I went to Ivitachuco and joined the Paramount Chief of Apalachee Don Patricio Hinachuba, who was bound with his people toward Potano Province in Western Timucua. Because he feared prosecution by the Spaniards for his lack of support during the last days of San Luis, Don Patricio thought it unwise to accompany the Spaniards to San Augustín.

We found an abandoned Potanan village named Abosaya, half a day's walk from the old Misión San Francisco de Potano. This was familiar territory to me, close by Utina Province where I was born. While Don Patricio's people built their houses, I traveled about in Potano and crossed the river into Utina Province looking for some sign of my family.

There was nothing left of Laguna Oconee, where I was raised. Santa Fé still exists, but only because there is a military garrison there, and some degree of safety against the Yamassee and other outlaws who travel freely about with their English muskets, taking slaves for Charles Town and shooting anyone who resists.

I traveled all the way to Ayacouta before I turned back to Abosaya. In seven days of wandering about, I encountered no more than ten people who spoke the language of my birth, Timucuan. I gave up on my quest to find family.

In my absence, Don Patricio had received a letter from Manuel Quiñones urging the chief to come to San Augustín where the well-armed fortress would provide safety from the Yamassee raiders. Quiñones also asked about my whereabouts, and said that he had work for me and a place for me to stay if I would come. With Don Patricio's encouragement, I set out for San Augustín.

It is a painful thing to recall, and write down the memory of, what befell Don Patricio. The village he chose had no natural defenses, such as a deep river or swamp, and proved vulnerable to attack. In the winter of 1705-6, he gave up and moved his people to another village closer to San Augustín, where he thought they would be safe.

On a cold night in the winter of 1706, the new village was attacked, and Don Patricio Hinachuba died. Some people survived the battle and lived to tell the terrible story. The attackers were a mixed army of Yamassee warriors and renegade Apalachee. They were people who had once honored Don Patricio as their chief, and now their hearts had turned so bad that they set out to kill him.

Some of the Spaniards of Misión San Luis fared no better than the Apalachee. Two men in particular paid a dear price for the sins they had committed. Francisco de Florencia, the most violent of all of them, and the one who was responsible for the deaths of 16 Tasquiqui Indians, died of an epidemic within a month of his arrival at San Augustín.

Lt. Jacinto Roque Pérez, who was Deputy Governor of Apalachee Province three times, died in the same contagion. In my early years at San Luis I looked upon Roque Pérez as an honorable man, but in time I came to know that he was no better than the rest of the Florencias.

———— —— ——

I had been in San Augustín for a month when I encountered the widow Juana Cathalina de Florencia. She was dressed all in black, and was shopping in the vegetable market with four of her ten children, on a crisp fall Saturday morning.

At my age I have no secrets, even from myself, and I can say what sometimes burdens my heart. When I approached her to express my condolences for the loss of her husband, she did not recognize me. I realized, perhaps for the first time, that I was never an important person in her life. She was the reason I never married. I had the strongest of feelings toward her, but they were never returned.

I take no pleasure in recounting the rest of her story. As a Florencia, Juana Cathalina was once a wealthy woman, honored and respected by her people. Only the Apalachee who had suffered the cruelty of her sharp tongue and harsh treatment saw her differently.

After the death of her husband and her brother, Juana Cathalina went on a sea voyage bound for Pensacola where she intended to make her home. Her ship was attacked by French pirates, and they took her possessions, including her gold and precious jewelry. They also robbed her of her dignity.

Juana Cathalina lived on the charity of others in Pensacola. When last heard of, she was living in Vera Cruz, in Mexico. The governor there provides a stipend sufficient for her to live.

———— —— ——

By far the greatest number of Apalachee went to the west, stopping for a time near Pensacola before moving further to the French town of Mobil. There were 400 people led by Bip Bentura. Almost all of the people of Talimali were with him, and many from Cupaica and other villages.

Many of the cattle they had with them survived, and Bip even loaded small pigs in a wagon so the people would have pork to eat along the way. In my employment as scribe to Governor Francisco Córcoles y Martínez, I am in a position to see many of the archived reports and official letters that come from other colonies. There was one such report from Pensacola that marked the arrival of Bip Bentura and his people, and another reporting his departure to Mobil. Since then I have not heard or read a word about my friend, Bip. I pray that he is well and happy living among the French, and that some day we might meet again.

I live in the household of Sr. Quiñones. I described him as a fair man, but that word does not do him justice. His more notable qualities are his generosity and his love of his fellow man. Perhaps I should say more about the circumstances of my present condition.

Sr. Quiñones was once wealthy, and his house the finest in all of San Augustín, as might be expected of the king's fiscal officer. The mansion consists of eight rooms, with a stairway leading to an upper floor. There is a bedroom downstairs that is occupied by Sr. Quiñones and his bedridden wife. I have an adjoining room that was once a pantry or cupboard, but it is fully sufficient for my needs.

There are four bedrooms upstairs that once accommodated all of the Quiñones children who have now grown up and moved away. Now there are eight Indian orphans who live there.

Because Misión Nombre de Diós is so impoverished, there is no way to feed or care for the orphaned children of San Augustín, except for the generosity of Sr. Quiñones. I live in the house without charge, but give to Sr. Quinines half of my earnings to support the orphans. The mission no longer has the funds or teachers to educate Indian children, so I teach them to read and write in Spanish.

Some of the children are Guale, whose people fled from the Yamassee 10 years ago but died soon after they arrived here. Others are Timucuan and Surruque. One twelve-year-old girl, Maria Cavale, was a princess whose aunt was a Mocaman *caciqua*. I believe she is the only full-blood Timucua among the orphans.

The expense of raising the children has left Sr. Quiñones a poor man compared to his former state, but the blessings he and I receive every day from the children's laughter is worth more than gold.

Although San Augustín is no longer a rich town, there are still Spaniards who wear new clothes, send their children to Havana for an education, and live in fine houses. Claudio de Florencia is now the leader of the Franciscans, and lives in the monastery. His younger brother, Diego, is a wealthy merchant and ship owner.

I do not begrudge these two Florencias their success. They are more like the patron of the family, Juan de Florencia, who cared deeply for the welfare of the people of Apalachee. The worst of the Florencias are gone. Francisco and his brother-in-law Jacinto Roque Pérez are dead, and Juana Cathalina all but erased from my memory, living in Mexico. Perhaps I can now let go of my hatred for what they did to the people of Apalachee.

There were three visitors sent by the governors to address and correct the abuses we suffered. The first was

Joaquín de Florencia, a member of the family, who has since died.

The second visitor was Juan de Ayala Escobar, who was related by marriage to the Florencia family and gave us no relief from our suffering. Ayala had Sr. Quiñones with him, but was deaf to what Quiñones had to say. Ayala is still here, strutting around in his fine Spanish clothing, with his nose in the air. Some say he is the king's favorite, and destined some day to be governor.

The last of the visitors was Bernardo Neito Caravajal who betrayed his oath for a bribe of ham and a piece of dried beef. He is still here, also. When I see him in town I taste the bile that rises in my throat, the same anger I feel when I see Ayala.

It has been so long since I thought or wrote about the past, it surprises me that my mind is full of old poison. I will pray on it and ask God to give me a forgiving heart.

Chapter 44

San Augustín
June 2, 1711

*T*oday is a day of great joy in the Quiñones household. Indian girls and young women flit about, all grown up in silk blouses under tightly laced corsets, with bonnets and bright colored skirts. Boys strut self-consciously, freshly scrubbed clean, and dressed in crisp, starched linen shirts and breeches, each with a fancy silk sash around his waist.

I have not seen my love Maria since early this morning when she disappeared into the master's bedroom with her gaggle of giggling helpers, locking the door lest I should intrude and spoil the surprise of how she will look on her wedding day.

Sr. Quiñones was so concerned about my nervousness that he set me down at the desk in his study and ordered me to fill my mind and my time by writing a description of this extraordinary day.

I scarcely can believe the day has come. At the age of 63, I will marry for the first time in my life and to a woman one-third my age. Neither of us could be happier.

The vows will be given at the doorway of the church at Nombre de Diós, with the mission priest performing the service. Sr. Quiñones will stand with me, and my employer Governor Francisco Córcoles y Martínez has promised to attend unless affairs of state interfere.

My wife-to-be and I have chosen to live in a manner traditional for Timucuans. Although she has no living family, she is White Deer by birth and we had decided that she will be the matron of the clan. If we have children, they will be White Deer, also. In earlier times, our offspring would be the stock from which chiefs and *inijas* would be chosen. In modern times there are so few Indians left that there is no need for leaders of that stature, only for those who serve as village leaders.

So it is a fiction we tell ourselves, but it is done with the best of intentions, to honor those of our race who have died through the centuries, leaving us who remain, in our pitiful state.

Our first thought was to be married by a shaman in the traditional Timucuan way, with ancient incantations and petitions to the ancestors to bless our union and make it happy and fruitful. As Christians, of course, we would also seek the blessings of the church.

Search as we might, we could not find a single remaining Timucuan shaman in any village surrounding San Augustín. There was one man who claimed such powers, but he was a fraud who preys upon other people's yearning for the old life. Another was Guale, but he had no knowledge of Timucuan ceremonies.

The time is drawing near, and I can hear the familiar voice of Sr. Quiñones greeting the celebrants as they arrive at the door. We will all go together to the church. Inwardly I feel calm, but the problem is my hand. It sweats so profusely I can scarcely hold the quill.

———————

San Augustín
September 24, 1713

"Juan Alonso Cavale, the first child born to Maria Cavale and Juan Mendoza of San Augustín, was welcomed into this life on the winds of a hurricane that has blown for two days. When the storm departed, it left behind our flooded roads and houses, thatched roofs ripped asunder, and one beautiful, smiling, fat-cheeked Timucuan boy."

Those were the flowery words penned by Sr. Manuel Quiñones and posted at various message boards throughout the town.

The child was named by his mother. She named him Juan, after me, ignoring my urgings that he be called Manuel in honor of our benefactor, Sr. Quiñones, or Coya, in remembrance of my father who was a great Timucuan chief.

Alonso is a name intended to honor the memory of Fr. Alonso Leturiondo who was Protector of Indians for many years and used his pulpit to denounce the cruelty inflicted on the Indians of La Florida. Cavale, of course, is the family name of the child's mother.

I settled in with the sound of the name: Juan Alonso Cavale, a good name, a strong name. I vowed before God to make him into a devout Christian and a man proud of his heritage. I will teach him the lessons taught me by my father, and the stories I heard as a child.

I built a small house next to the large one owned by Sr. Quiñones, and moved my family into it. When Maria is recovered from the child birth, we will find room for one or two of the orphans, and raise them as our own.

April 22, 1718

A remarkable thing has occurred in San Augustín. Lately we have heard rumors of conflict between the Yamassee and their English sponsors at Charles Town. For years the Yamassee have been armed and sent to attack the peaceful Indians of La Florida. They destroyed Apalachee, in concert with the Chiscas, and they laid waste to most of Utina, Potano, and even Yustaga, leaving no safe, habitable towns west of the River San Juan.

The Yamassee were the ones who destroyed the province of Guale and the missions in the coastal land formerly occupied by the Timucua who speak the Mocaman dialect. Untold thousands of people were murdered by them, and as many taken to the slave market at Charles Town.

As we hear the story, the English decided to take Yamassee as slaves also, and they began to treat them as harshly as the Spaniards treat the rest of us. Being bloodthirsty savages by nature, the Yamassee rose up quickly and declared a war against the English.

Now our former enemies, the Yamassee, flock to San Augustín like so many birds fleeing the shotguns of hunters. Day by day they come seeking the protection of the cannons at Castillo de San Marcos, begging for a sanctuary they never granted to Apalachee, Timucuans, or Guale.

The governor grants them amnesty for their crimes, takes their English weapons, and provides them a place to stay at the council house at Nombre de Diós. He is a kind, forgiving Christian. Unfortunately, some may not be so forgiving. In the past fortnight, seven Yamassee have been killed, and their bodies found floating in the bay. The governor has no idea who might be doing the murders.

February 2, 1719

For fifteen years Sr. Quiñones has been bothered by the events that led to the destruction of Apalachee Province. When we are alone, with no other Spanish ears to hear, he speaks of little else. The ill treatment by the Florencias was greatly to blame, he says, but the worst of them are now gone from this life and no doubt trying to justify themselves before a vengeful God.

Juan de Ayala y Escobar, the official visitor who came to Apalachee with Sr. Quiñones in 1701, has yet to meet justice for his treachery on behalf of the Florencias, and for his sins against the people of Apalachee. Ayala had always been immune from justice by virtue of the high offices he occupied for many years. Most recently, he served a term as governor.

"We have a saying in Spain," Sr. Quiñones said to me today, when he returned from the presidio and we sat in his den. "'Every dog has his day.'"

A new governor has been appointed by the Council of the Indies, Antonio de Benavides, and Sr. Quiñones met with him today. Governor Benavides's first duty will be to convene a residencia investigation of Ayala y Escobar's conduct.

"I intend to present evidence of seditious misconduct on the part of our former governor." Sr. Quiñones reached into a drawer and pulled out a stack of papers two inches thick and dropped them on the desk. He was smiling when he said, "Juan, you are not the only one capable of writing down historical fact."

August 14, 1719

"The Quiñones Manifesto," as his papers came to be known, hit San Augustín like a barrage of artillery from heavy cannon. Legal objections were filed by Ayala y Escobar, complaining that his services as official visitor to Apalachee occurred years before he was appointed governor, and thus should not be the subject of a residencia proceeding.

Governor Benavides deferred to the decision of the Council of the Indies. In June the Council ruled that the accusations were of such a nature that Benavides should hold the hearing and make his findings of fact even if, technically, the offenses occurred before Ayala y Escobar became governor.

Benavides agreed to keep me on as his official scribe when he took office. When I told him that I planned to testify at the Ayala y Escobar residencia, he said that I could not serve as both scribe and witness in the same proceeding. That made sense to both of us, so he sent to Havana for another scribe. To my delight, the new scribe is Alfonso Garza, the man who served with me at the trial of Calesa many years ago.

When Sr. Garza came ashore, he was happy to see me. "You have not aged a day," he said when we embraced. I know he was lying. Sr. Garza was now an old man with sparse white hair and a wrinkled face. I went to my house and looked carefully into a mirror. I too showed my advanced age of 70 years. I also noticed for the first time that my eyes were obscured with a thin white cloud.

————

Sr. Garza was not the only person from my past who came for the residencia. Friends of Sr. Quiñones in Pensacola went to Mobil and found the Apalachee *inija*

Bip Bentura and arranged for his passage by boat to San Augustín. He arrived during the second day of the hearing. Bip's memory, if not his health, was good.

He spoke about Sr. Ayala y Escobar's failure to listen to the truth about the way we were treated in Apalachee. In every detail, Bip's testimony matched mine, and our words confirmed all that Sr. Quiñones had to say.

On the last day, a surprise witness appeared. It was the old Spanish soldier, Federico, who had worked at San Luis for 10 years before it fell to the English. He was the man who loaded down the pack horses with hams, lard, and beef: the bribes with which the Florencias purchased the silence of the last of the official visitors, Bernardo Neito Caravajal.

In the end, Governor Benavides issued a strong denunciation of the official visitors and the governors who accepted their fraudulent reports. He sent his findings to the Council of the Indies for a decision on who was to be prosecuted.

Bip Bentura stayed with us for seven days after the hearing. He told me of the misfortunes his people had experienced since they left San Luis. Many of the cattle were lost at river crossings, but a few of the pigs thrived in the boggy country near Mobil. One hundred of the four hundred people who set out from Talimali died on the trail to Mobil, or shortly thereafter, from sickness for which they had no cure.

"Now we are doing well," he said. "The French treat us better than the Spaniards did at San Luis, but we still get sick from the wet climate."

When I walked Bip to the boat on the last day, he was coughing so hard he could barely speak. I went directly to the chapel and prayed that he live to see his family.

San Augustin

Convento de Santo Domingo

Guanabacoa, Cuba
June 2, 1769

To: Monseñor Pedro Agustín Morell,
Bishop of Santiago de Cuba
Havana

Your Excellency,
As always, your brothers in Christ send their warm greetings and hold you in their hearts and in their prayers. May your service be long and fruitful, and pleasing to Our Father in Heaven.

The manuscript submitted to you today concerns events in San Augustín, La Florida, between the years of 1730 and 1763. It is the final volume, but it may be more interesting from an historical standpoint than the earlier writings, although I leave such judgments to you and others more qualified.

Of particular interest are the numerous references to Your Excellency. The Indian, Juan Alonso Cavale, wrote effusively of your official visitation to San Augustín in 1762, of your stalwart defense of the Indians against the English slavers, and of your spiritual guidance and inspiration that sustained the beleaguered people of San Augustín.

Being mindful of my commitment to you to refrain from any edit or abridgment of the manuscript, I must admit that there are 40 pages, front and back, that have not been copied. They consist of nothing more than penmanship exercises: endless repetition of the symbols of the Castilian alphabet. They appear to be in the unschooled style of other writings which I have

Fredric M. Hitt

identified as having been authored by Juan Alonso Cavale. Those 40 pages are being retained here with the rest of the other original documents, pending your instructions for their disposition.

My work is almost done, unless there is some other service that you wish me to perform. There is one other task I have undertaken: an account of the life of the deceased, Juan Alonso Cavale, which I have appended to the end of the manuscript. The church records are sparse, since he seldom darkened the doorway of the church, but there are friends and acquaintances of Cavale who knew him in San Augustin who tell us of his family, background, employment, etc.

With this transmittal, you now have in your possession the entire transcribed record of what we now refer to as the Cavale Timucuan Indian Manifesto. That, of course, is not an official name. We leave it to you, if you feel it is necessary or appropriate, to apply a name to it.

As our Lord and Master said on the cross, "It is finished."

I kiss your ring.

Fr. Manuel de Soto

Chaplain, Convento de Santo Domingo

Chapter 45

San Augustín
October 17, 1730

My father Juan Mendoza, Scribe to the Governor of La Florida and friend to Indian and Spaniard alike, passed to his reward a year ago today.

For most of his life my father wrote down the history of our people, as his father did before him. In so doing, they were not unlike the old storytellers, except that the storytellers did not know how to write, and so kept the stories in their memory and not on paper or parchment stored in a leather box.

My father spent the last years of his life, even after he became blind, teaching me to read and write. His two ambitions for me were that I follow him as scribe to the governor, and that I honor the family tradition of recording the history of our people.

When he was on his deathbed, I promised him that I would write history. Now that the Timucuan year of mourning has been observed, it is time for me to honor his wishes and redeem my promise.

Every day, for the last years of his life, father would be with me, encouraging me in my writing exercises. "A man who can write with his hands will never dirty them in the fields," he would say, "and when you are trusted by the governor, you will be respected by Indian and Spaniard alike."

Juan Mendoza achieved his position of honor as a scribe because of his talent with a quill and pen, and because of his long friendship with Sr. Manuel Quiñones who recommended him to the governor.

When he lost his eyesight four years before he died, father was dismissed from his employment in the office of the governor.

In the beginning his eyelids swelled. Later his eyes would be encrusted when he awoke in the morning, and he would have to pry them open with his fingers. A thin white cloud appeared at the centers of his eyes. It was so gradual, and father so addled by age, and absentminded, that he did not know when he became blind. His father, Coya Ayacouta Utina, suffered the same malady.

Because he was blind, Father could not see the poor quality of my writing. I remember how he stood over me while I did my exercises, complimenting my work and pretending to read what I had written on the tablet. He did not know that my work was below the standard required for documents bearing the signature of the governor.

I cannot forget Father's reactions upon hearing that Governor Antonio de Benavides had chosen an educated Spaniard over me. First he said that the governor was prejudiced because I am Indian. Later my father told me that a little hard work in the fields would be good for me, and that I could learn to grow crops or catch fish for a living. "Besides, the most important thing for you is the writing of history, not the scribbling of letters for the governor's seal."

Before his own death, Sr. Quiñones secured for me a position as clerk to the sergeant major. It is not what you would call an honored position, and pays barely enough for food, shelter, and an occasional sip of rum.

For the most part, Father wrote in the Timucuan language. I understand that tongue when it is spoken, and can read it with some difficulty, but Father only taught me to write in Spanish.

"There are so few of us left alive, it is a waste of time to learn to write a language nobody can read," he would say.

The friars who once taught the Indian children at the mission school no longer have enough students to make it worth their while. Sometimes they try to form a class, but the parents do not understand the importance of education. Father said that most of the Indians in San Augustín are now drunks and poor examples for their children.

———

My father's death was a devastating blow for a boy of 16 years with no other family. Lately, there has been little work for me. When there is no copying or filing to be done, sometimes the sergeant major sends me home. But with no father or mother, the place I live in is no home, and I spend my spare time wandering the streets of San Augustín, visiting with the vendors in the market and occasionally using what little money I have to buy rum.

As I look through my sole inheritance, a manuscript which my father kept in a leather case, I note that Father wrote very little about my mother Maria Cavale after the account of my birth. Nor do I remember him speaking of her. It is as if he had forgotten her.

The truth is that my mother is still alive and was last known to be living with her new family in Spain. I know this only because it was told to me by a priest. Maria gave birth to a mestizo child while I was still an infant, and to cover her shame she left San Augustín with the father, a Spanish soldier.

Father was already an old man when he married. It is not surprising that my mother went with someone younger. Sr. Quiñones said to me that the only reason they married was that there were so few pure blood Timucua Indians left, and that my father believed in keeping tradition alive.

Juan Mendoza did not love Maria Cavale, and did not miss her when she was gone. There was only one woman whom my father loved in his lifetime, and although he never spoke of her, she is mentioned in his writings. She was a Spaniard.

I have learned something about blindness from having cared for my father. When God takes a man's eyes, be compensates for the loss by sharpening the remaining senses. Juan Mendoza's hearing was always good. He could hear the footfalls of anyone approaching from behind, and recognize the call of every bird in the woods. But his sense of smell was even more remarkable.

In the last two years of his life, he was too sick to leave our house. Still, he could almost mark the day of the year by the air that came in through the window.

"Is it the first of May?" he asked me one morning.

When I asked him how he knew, he said that the swamp mallow usually bloomed around that time, and its scent was on the breeze. I went outside and looked around and could see no swamp mallow anywhere near. Two days later they were abundant down by the creek.

Another time he complained of the cloying smell of hibiscus, which he found unpleasantly sweet. The only hibiscus in bloom was outside a neighbor's house, a great distance away. I went there in the night time and pulled up the bush and threw it away.

Each day, father would remark on what the breeze told him. He had his favorite smells, and I made sure to plant the proper seasonal flowers in the yard outside our house.

On his last day, father awoke from a deep sleep. "Are those October Daisies I smell?" It was a strange question. To my nose, that flower is odorless.

I walked out the door and saw that a tall stand of the bright yellow flowers had bloomed over night and now stood at the edge of a swamp. I went near, and still could not smell them.

"They are there," I said when I went back inside the house, "but for the life of me, they have no smell."

"Show them to me," he said. I helped father off of his bed and he leaned on my arm as I took him to the window. He breathed in deeply, and slowly let the air escape from his lungs.

"Tell me, are they nodding their heads in the breeze and watching the sun as it moves toward its resting place?" he asked.

When I said that they seemed to be bowing to the Sun God, it made my father smile as if he could see it in his mind.

"Not everyone can smell them. They have an earthy smell – not sweet, like some other flowers. Would you like to hear the legend?" he asked.

"Shaman say that because the swamp daisy is the last to bloom, its gentle breath signals the approach of death."

What he said upset me, and I moved toward the door to go outside and pull them up by the roots.

"Where are you going?" he said. "I did not say it was an unpleasant smell. Leave them alone. They have waited a long time. It is their season."

Those were the last words he spoke to me. Father lay down on his bed and went to sleep. During the night I heard him talking with the spirits. In the morning he was gone.

Chapter 46

San Augustín
March 10, 1731

L ooking at what I wrote down last year, and comparing it to my father's writings, I am persuaded that writing history is not as easy as I first believed. My writings are emotional and personal, and deal with the loss of my father and mother. My father's stories were of great events and strong men, and of their resistance against evil enemies, with the survival of our people at stake. My father wrote of important events; I write of inconsequential matters of no interest to anyone other than myself.

Juan Mendoza would be as unhappy with my efforts as a writer of history as he was with my failure to become a scribe.

Let me start over. Something important has happened in my lifetime that I can remember.

War came to San Augustín two years ago, or rather to Misión Nombre de Diós. I was a witness to what occurred, and lived to tell the tale.

In my father's writings he tells how the Yamassee plotted with the English the destruction of every mission town between Guale on the coast and Apalachee in the far west. Thousands of innocent people were murdered and ten times that number were herded like cattle to Charles Town where they were sold as slaves.

When I was two years old, the Yamassee and the English had a falling out, and the Yamassee declared war on their masters. The English joined with the Creek Indians and chased the Yamassee south, and they ended up here in San Augustín where they have lived ever since, under the protection of the guns of the Castillo.

Now, those who live in the village served by Misión Nombre de Diós are mostly Yamassee. None of the rest of us feel safe there, even while attending Mass.

Colonel Palmer and his Creek allies must have long memories. Two years ago they came in search of Yamassee, to punish them for betraying the English.

When the English approached Nombre de Diós, the Spanish governor removed the friars and the people of San Augustín to the Castillo, along with most of the Indians. There was no room for the Yamassee.

The Spanish soldiers retired to the safety of the fort, and watched through their looking glasses as the English soldiers and their Creek allies raided and burned the mission, killing 40 Yamassee. Not once did the Spaniards turn their cannon on the English, or go to the defense of the Yamassee.

Governor Benavides later said that he gave the order not to fire the cannons because he did not want to destroy the mission and have to rebuild it later. Of course, the English burned the mission to the ground, and Nombre de Diós was rebuilt in the spring.

Fredric M. Hitt

That all happened two or three years ago and perhaps I should have written about it then. Sometimes it is hard to recognize history when it happens. With the passage of time, it is easier to understand important events.

————————

Pueblo de Timucua
September 1, 1735

After my father's death I left the house in which I was born, next to the larger one owned by Sr. Quiñones. Because of my work at the presidio, I was unable to tend to the two orphan children who lived with me. It was Sr. Quiñones decision that I find another place to live. He had a Spanish man and his wife who would take my place and provide for the children.

I lived for a time with a Timucuan man and his wife in a small house near the convento at Nombre de Diós. It was only a short walk from the office of the sergeant major where I am employed as a clerk, and would have been a good place to live were it not for the Yamassee who constantly caused trouble.

Life was almost intolerable for civilized folk. Two times, I was robbed while coming home after dark, and the second time I was badly beaten. The Yamassee are a wild breed, and they steal whatever they can get their hands on, whether it belongs to a Timucuan, an Apalachee, or another Yamassee. Many crimes were reported to the governor, and the jail was always full of Yamassee thieves.

The governor had mercy on us, and set aside a place for a new Timucuan village, west of town, on a small creek. The water is filthy and holds no fish, and corn will not grow in the sandy soil. But there are no Yamassee to make our lives miserable.

Sr. Quiñones had heard from a priest about a crippled man who lived at Pueblo de Timucua. He said it would be a service to God for me to move in with him and give him whatever help I could. His name is Manuel Riso, and Riso was neither pleased nor displeased to have me, until I told him that I earned seven pesos each week, and would give one of them to him and weed his corn patch for a place to sleep.

Although he bears a Spanish name, Riso is pagan and does not go to Mass. Nor does he speak much to me or to anyone else. From morning until nighttime we go about our lives with hardly a word for each other. When he does speak, it is in the Utina dialect of the Timucuan people. It is the same tongue my father spoke.

Riso is hunchbacked, with a stiff neck that will not turn far to the left. He walks slightly sideways, as if he is creeping up on someone. He suffers, but mostly in silence. At night I hear him groaning when he tries to roll over in his sleep. On the day I moved into his house, I asked Riso how he came to be a cripple. He is a very private man, and he got up from his cot and walked outside without answering me.

There are 19 houses in Pueblo de Timucua. Most of the people come from Santa Fé or San Francisco, west of the river. It is a farther distance for me to travel each day to my work, but at least I do not have to worry about my rum being stolen while I am away.

Chapter 47

San Augustín
April 30, 1738

For five years after my father died I tried to honor his wishes and write down history. Twice the English came to San Augustín on their slave raids, burning the churches and other buildings, and hoping they could lure the Spanish soldiers out of the Castillo to fight. There were ongoing squabbles between the Timucua who live here and the Yamassee who came to push us out of our rightful place, but nothing that meant very much, or lasted long, or changed our lives. Sometimes I would try my hand at writing them down, only to tear up the pages or burn them later.

Now I realize what a fool I have been. Within the past three months, events have occurred that have proved to me that my mind has been as blind as my father's eyes. I have undergone what the priests might call an epiphany, a sudden awakening to the truth.

I will tell it as it occurred. It began on a Sunday in January.

I went to Mass at Nombre de Diós. Sunday morning is a good time to go to the mission, since many of the rowdiest Yamassee who live in the town have not awakened from their drunken parties of the night before. It is safer to go with another person, but my friend, Manuel Riso, has never accepted Christ and refuses to enter a church.

When the service was near its end, two new priests were invited to the pulpit to make an announcement. They were peninsulars, or priests educated in Spain, and they were new to San Augustín. The friar at Mass is a Creole, or one who was born and received his training at the Catholic schools in Mexico and Cuba.

It is said that the peninsulars and the Creoles have little respect for each other. Creoles look upon peninsulars as being upstarts with no knowledge of life in La Florida. Peninsulars look down their noses at Creoles, saying they are poorly educated and ignorant of church doctrine. Sometimes they do not even speak to each other, so it was unusual to see both kinds of priests at the same service.

Fr. Pablo Rodriguez and Fr. Antonio Navarro were the speakers, although Fr. Navarro did most of the talking. He asked for a showing of hands of how many people were of the Timucuan nation. I held my hand up and I looked around. Of 150 people at Mass, there were fewer than 30 hands in the air.

He then asked if there were any Apalachee present. This time only six hands were lifted. The two peninsulars looked at each other, and from their expressions they seemed disappointed at how few Timucua and Apalachee were there.

Fr. Navarro then said that 130 years ago the first Franciscan mission was established on the west side of the River San Juan, and that in time more than 50 mission churches were built, stretching through Potano, Utina, Yustaga, and throughout Apalachee.

"God led us to 28,000 pagan souls in need of salvation," Navarro said, "and many of them were your fathers and mothers and your ancestors."

"Praise be to God," Fr. Rodriguez said in a loud voice, crossing himself.

"Praise be to God," someone answered from the congregation. That seemed to please the priests and they smiled at each other.

A festival was planned, Fr. Navarro said, to celebrate the anniversary of the establishment of the first church west of the river and to commemorate the brave friars who had given their lives to God's work, and the Indians whose labor and acceptance of the friars' teachings had made it all possible.

"It will be called The Prieto Festival, in honor of the first brave Franciscan missionary, Fr. Martín Prieto," Navarro said, "and it will begin with a dance that will take place on Saturday evening, March 18. Mass will be celebrated the next day at the regular time. It will be exactly 130 years to the day from the first Mass celebrated in Western Timucua."

The friars seemed very proud of what they had planned, and promised that within two weeks an announcement would be made on other details of the festival.

"We look forward to hosting as many as 1,000 Timucua and Apalachee," Fr. Rodriguez said.

I watched the face of the Creole priest. He smiled, but it was more of a smirk from where I stood. My impression was that he thought the peninsulars to be fools.

The *Cacique* of Pueblo de Timucua is Alcutesa, an 80-year-old Potanan who came to San Augustín from Santa Fé when that village and mission was overrun by the Yamassee 30 years ago. As far as anyone knows, his mother was not of the White Deer Clan, and he has no training as a chief. We are a small farming village with barely 20 families and have no need of a chief or a council house. Since Alcutesa is too old to tend his own fields and we would have to do it for him anyway, we decided to name him chief and take care of his needs.

He sent a boy to fetch me when I arrived home from the presidio. Chief Alcutesa's house is smaller and dirtier than the one Riso and I stay in. He invited me to sit on a mat across from him. A small fire between us cut the chill of the winter day.

Alcutesa did not "beat around the bush," as the Spaniards say, but came directly to what was on his mind. He had received instructions from the governor to cooperate with the peninsular priests in planning the festival that was to occur in March.

"I am 90 years old, and too sick to be bothered by such foolishness," he said. "You are the only one in the village who reads and writes the Spanish language. I told the governor that it was your responsibility." Alcutesa rolled over on his side and closed his eyes, pretending to be asleep.

Alcutesa lied about his age to improve his argument, but he was right that there was no one else in Pueblo Timucua who could work with the Spaniards. I also knew that if I refused, it would go badly for me with the governor and with my employer, the sergeant major.

I had neither the time for, nor the interest in, being involved in this crazy scheme of the peninsulars, and I decided that the next day I would go to the larger Timucuan village, Palica, and meet with their Chief Juan Ximenez. He is known as a crafty person, and I knew that if there was a way to avoid getting involved, Juan would already have a plan.

———

Palica is a village of 100 people. They are mostly Timucua from the coast. None of them has ever lived west of the river. Being an old village, Palica has a council house that is still in use. Unfortunately, it seats only 150 people. When floor benches are removed, there is room for 250 people at a dance.

"It would not be nearly large enough to host 1,000 people," I said as Ximenez and I walked around inside.

He laughed and slapped me on the shoulder. "Relax, Alonso, we can put on a proper dance. We have musicians to make music, if we want any, and if the dancing spills outside that will not be a problem."

"You mean to say that you favor this plan by the friars?" I asked.

"Do we have a choice?" Juan Ximenez asked.

Two days later, Juan Ximenez and I went to the monastery and met with the peninsulars, Fr. Navarro and Fr. Rodriguez. They were pleased at our willingness to help with the festival, and after they led us in prayer, the four of us sat in the convento and planned what was to occur.

Juan Ximenez, as *Cacique* of Palica, would provide the council house, the musicians, and three strong men to insure that the people were decent and well-behaved.

"The dance should end by 10 o'clock at night, so the people are well rested and ready for Mass in the morning," Fr. Navarro said.

Ximenez immediately agreed, saying that many of the older people would be home in their beds much earlier than 10 o'clock. I thought that was strange, since I had heard that the dances at Palica sometimes go all night long.

"And no rum and no wine," Fr. Rodriguez said.

Again, Juan Ximenez agreed to the condition. "We will have cassina on the boil for the men, and berry juice, and fresh water. Nuts and cakes will be there for people to eat."

I had remained quiet, somewhat puzzled at the ease with which the plans were made. Finally, I had something to say. "I cannot imagine that there would be 1,000 people there, as you expect. Between my town Pueblo de Timucua and Palica, there are scarcely 200 people. Perhaps a few live in San Augustín, but they are mostly servants in the Spanish households."

Juan Ximinez gave me a scornful look. "There are many more in the other villages. I am sure when the word spreads, they will all come for such a wonderful event. I know of at least 30 Apalachee who will want to attend. We could also invite the Yamassee who live nearby."

Navarro turned to me. "Since Chief Ximinez will be busy with the facilities, entertainment, and sustenance, may we count on you to go to all of the towns and invite the people to attend?"

Before we left, the priests offered another prayer to God that he bless the Prieto Festival. I silently prayed for what would have to be a miracle: an evening of dancing by Timucua and Yamassee that did not result in a war.

I spoke as clearly as I could, not wanting to be blamed: I had invited none of the Yamassee who appeared at the Prieto Festival dance at Palica. I testified to that fact under oath when I was summoned to the governor's inquiry into the stabbing death outside the council house.

Nor did I know beforehand that after the friars left the dance to return to the monastery, two kegs of rum and a plentiful supply of wine would be made available for sale to the dancers by Chief Ximenez's people.

The dance went for many hours beyond 10 o'clock and would have lasted until sunup if it had not been for a knife fight between an Apalachee and a Yamassee. I have heard it whispered that the Apalachee caught the Yamassee cavorting with his wife in the dark outside the council house. The Yamassee died of his wounds, and his body was tossed into the water.

No one admitted seeing the fight and the killer was never identified or brought to justice. To the Spaniards, it was just another Indian knife fight.

The next morning, fewer than a dozen people went to Mass, and some of them, like me, were sick from mixing wine and rum.

The peninsulars were ridiculed by the Creoles for trusting the Indians to behave as proper Christians, but in the long run the two groups found common ground in placing blame on the Indians. When Governor Manuel de Montiano wrote his report on the condition of the mission effort at the end of the month, both the Creoles and the peninsulars agreed with his conclusions.

As a file clerk, I made a copy of the report Governor Montiano sent to the Council of the Indies. He wrote that the Indians of San Augustín were, "Christians in name only," and that they were, "a little worse in their conduct than the gypsies in Spain, with their stealing, cursing, blasphemy, and gambling."

He never explained the reference to gypsies, but from the context of the report it sounds like gypsies are not a well-mannered tribe.

Finally, Governor Montiano said that all of the adults among the Indians living at San Augustín are addicted to alcohol, and that they set poor examples for their children. It was the same thing my father said 20 years ago. The Governor's census counted fewer than 400 Indians in the villages surrounding San Augustín. Two hundred others have fled to the south within the past year, and more than one hundred others perished from plagues.

———————

I said that I had experienced an epiphany.

When I read what Governor Montiano had to say about the Indians, I was at first insulted, and then angry, and as the truth began to settle in my brain I felt bad and went looking for rum to drink. I could find none. Strong drink is now forbidden to Indians, and it is getting harder to find and more expensive than I can afford.

I returned to my house and read all that was written by my grandfather, whose full name was Coya Ayacouta Utina, the *Holata Aco* of the Nation of Utina. He was for many years the most powerful chief in all of La Florida.

Coya deserved his honors, and he was beloved by his people and respected and feared by anyone who would be his enemy. One hundred years ago, Coya had but to snap his fingers and four thousand warriors would follow him into battle.

I also spent a long time reading what was written by my father. Juan Mendoza was an honorable Indian who distinguished himself among both Timucuans and Apalachee and, because of his good character, was given authority over others. In Apalachee he sometimes presided at meetings in a council house so immense it could seat 4,000 men. That was only 40 years ago.

Now there are neither armies of 4,000 men, nor council houses grand enough to hold them. We are reduced to a tenth of a tenth of our former number. Leaders of character, honesty, and wisdom no longer exist. They have been replaced by charlatans who sell the rum that poisons their people.

We, the Timucua, the Apalachee, and all the other Indians of La Florida are dying, and we are dying without honor. That is my sad epiphany.

Chapter 48

Pueblo de Timucua
November 12, 1753

M y days do not vary much, one from another. Of a morning, I make my way half a league to the presidio where I sit at a work desk until late in the day, sorting documents and putting them in the proper box where they belong. I am paid as a clerk, but sometimes the sergeant major gives me work that is more appropriate for a scribe, such as copying official orders, auditing shipping manifests, and writing letters.

When my work is done, I retrace the path to Pueblo de Timucua and go to bed soon after sundown.

Yesterday was different. Riso got his hands on a jug of rum and drank half of it before I got home. I found him sitting outside with his back to a tree. He was more talkative than I have seen him, and I took advantage of his condition by sitting down and asking once again how he became crippled.

"You want to hear that story? That old story?" he asked. Before I could answer he commenced to tell it.

As a young man with no education, Riso worked for a time building the Castillo. He was strong, and a good quarry man to dig out the coquina on the island. In time, he apprenticed himself to a Spanish stonemason and learned to grade the coquina and shape it, keeping the good rocks and leaving the bad. With hammer and chisel, he fashioned the foundation, the walls, and the lintels.

When he was 20 years old the work on the Castillo was finished, and Riso needed other work to do so he could eat. A soldier convinced him to join a caravan of men who carried supplies for the soldiers at Santa Fé and Apalachee. Walking in the woods could not be nearly as hard as quarrying, Riso decided, so he signed on to the work.

The sergeant that went with them treated the five Indians more harshly than had the soldiers in San Augustín. He cursed the men and whipped anyone who fell behind because he was not strong enough for his load. A middle-aged man, a Potanan, befriended Riso, and because Riso was young and strong he lightened the man's burden, taking the extra weight on his strong back.

Six days out from San Augustín they came to a creek where a fallen tree served as a bridge. Riso lost his balance and fell into the water striking his head and shoulder on underwater cypress knees. He was pinned down by the burden on his back and would have drowned if the other men had not jumped off the log to save him.

The sergeant cursed Riso and blamed him for the supplies getting wet. When Riso could not stand up to climb out of the creek, the Spaniard commenced to strike him about the face and head with a leather whip with metal barbs.

Riso's shoulder was broken in the fall, and the bones in his neck, also. The men pulled him back to the trail and laid him under a tree with a calf skin of creek water and a few corn cakes.

"If he is still alive when we come back this way, I will decide what to do with him," the sergeant said. "If he is dead, we will dig him a hole."

The Potanan did not want to go on, but said he would stay with Riso and carry him to Santa Fé which was only a day's travel. The sergeant cursed the Potanan and began to whip him. Finally, Riso told the Potanan to do as he was told by the soldier. He said that he would be all right for a few days, left in the shade of the tree.

It was eight days later that the men came back for him. Riso had eaten the last of his bread three days before and had not had a drink of water in two days. The sergeant was not with them. The men fashioned a travois and halter and took turns dragging Riso until they reached Santa Fé.

"I recovered my strength at the mission at Santa Fé," Riso said. "In a month I could stand. In two months I could walk around the mission with a crutch. It was half a year before the friar would let me travel, and I came home to San Augustín. As you can see, my shoulder and neck did not heal properly."

Riso perched the jug on his right shoulder and took a long draft of rum. The sun was setting and the sky was lit a bright orange with streaks of blue. The October daisies stood as high as the corn and turned their yellow heads to follow the course of the sun.

Riso offered the jug to me and I took a drink.

"That is the first time in 30 years or more that I have told anyone about how it happened," Riso said.

I took another swallow of the strong Cuban rum and handed the jug back to Riso. "What happened to the sergeant?" I asked.

Riso paused, squinting his eyes at the colorful display in the western sky. "I do not know. I wasn't there," he said.

Sensing that the conversation was over, I stood up to go inside the house to gather the corn and dried venison we would eat for our dinner.

"I can tell you what the Potanan told me," Riso said. "He said that there was one dangerous creek to cross the day before they got back to where I was laying beside the trail. The stream was flooded with the spring rain. The sergeant fell in, and he must have been a poor swimmer. Before the others could get to him he was gone. They never found his body."

I did not ask him about it, because it was none of my business, but there is a leather whip that hangs suspended from the roof in Riso's house. When I went inside to fix the meal I looked at it. It has metal barbs attached to the leather thongs.

October 18, 1754

Sometimes I think it was a mistake to become Riso's friend. For the first 14 years we lived together he hardly spoke to me except to complain about my cooking or housekeeping, or to accuse me of stealing his rum. Since the day he got drunk and told me about how he was crippled, I scarcely have an hour of peace when I am with him. Now he talks too much, even when he is not drunk. It is as if he has 80 years of words stored up, and he needs to get them out before he dies.

One day it occurred to me that because of Riso's old age, he might have something worthwhile to say, that he might know some history that should be written down. I began to listen more closely to his stories of his life in the villages around San Augustín.

His mother moved from village to village, staying nowhere very long. He did not say it, but I believe she must have earned her living as a prostitute. She kept him away from the mission churches, and I guess you would say he is pagan, except that he doesn't know anything about the beliefs of the Indians before the friars came here. Riso never learned to read or write.

Before he became a stonemason he was a thief. He still steals things sometimes, but they know him in the market as a pickpocket, and the merchants and soldiers chase him away. Sometimes he leaves the house at night and comes home with a jug of rum. I never complain about it or ask him where he got it.

Riso never talked about his father until recently. I started writing what he had to say, but Riso stopped talking until I put away my paper and pen. He loved his father but did not want the story to be written down for other people to see. I promised him I would not write down the story, but I will say a little on the subject to explain what I learned next.

Riso's father went to prison for murder, and died on the island of Cuba where they sent him. Riso was a small child when it happened, and he heard about it from his mother. It was a shameful story, whether you believed what Riso had to say about his father, or what the Spanish accused him of doing.

The man's name was Carlos, and he was Utinan, as were my ancestors. Riso said his father was a warrior, a brave man who bedeviled the Spaniards 80 years ago. In the old days he would be honored as *Noroco* because of the number of enemies he killed in battle, but to the Spanish governor he was a murderer.

The story was both familiar and strange to me, as if I had heard it before, but told differently. Then Riso said his father was born in a tiny village called Oconee. My own father, Juan Mendoza, came from a place he called Laguna Oconee. Neither of those names can now be found on a map, but the coincidence bothered me and made me wonder.

I began to read again the early accounts written by my grandfather, Coya, and my father. There was a boy named Carlos who was my father's younger brother. He attached himself to a band of *cimarrones*, and became an outlaw. Father wrote about a trial in San Augustín that happened in 1677, where his brother was convicted of killing five innocent people. Carlos had a woman with him, and she carried with her a male child of about four years.

Today, if he still lived, that child would be 80 years old. I asked Riso his age.

"I never learned to count the years," he said, "but my mother told me I came in the year 1673."

I said to Riso that I needed to go for a walk, and I got up and went outside.

I carried with me a piece of paper and a pen to do my ciphering. As many times as I tried, and as many numbers as I put down on the paper to subtract and add, there was no escaping the truth.

Riso is 80 years old, and I am 40 years old, and yet Manuel Riso is my cousin. His father Carlos (or Calesa as he was sometimes called) and my father were brothers. If this were another time, we would be clansmen, family.

It is something I will never say to Riso. He would not be able to understand or accept it. The truth of it, that his father was a vicious killer and not an honorable warrior, would be upsetting to him at his age. If he ever asks me about my family, I will make up a lie. I pray that a merciful God would forgive me.

Chapter 49

*T*he new sergeant major is not ordinarily a friendly man to the few Indians who come and go at the presidio. He is by no means abusive, but he is by nature reserved and proper in his relations with his inferiors. That is why today I was so surprised when he walked out of his office and sat down in the chair next to the table where I was sorting through a ship's manifest, looking for supplies that we had requisitioned.

"Juan? That is your name, is it not?" he asked.

"Juan Alonso Cavale, sir," I said. "I am commonly called Alonso."

"Alonso, would you mind taking these dispatches to the governor? And ask him if he has a response that he wants you to carry back to me."

I stood up, and he handed me a thin stack of papers bearing official seals.

"Do you read the correspondence when it is entrusted to you?"

It was the sort of question a clerk hates to hear. If I answered yes, he might have thought I was presumptuous. If I said no, he might have considered me a liar.

"Yes. I read everything that comes my way, unless my superior tells me it is confidential."

The sergeant major leaned back in his chair and laughed out loud. "Then since you know what goes on anyway, sit back down and read what I have given you."

My training is such that it takes me only a moment or two to understand what is in a dispatch. I look first to see who received it, then who sent it, and the subject of the correspondence, which usually appears above the salutation. If it interests me, I usually read the rest of it. If not, I simply set it aside or file it in the proper place.

These must have been important, I decided, and the sergeant major was watching me carefully, so I took my time and read each one. The first one originated in Madrid, and was forwarded from the Governor of Cuba. The second was from Santo Domingo's sergeant major, and the last one from the Governor of New Spain. They each dealt with a war between France and England, and how it might affect Spanish interests in the new world.

"What do you think?" said the sergeant major. He had a broad smile on his face, but I have learned that sometimes a smile can mask a sinister intent, so I considered my words carefully.

"I do not understand much of it," I said. "There are so many wars going on, and so many foreign countries, that it is very confusing to an Indian."

"Allow me to explain it so you will understand," he said.

For the next half hour he lectured me on the politics of European wars and the reasons they happened. He spoke of a war between France and England, and another involving England and other countries, whose names sounded strange to my ears.

"There are no less than five wars going on at this moment," he said.

I answered him with a Spanish phrase I had heard spoken many times by his predecessor, the old sergeant major. "The whole world has gone crazy," I said.

Again, he laughed out loud and leaned so far back in his chair I feared it would crash to the floor. "Precisely!" he exclaimed. "But would you like to hear what it means for us here in San Augustín? It means that we are safer now than we would be if there was peace in the world. As long as England and France are bloodying each other, they will have no time to worry about La Florida, Cuba, New Spain, or the rest of our possessions. I hope they fight on until they bleed each other to death."

All the talk of blood and death had him in a jubilant mood, and the sergeant major stood up. "Never mind," he said. "I'll take these to the governor, myself. Have a nice day." He strolled out of the room and closed the door behind him.

———

Three years ago Pueblo de Timucua was abandoned on the orders of the new governor, Alonso de Cardenas. He said that it was too far from the village to the Castillo, and that it would be impossible for the soldiers to protect us if we were attacked. There were only seven of us still living there, so we followed his orders and moved to Nombre de Diós where there were many vacant old houses in which we could stay. Most of the Yamassee who lived there have died or moved away, and it has proved to be a good place to live, and convenient to my work at the presidio.

There are fewer than 60 people living here. Five of us call ourselves Timucua. The others are Chiluque, Guale, Apalachee, Surruque, and a few Yamassee. For the most part we live in peace with each other until someone gets drunk and starts a fight.

I still live with Manuel Riso. He is strong and healthy for a man of 88 years, but his memory is so bad he forgets to bathe, or change his clothes when they get dirty. If I did not prepare his meals, he would likely forget to eat and would starve to death. I do not think that he remembers that we left Pueblo de Timucua, and sometimes he steps outside and seems to be lost and confused by what he sees.

We have a larger house than the one we lived in for all those years in Pueblo de Timucua. It was once lived in by a Mocaman *inija,* when we had such people.

My only complaint is that nothing grows here. I like to plant flowers, and to fertilize them and water them and watch them grow and blossom in their season. Pueblo de Timucua was near a swamp and there were always azaleas or mallow or scarlet hibiscus to scent the air. I even succeeded in growing a tall stand of October daisies when most of the other flowers had died off.

The soil here is so sandy and poor that nothing lives very long. The heat of the sun withers the leaves and the petals fall off. After that, they do not come back the next year, but I keep trying and being disappointed.

There are a few children who live here, but they are a wild, unruly bunch. Sometimes they sneak into my house to see if there is something to eat or to steal. Riso's mind is so addled that they pay no attention to his threats. By the time I get home he has forgotten that they came there at all.

There is a mission church, but the friar does not teach the children. Mass is celebrated on Sunday, but fewer and fewer people attend.

Most of the women work in San Augustín in the houses of the rich Spaniards, while their husbands go fishing, gamble, or get drunk during the day. Some of the men work as carpenters or maintain the fort, but for many there is no work to be found.

Tolomato is the only other village that still holds people. They number forty or fifty, and are mostly Guale and other people from that part of the country. The other villages, including Palica, have been closed down for years and no longer exist.

Spaniards outnumber Indians by more than ten to one around San Augustín. Because I work at the Presidio, some of the Spaniards are friendly to me, and inquire as to Riso's health, and greet me on the holy days. Our houses are within sight of each other, but we live our separate lives.

———————

Some days ago I opened the leather trunk and began to reread the stories told by my father and grandfather. They are entertaining tales, much better than any I could write in this modern world where nothing interesting ever happens. One day I was reading about a Spaniard, a soldier with whom my father worked on a cattle ranch. A black stallion had been beaten by the man, and the horse fought back, killing the soldier with his hooves. It was such a good story that I could see it in my mind.

I rummaged among the papers and found a clean piece of parchment that had not been written upon. Using charcoal, I drew a picture of the fight between the horse and the man, as I imagined it happening. I even drew the whip lying on the ground in the corral. I showed the picture to Riso, and although he cannot read, he understood the story. "The bastard got what he deserved," he said.

Since then, I have drawn other pictures. One was of a council house in Apalachee that my father said was so big it could hold 4,000 men at one time. I have seen smaller council houses, but it is hard to imagine one so large.

Fredric M. Hitt

If I have no talent at writing history, perhaps I can draw pictures to illustrate what my father and grandfather saw with their own eyes, before they each went blind and died.

Chapter 50

Presidio de San Augustín
October 14, 1761

A dispatch arrived today on a neutral Dutch merchant trader that anchored beyond the bar. When the ship's captain came to the presidio, he asked to see Governor Cardenas personally. He would not even show the document he was carrying to the sergeant major.

The sergeant major accompanied the sailor to the governor's house, and he asked me to go with them in case they needed my services. We were taken into Cardenas's study, a room filled with rich mahogany furniture and with portraits of former governors on the walls.

Governor Cardenas sat behind his desk and welcomed us. He used a silver letter opener to break the blue seal on the document. He opened it and laid it before him. I watched his eyes as they moved over the paper. He frowned, and the creases around his mouth and on his forehead deepened.

"Stupid!" he said. His fingers curled around the parchment and crushed it into a ball which he hurled across the desk. It bounced off the chest of the sergeant major and fell onto the floor.

"We are doomed," Cardenas said. "Spain has met with the French ambassador in Paris and has agreed to join with them in making war on England."

The sergeant major was standing next to me, and I heard the sigh as air escaped his lungs. He appeared shaken and unsteady on his feet. I caught his arm and lowered him into a chair.

When he had recovered his senses, and the sailor had been sent back to his ship, the three of us sat in the governor's study for a long time. They were so engrossed in their conversation that they forgot that I was there. Cardenas felt a chill and had a servant start a flame in the coquina fireplace. It made the room uncomfortably warm.

The governor asked the sergeant major to give his appraisal of the dangers facing La Florida.

"As long as we control Cuba and Santo Domingo, and the islands of the Caribbean, we should be safe from the British fleet," he said, "but if the Straits of Florida is breached, we are vulnerable to attack with no hope of reinforcement."

March 14, 1762

I have the office to myself nowadays. The sergeant major and Governor Cardenas come and go on their visits to inspect the readiness of the soldiers at the block houses on the coast, where they watch the horizon for the sails of British ships. The two soldiers who once worked here in this officee are now on patrol outside of the town. The

Spaniards are worried about an attack, although there have been no sightings of hostile ships in many months.

I get bored sitting around with nothing to do, and I asked the sergeant major if I could use a few sheets of his paper to practice my writing. He said it would be all right, if I did not waste the paper, and that I should write on both sides of each sheet. He also said that if Governor Cardenas comes in the door, I should put away what I am writing and try to look busy.

This morning I got very busy. A trader sailed into port just after high tide. When he got ashore he ran all the way up the hill to the presidio. He said he had terrible news for the governor. About that time the governor and the sergeant major walked in the door, having just returned from a trip to the village of Nocoroco, and the governor received the trader.

"Terrible news! Terrible news!" the man shouted. He was a simple sailor, and knew none of the etiquette of addressing an important person like the governor. He had not bathed, and the room was filled with his stink.

Before the governor could be seated, the man was in his face, talking louder than the sergeant major thought necessary or proper.

"Sit down," the sergeant major ordered, grabbing the man roughly by the arm and pushing him into a chair. But the man was so excited he jumped back to his feet.

"They have taken Cuba," he said. "The port at Havana is closed, and a British man-o'-war fires its cannons at anyone who comes near."

"Sit down" the sergeant major repeated.

The sailor ignored him and continued to address the governor, who had moved away from the smell of him toward an open window.

Cardenas turned to face the man. "Impossible," he said. "There are five Spanish war ships guarding the

Cuban coast. No Englishman would risk an attack on Havana."

"Nevertheless, it has happened. The Earl of Albermarle reconnoitered the island of Hispaniola, as if Santo Domingo was his target. Four days ago the Spanish ships left Havana and headed east, and when they were gone, the Englishmen descended on Havana from the west."

Governor Cardenas ordered me to take the man into another room and calm him down and have him write down his statement. "If he cannot write, do it for him" he commanded.

As I pulled the sailor through the doorway into the next office he shouted over his shoulder, "Who is going to pay me for the damage to my schooner?"

Presidio, San Augustín
April 10, 1762

Governor Cardenas ordered that all of the Indian men of San Augustín be brought together so he could speak to them after the evening meal.

"There are fewer than one hundred and thirty Spanish soldiers to guard San Augustín," the governor said to the men gathered in the mission church at Nombre de Diós. "If the British come, we will be outnumbered three to one.

"For that reason we need able-bodied men to step forward. Already, almost a hundred civilian Spaniards have taken up arms in defense of their homes and families. These are not volunteers. I consider it the duty of all the citizens of San Augustín, Spaniard and Indian alike, to stand as men to fight the slavers who threaten us. Those of you who are skilled with modern weaponry will be armed with muskets, shot, and powder. Others will use their bows, arrows and spears – and knives, if nothing else is available."

It was a good speech, one that he had dictated to me and I had written for him earlier in the day.

There were only 30 Indian men to hear it. That was all the sergeant major could find living in the villages of Nombre de Diós and Tolomato. I looked at their faces and knew that there were many others who must be hiding in the woods.

Later, Cardenas and the sergeant major calculated that even if all of the Indians and civilians were ready for war, there would be twice that many Englishmen in a single regiment. A Cuban spy had reported that there were at least two regiments resting in Havana.

Four days after news of the blockade of Havana harbor came to San Augustín, a second boat came into port. It was a packet boat, a mail and supply vessel used between the islands. It was light enough to cross the bar even at low tide, and because of its shallow draft, the captain ran it up on the shore near the Castillo.

Its passenger was a priest, Fr. Manuel Pacheco, from Havana, and he told an interesting tale of his escape from Cuba to Santo Domingo, and how he persuaded the man who ran the packet boat to cross the dangerous waters of the Gulf Stream to San Augustín.

Even more interesting was the story he told of what occurred in Havana. He spoke later that day in the main church in San Augustín. The governor was there, and the other officials and all of the leading citizens of San Augustín.

When the Englishmen blocked the harbor and invaded Havana, the meager Spanish force was soon overcome. Spanish officers were imprisoned in their own jail until all the soldiers put down their weapons.

Only one brave man opposed the orders of the English Earl, and he was a priest. His name is Pedro Agustín Morell, and he is the Bishop of Santiago.

Fr. Pacheco said that on the third day, the English levied taxes against the property of everyone, including the church. They took gold and put it in their ships and burned the houses of anyone who refused to pay.

Through it all, Bishop Morell sat on his Episcopal chair in the cathedral and refused to answer questions about where the wealth of the church was stored.

"I answer only to my Cardinal, to the Pope, and to God in Heaven," said the bishop. "Since you are none of the three, but only a mercenary slaver, and an enemy of God and all that is good and holy, I command you to leave this church."

Everyone in the church at San Augustín was hanging on every word of Fr. Pacheco's amazing story. Not a sound was heard except for the voice of the priest.

"The Englishman must have feared that God would strike him dead if he plundered the church with a bishop looking on. When the bishop refused even to stand in the presence of the soldiers, their captain commanded that he be carried on his chair to a man-o'-war waiting in the harbor. Bishop Morell sat erect and with great dignity as he was carried through the streets of Havana to the cheers of a multitude of Spaniards who loved him so. All the while, Monseñor Morell was praying out loud for the souls of the Englishmen."

Fr. Pacheco dropped his head, and when he lifted it again his tears rolled down his cheeks. "They exiled him from Cuba. They took him to Charles Town. Beyond that, we know nothing of his fate."

A special Mass was held that evening, and into the nighttime. It was well attended by the Spaniards.

Chapter 51

Misión at Solomototo
November 23, 1762

I left the presidio two days ago before the sun was up. I asked a woman who lives at Nombre de Diós to watch after Riso until I return. She promised she would feed him and make sure he bathed. Not knowing how long I would be gone, I left her with four pesos.

I had my orders, and two other men had theirs. I was to go to Tocoi crossing on the San Juan River. I carried an order authorizing me to commandeer a large canoe and the services of a man familiar with the river. I was to go north, stopping at every inhabited village.

Another man was to cross the river at Tocoi and continue to the west along the Royal Road, into the land where the Potano Indians once lived. A third man was ordered to go south on the coast to Nocoroco and as far as whatever Surruque and Ais villages might still exist.

Our orders were to conscript every able-bodied man and boy, to take their names, and to order them to go to San Augustín. No slackers would be tolerated, we were told, and if anyone failed to do his duty and appear at San

Fredric M. Hitt

Augustín, he would be hunted down and punished as a traitor.

I found a canoe man at Tocoi, and he obeyed the orders and took me north to this old, abandoned mission village, Solomototo. No one lives here anymore. Not a single house is occupied.

It rained during the night, and the shelter we slept in leaked water all over our bedding. Unable to sleep, we lay awake talking, and I told my canoeist what I had heard about the events on the horizon. I told him that some of the Indians were terrified that the Englishmen would take them for slaves.

I must have been persuasive in whatever I said to the man. When I awoke, he was already gone. He left me the canoe, and two paddles, and all of the food. I have never paddled a canoe, and do not know the river. Worst off all, if I fall out I will drown, because I never learned to swim. As I see it, I have no choice but to continue on, trusting in God.

I will go north and east on the river to where it meets the ocean and make my way south between the islands and the coastline until I find San Augustín. I am almost 50 years old, and I have none of my father's knowledge about surviving in the wilderness.

It is time for me to put away this paper, drain the rain water from the canoe, and begin my journey.

Misión Nombre de Diós
December 4, 1762

I have returned without finding more than four Indians who said they would come to San Augustín for the fight. Still, I was greeted as a hero. God looked down from Heaven and placed his hand on me. He used me to

332

his purpose here on earth. There is no other way to explain what happened.

The canoe did not tip over, and I did not drown, which is a miracle in itself. The current was slow but steady, and I learned to sit in the back and use the paddle to control the direction, and not to worry about going faster than the river wanted to carry me. That gave me time to study the shoreline, looking for smoke from campfires. It also allowed me to rest my hands which were badly blistered on the first day when I tried to manhandle the canoe.

I encountered so few people that I suspected that they knew of my mission and hid away in the woods. After two days of seeing no smoke, I became convinced that large villages with many people simply did not exist on this part of the river.

When I left the San Juan and entered the salt water, I steered south inside of an island, with a nice breeze at my back to move me along. I saw three fishermen and I gave them their orders. When I said they would be hunted down by the soldiers if they did not go to San Augustín, they laughed at me, saying that this was not their fight, and that they preferred the company of Englishmen to that of Spaniards. When I lost sight of them they were going north, and not south.

Later that same day I went ashore to bathe the sweat off of my body and rest in the shade of a tree. I was near sleep when I heard the sound of palmetto leaves rattling behind me.

A tall man stepped from behind a tree. I knew he was a priest of some kind, because he wore a tattered robe, but it was the color of ripe plums, and not gray or brown as the friars wear. His eyes had a strange look, as if he were ill, and he mumbled and made no sense when he spoke. His face was badly burned by the sun and covered with bug bites.

I put him in the canoe, and he lay down in the bottom and slept for the rest of the day and all that night, as I moved as quickly as I could to the south.

On the morning of the second day, he awoke, and after I fed him and let him bathe himself at the mouth of a small river, he was refreshed.

"Can you take me to San Agustín?" he asked. When I said I hoped we would be in San Agustín before dark, he lifted up a prayer to God in a powerful voice.

"Are you Christian?" he asked, when he was done with his prayer.

I told him I was a good Catholic, and that seemed to please him.

He never said his name, and I did not ask. When we arrived at San Agustín, and I delivered him to the monastery, the priests fell to their knees in front of him, crying out and washing his feet in their tears.

His name is Pedro Agustín Morell, and he is the Bishop of Santiago de Cuba. He is the man who would not leave his chair to please an Englishman.

He said to the friars that the British at Charles Town grew weary of his obstinacy and put him ashore at Guale. He had walked for four days before I found him. "I knew that if I kept the ocean on my left hand, God would deliver me to San Agustín."

San Agustín
December 31, 1762

The Spaniards look upon the coming year with dread and apprehension. Their fate, and the future of the colony of San Agustín, seem precarious. From a watchtower on the island, reports are received at the presidio almost daily of British ships venturing nearby. Because there is no formal blockade of the port, Governor Cardenas has described the situation as "an uneasy hell, between peace and war."

Today a communiqué arrived on the packet boat, which now makes regular stops at San Augustín after navigating a circuitous route from Santo Domingo so as to avoid the English at Havana. It was from the secretary of the Council of the Indies, and it ordered the governor to avoid any provocative actions against the enemy, but to take a defensive position to protect Spanish subjects and property. The message told of a peace conference taking place in Paris between England, France, and Spain.

Governor Cardenas spoke to the men of San Augustín today on the eve of the New Year and said that the negotiations would be very complicated because the war has raged for seven years and involves far more than British incursions and threats to Cuba, the West Indies, and La Florida. Powerful countries are arguing about who should dominate weaker ones all over the world.

"When they have divided the spoils," he said, "as an afterthought they will decide what is to become of us."

The coming of Bishop Morell has been a singular blessing to the Spaniards of San Augustín. He makes light of his predicament of being separated from his subjects at Havana, and says that his exile from Cuba must be the will of God, or it would not have happened. He has declared his presence to be an official Episcopal Visitation to the people of La Florida.

In the three weeks since he arrived, he has revived the spirit of the Spanish people of San Augustín. Whereas the priests had become distracted from their duties by the uncertainties of the future, Bishop Morell has again focused their minds on the task that is theirs. He has confirmed more than 200 people in the faith, and many more await baptism. His immense Godly spirit has strengthened the faith of priest and parishioner, alike. Of those confirmed in the faith, only a few were Indians and the rest Spaniards.

———————

San Augustín
April 11, 1763

A small ship arrived in port 10 days ago. It was sent by the priests of the See of Santiago de Cuba, and it came to carry Bishop Morell home to his cathedral. It is the first confirmation of the rumors that a peace treaty has been agreed to. No one has yet seen a written copy, but the governor says that England will withdraw from Havana. In turn, King Charles III of Spain will relinquish any claim to San Augustín and all of La Florida.

When be boards his boat tomorrow morning, Bishop Morell will carry with him a new Episcopal chair built by the artisans of San Augustín to replace the one stolen by the English. It is God's will that he go home, but it brings great sadness to the people here.

He conducted his final Mass at the church in San Augustín this morning. For his scripture, he read from the fourteenth chapter of the Gospel according to St. John: "I go to prepare a place for you."

Chapter 52

The Presidio, San Augustín
July 20, 1763

Today a regiment of British redcoats marched through the plaza of San Augustín. Some of us who were busy packing our belongings, or already carrying bundles to the boats, stopped and watched. The bright sunlight glinted off the shiny buttons of their tunics. For a race we all know to be bloodthirsty slavers, some of them had young, innocent looks about them. As they passed by, those of us who were downwind were reminded that the English do not often bathe.

I watched the angry, red faces of the Spaniards. One or two of them shouted insults and curses, but they spoke Spanish and the English did not answer back. The few Indians who were there looked fearful, and hid themselves behind trees and in the alleys.

I was at the harbor when I heard the bugles, flutes and drums from the ceremony where the governor surrendered the Castillo de San Marcos to the British.

———————

I am sitting alone, for the last time, in the presidio office of the sergeant major. He was here earlier, and he was drunk on rum. I asked him if I could have a piece or two of paper to write down what had occurred on this historic day. He told me to help myself to all the paper, and take it with me. He thanked me for my service, shook my hand, and walked out of the door.

We have been ordered to board the boat at midnight. Four heavily laden ships will sail with the morning tide. Three thousand Spaniards and eighty-nine Indians will make the voyage to Cuba. None of the Indians of San Augustín chose to stay and risk being enslaved by the Englishmen.

When I finish this page, I will walk the path to my house at Nombre de Diós for the last time, and fetch Riso to take him to the harbor. I told him we were going to Cuba, and that we would not be coming home again. His understanding is not good, and Riso seems more worried about getting out of bed in the middle of the night. When I told him we would go for a boat ride, his mood brightened and he was content.

Our baggage is light, and most of it is already on board. I packed a variety of flower seeds, not knowing what flowers grow in Cuba, and put them in the same bundle with our clothing. If everything is stolen, or the boat sinks in a hurricane, it will not be a great loss.

I will carry with me only the leather case containing my writings and those of my father and my grandfather.

J. Alonso Cavale

July, 1763

Guanabacoa, Cuba, 1767

Epilogue

Convento de Santo Domingo
Guanabacoa Cuba
June 2, 1769
To: Monseñor Pedro Agustín Morell
Bishop of Santiago de Cuba
Havana

A short addendum, Your Excellency,

Once again I have researched the attendance records of The Church of Our Lady of the Ascension, and although such records are notoriously inaccurate, I have discovered that Juan Alonso Cavale attended Mass on only one occasion: the Funeral Mass for his friend, Manuel Riso, who died shortly after his arrival in Cuba in the summer of 1763.

Sr. Cavale made no demands upon the church for services, and volunteered none of his time to our programs. Seemingly, our only contact with him was through the widow we sent to look in on him from time to time.

None of the Indians who immigrated to Havana from La Florida claim to know him well, but they said he was well-behaved and made no trouble at Nombre de Diós. If he was addicted to alcohol in San Augustín, no one made note of it. It is my belief that he began to consume alcohol to excess when he left his homeland.

His employment in San Augustín was as a clerk to the sergeant major at the Presidio. His father before him served for many years as scribe in the service of several governors of his time.

Sr. Cavale's only hobby was the raising of flowers, and, when I went to claim his body, I discovered a prodigious growth of a flower identified as October daisy near his house.

Fredric M. Hitt

When I returned recently, the flowers were gone. I can only assume that this plant does not flourish in the soil of Cuba.

I have also concluded that Cavale was the artist who created the illustrations that were found with the writings.

A careful inspection of the church records discloses that Juan Alonso Cavale was the last surviving Timucuan who immigrated to Cuba. If it is likewise true that there are none left in La Florida, his passing is indeed a sad event for us all.

Your brother in Christ
Fr. Manuel de Soto

Author's Note/
Acknowledgments

When Juan Ponce de Leon set foot on this continent (arguably, south of Melbourne, Florida) it was Easter time, April 2, 1513, and he named the land La Florida because of the lush profusion of flowers. Later in his voyage he encountered indigenous people further south along the coast, and he and his party were met with spears and arrows and driven away.

Ponce returned on another voyage, and other adventurers followed him. French Huguenots established Fort Caroline at the mouth of the St. Johns River, near present day Jacksonville, in 1564 and led an uneasy, short-lived existence with Timucua Indians as their neighbors. Eighteen months later, the French were routed by the Spanish and Pedro Menéndez de Avilés founded St. Augustine.

In the beginning, Ponce and Menéndez were looking for riches to rival what the conquistadors had discovered in Mexico and Peru. Over time, when they found no precious stones and metals in Florida, the Spaniards stayed for two purposes: to guard the shipping lanes between Mexico and Spain, and to convert the natives to Catholicism.

Fredric M. Hitt

Could Ponce or Menéndez have guessed that their efforts in Florida would lead to the extinction of a race of people? That exactly 250 years from Ponce's first landing, a society that numbered approximately 300,000 souls would cease to exist? It's unlikely they could have anticipated the wholesale deaths that would be caused by contagious diseases carried by the Europeans, or that their own ineptitude and insensitivity would drive the natives away. Or that continuing slave raids by other European powers would decimate the Spanish mission system, which at its apex had baptized 28,000 so-called pagans into Christianity.

Nor could they have foreseen the negative consequences of robbing a people of their roots; their legends, games, ceremonies, and beliefs that had for 10,000 years explained to them their place in an uncomplicated world.

Spanish records demonstrate that Juan Alonso Cavale was, in fact, the last full-blooded Timucuan. His death in Cuba in 1767 marked the end of a society. Undoubtedly, many Timucua intermarried with the Spanish and French, and with other indigenous peoples, such as the Creek and Apalachee.

The Apalachee Indians were also assumed to have met extinction, until decedents of the survivors of Talimali were found living in Rapides Parish, Louisiana.

The current Apalachee Chief, Gilmer Bennett, and his family have visited the magnificent reconstruction of Mission San Luis in Tallahassee, Florida, and have stood in amazement in the council house that accommodates 3,000 people. They have prayed in the mission church, a replica of the one their ancestors worshiped in more than 300 years ago.

If the Apalachee survived, why not the Timucua? Do you think it might just possible that . . .?

My heartfelt thanks to everyone who helped me along the way on this painful, yet rewarding journey of discovery of the early Florida Indians. My first book, *Wekiva Winter*, won the Florida Historical Society's Patrick D. Smith Award as the best Florida historical novel for 2006.

The identical honor was bestowed on *Beyond the River of the Sun* for 2008. Now, with the publication of *The Last Timucuan* the story is done, the trilogy completed.

I have thanked most of my contributors and collaborators in the other books, so I'll make this short: Thank you Dr. John Hann, Dr. Bonnie McEwan, David White Wolfe, Bill Belleville, Charles Tingley, Fr. Pareja, Marehootie, Bip Bentura, Tom Wallace, Juan Mendoza, and Juan Alonso Cavale.

A special word of thanks to Florida's "Cracker Tenor" Benjamin Dehart who has written a ballad, "Timucuan Eyes", inspired by my books and characters.

And of course, my wife and artist-in-residence Linda Silsby Hitt, and all the other sweet spirits, living and dead. I have listened to each of you.

Fredric M. Hitt
December, 2008

LaVergne, TN USA
14 November 2010
204640LV00004B/6/P